To June, you have the patience of a Spartan. I hope you enjoy this wild ride.

John Barton

THE LAST SPARTAN

PRESS
A Superior Publishing Company

P.O. Box 115 • Superior, WI 54880
(715) 394-9513 • www.savpress.com

First Edition

Copyright 2008, John F. Saunders

First Printing
08 09 10 11 10 9 8 7 6 5 4 3 2 1

All rights reserved, including the right to reproduce this book or portions thereof, in any form, except for brief quotations embodied in articles and reviews, without written permission from the publisher. This is a work of fiction. Any resemblance to real persons is purely coincidental.

ISBN 10: 1-886028-88-5
ISBN 13: 978-1886028-83

Library of Congress Catalog Card Number: 2007943484

Published by:

> Savage Press
> P.O. Box 115
> Superior, WI 54880

Phone: 715-394-9513 or 800-732-3867

E-mail: mail@savpress.com

The author can be emailed at: HnrSpartan@aol.com

Website: www.savpress.com

Cover design: Debbie Zime

Printed in the U.S.A.

THE LAST SPARTAN

John F. Saunders

Dedicated to:
My wife, Lynn—beautiful, wise, and kind;
My two sons, John and Jake—men, warriors, friends—
stay strong, stand tall;
And to anyone who realizes the world is a cold, dark place
but chooses to live with honor anyway.

Stand straight in the front rank with your shield before you
and see your life as your enemy; the darkness of death
should be welcome as the light of the sun.

>Tyrtaios, Spartan poet (685–668 BC)

Prologue

Frank Kane was dying. He was wounded to pieces. At six feet, four inches and close to two hundred and twenty hard muscled pounds, that took some doing. He tried to prop himself up against the tree but found his legs weren't working anymore. He stared down at his blood-soaked shirt. The bullet holes were barely noticeable now. Just small innocent looking punctures. They seemed to have stopped bleeding. The blood still seeped steadily from the knife wound in his abdomen. He pressed harder with his right hand, trying to slow the bleeding. A thick, pink loop of intestine slipped out between his fingers, and he carefully tucked it back inside. His thin leather gloves were stiff with blood. He had meant to discard them after the wet work like always. Now, it didn't matter.

He looked over at the motorcycle. It was a BMW, one of the 1200 series, painted a deep, metallic, ocean blue. His drying blood had stained the gas tank and sides with long, dark streaks. It was a sweet ride. One hundred BHPs. Twelve hundred CCs. The bitch was super fast, that was for sure. He didn't know how far he had gotten before the tank finally ran out, but then, it wasn't his bike. It belonged to Spanish Johnny. It was the first one Frank had found outside the safe house with the keys still in the switch.

Spanish Johnny, now there was a piece of work. Frank wondered what Spanish Johnny meant when he whispered, "For Aphrodite?" It was hard to know with Spanish Johnny.

God, he felt tired. Exhausted. Frank wanted to close his eyes and sleep, maybe for a thousand years. He was beyond pain now. His body felt numb, somehow dulled, even a little cold. He knew his body was going into shock. At least it didn't hurt anymore. Well, just a little.

The Spartans had enjoyed a good run. For nine years they had been the most powerful motorcycle gang on the East Coast. Nine years of taking names and kicking ass. They were so small when they started, no one even noticed them. Cyrus had named them. He had taught them, showed them the way. His vision had guided them. He had made them strong, relentless, feared. Like a modern day Lycurgus, he had molded them on the design of ancient Sparta. At their peak no one dared to oppose them. They worked with impunity, even filling the niches for the big boys in organized crime.

It couldn't last. They had known that from the start. It was all over now. Their strength had doomed them. The government brought massive pressure from the F.B.I., A.T.F., D.E.A., and all the alphabet boys. Other East Coast bike gangs were tempted to try and reclaim their old turf. West Coast gangs moved in, probing for weaknesses so they could expand their own territories. The Spartans started to lose control of their affiliates, helots as Cyrus liked to call them, who began to revolt. Attacked. Infiltrated. Betrayed. That was what happened in Greece to the ancient Spartans, too.

Frank knew Cyrus was dead. He had to be, otherwise they would never have had the balls to try to burn Frank. Frank was the Spartans' chief enforcer. Too bad he was dying, he thought. There was a lot left undone. The hitters would be coming for him again. Soon. They had to. You couldn't leave a man like "The Hammer" alive. It would be suicidal.

He heard the engine off in the distance. Sounded like a truck. Old. Maybe a Ford F250. Probably four cleaners, maybe five counting the driver. He would have sent five. Just to be safe. Make damn sure he was down for good. Make sure Frank Kane never came back to haunt them.

He had dumped his twin Colt .45s at the scene. He still had a gun in his boot. It was a small double barreled derringer. It carried a couple of .44 magnum rounds in the pipes. The gun wouldn't save him, but it would send a couple of them to Hades before him. He tried to reach it. His left arm didn't seem to have any strength in it. He concentrated for ten seconds, forging the will. He tried to extend his left hand toward his boot again. The fingers stretched and the hand trembled, but the arm wouldn't move at all.

Frank sighed and leaned his head back against the tree. He gazed up into the bare branches of the tree. The sky overhead was clear and blue and pitiless, just like his eyes. His long, dark hair blew back in the cool breeze. He would have liked to have seen the ocean one more time. Smell the salt air. Listen to the roar of the waves as they broke on the shore. Drink a last cold beer with the sun warm on his face.

He pushed his swollen tongue over his lips and tasted the blood caked in his beard. It tasted like he had a mouth full of new copper pennies. Damn, there was a lot of payback out there needing to be done, and he wasn't going to make it. He closed his eyes and imagined himself like Odysseus adrift in a hollow ship on the restless back of the wine dark sea. He heard the truck closing in. Heard it skid to a stop before him. A gentle breath of wind brushed against his cheek. Frank wasn't afraid. Death reached out and took him then. He was the last Spartan.

THE LAST SPARTAN

Chapter 1

Frank Kane looked different. His hair was buzz-cut short. His beard was gone. He wore a long sleeved, blue work shirt over a red Under Armour nylon t-shirt. It was a vanity, and he knew it. The ancient Spartans had worn red battle cloaks. According to legend, the red was so that no enemy would ever see Spartan blood. Cyrus had them all wear red t-shirts in honor of that tradition. The t-shirts carried no logo or club identification. That wasn't important. It was the color that was important. Frank had over a dozen in long sleeve and sleeveless. The work shirt hid his Spartan tattoos and ritual scarring. He wore nondescript khaki pants and tan work boots.

Frank was a different man than he had been five years earlier. It wasn't just the time in prison, although that can change a man. It was deeper. He had been given a second chance. He had come back from beyond death and been reborn. He had been given a rare gift. He had been given a quest for redemption.

He wiped the Harley Davidson Soft Tail gently with the cotton rag. It was actually a baby's diaper. If it was soft enough for a baby's behind, it was soft enough to shine chrome. He polished until he could see his reflection. Perfect. The new fat pipes looked great. It really brought the big bike alive.

The client standing beside him was a stark contrast to Frank. The man was in his early fifties and wore a three-thousand-dollar, Italian, chalk stripped suit. His thick white hair was immaculately combed back and shone with grease. He exuded an air of quiet confidence. The man was an attorney named Charles Foster.

"Nice work, Frank," Foster said smiling. "You did a great job, as always."

"Thanks. She turned out real nice."

"That she did."

"These bigger pipes deepen the bass a little, too. Hints at unseen power."

"I like the way you put that. Power is important, Frank. The image even more so. I can't wait to give her a ride."

"You going to ride her back to your office?"

"No. I'll drop her off at home. I got something else I have to do first. I'll take her out for a spin tonight. Do you mind rolling her onto my trailer? It's on the back of the Escalade."

Frank turned to look out of the garage toward the parking lot. He saw the black Cadillac Escalade and the shiny trailer hitched behind.

"Glad to."

"Thanks."

Frank rolled the bike out and onto the trailer. He cinched the tie-downs to make sure it didn't come loose. He gave it a final rub with the soft diaper.

"Enjoy," Frank said, handing the man the motorcycle keys.

"I will. Hey, Frank, here's a little something extra for you."

Foster slipped him a fifty dollar bill wrapped around his business card. "I appreciate your good work. You ever need me, give me a call. I'm the best at what I do, too."

Frank smiled and nodded. "Yes, sir. I will keep that in mind. Hope I don't need your card."

He watched Foster climb into the driver's seat and pull away. He turned and looked back at the motorcycle shop where he worked. The large enameled sign above the garage said it all: "Elite Motorcycles" in bold three-foot-hign neon letters. And beneath it in smaller black block letters: "Sell, Repair, and Customize." It was a huge operation, easily the size of most car dealerships. In fact, it was laid out on that pattern. There was a central building with small private offices, a waiting room, an accessory store, and a central show room. There was an attached garage with a dozen bays that serviced and rebuilt motor-cycles with the latest equipment. Apart from the main building was a second garage for special order custom bike creation. Ever since the cable channels had started running all those shows about customized choppers, business had been booming.

Elite Motorcycles was a flat out money-making machine. They had to work hard to keep up with all the demand. Customers weren't just local. They came from all over. The company employed seven-teen people and was growing. There was talk of franchising the idea out.

"Hey, Anthony," Frank called as he walked back into the garage.

A young, skinny black man crowned with dread locks that would have made Bob Marley proud stepped out from one of the bays.

"What you need, Frankie?" he asked as he walked toward Frank, wiping his greasy hands on his pants leg.

"Little something for you," Frank said over the boom of the classic rock radio station being piped in, tossing the folded fifty to him.

"Damn, this is a Grant."

"Buy your baby something."

Anthony chuckled, looking at the money in his hands. "Can't be doin' it, Frankie. This is your tip, not mine. Wouldn't be right. Jah says a man must stay in the light in all things."

"Which one of us got a new baby?"

"Me, but..."

"No buts. I'm doing alright. You take it. Buy that little boy something from his Uncle Frankie."

Anthony beamed his gratitude as he folded the money in his hands again and stuffed it into his coveralls. "I appreciate it, Frankie."

"No problem."

As Frank left the garage, he glanced toward the curb as a Blue Bird cab pulled to a halt. Bob Seger was singing something about rock and roll never forgetting. A tall rail-thin man stepped out from the passenger's seat. He wore tight straight-leg blue jeans and an old white shirt that was freshly starched but frayed at the collar. The man was somewhere between sixty and a hundred-and-sixty years old with a face weathered by long farm work. He took off his green John Deere work cap and leaned back inside the cab. He picked up a manila envelope from the seat. He said something to the cab driver as he paid him. The man turned back toward Frank. The old man slipped his hat on and then off again and started to fumble with it nervously. Finally, he smiled and walked toward Frank. Frank didn't move. When the man reached him he stuck out a long- fingered hand.

"Frank."

Frank took his hand. "Lamar, what brings you here?"

The smile faded and the old man stared at the pavement. He didn't answer.

"Where's Sybil? Did she and Jenny come with you?"

"Naw. Just me. You know Sybil don't think much of flying. She's still not too sure what keeps them things up in the air."

Frank laughed. "That sounds like her. What about Jenny?"

Lamar looked up into Frank's eyes. "That's what I come about. She's run off. Is there some place we can talk, private?"

"Sure. I'm sorry. We can use one of the offices."

Lamar followed Frank into the main building. Frank found a small glass-walled office and closed the door for privacy.

"You want some coffee, Lamar? A soda? Glass of water?"

"No, thank you, son. Thank you for askin', but I'm fine."

Frank settled back into the leather chair. "What can I do for you, Lamar?"

"Like I said, Jenny's run off."

"Tell me about it."

"She ain't but fifteen. Just this side of sixteen. You know how it is. She's just a child, but she wants to be all growed up."

"Why did she run away?"

"I guess it all started with that tattoo she got. She got a little butterfly on her right wrist. It weren't much of nothing. Lots of kids got them things, but Sybil had a fit. Said it made her look trashy. No offense."

"None taken."

"Seems like they was always fightin' about somethin' after that. Who she dated, or where they went, or what time she come home. Jenny's a good girl, don't get me wrong, but she wanted more freedom, and I guess we was holdin' a little tighter than we should have. Trying to keep her our little baby granddaughter awhile longer."

"What finally made her go?"

"Well, sir, she run into a boy used to live on a farm near ours. He was a good bit older. Name of Vincent Street. He had left town when he was about Jenny's age and moved off to Atlanta. His mom had died recent and he had come back to town for the funeral. Anyways, he seen Jenny, and you'd a thought he'd never seen a pretty girl before. He wouldn't leave her alone. Said she had the prettiest eyes he had ever seen. 'Eyes like an angel,' he kept saying. Kept calling her 'Angel' all the time. Right embarrassing, if you ask me."

"She is a beautiful girl, Lamar. Boys are going to come around."

"I know that. It didn't worry me at first. Then he told her she ought to move to Atlanta and be a model. Said he knew people who could get her started. Said she would make lots of money. Says she deserved better than small town life."

Frank felt the hairs on his arms stand up, but he kept his face calm. Showed nothing to alarm Lamar.

"Did she run off with him?"

"No. He went back home to Atlanta. But then he started calling her all the time. Sybil put a stop to that right fast. He was ten years older than Jenny, and it wasn't right. Turns out he had been writing her, too."

"How do you know?"

"We found some of the envelopes where we burn trash. Jenny picks up the mail everyday after school, and she must have been sneaking his letters out."

"Did you talk with her about it?"

"Tried. Least ways Sybil did. It got pretty ugly. Hollerin' and doors slammin' and all. The next day she was gone with some of her clothes. And this little stuffed dog she liked to sleep with. You remember it. Called it Scampy."

"What did you do? Did you call the police?"

"Yes, sir, we did. They said there was nothing they could do for twenty-four hours. So we rode around trying to find her. We asked everybody, and no one had seen her or knew nothing."

"How long ago was this?"

"About a month. We had the boy's name and address, so we found us a, what do you call 'em, a private investigator to see if that was where she was stayin'."

"What did he find out?"

Lamar handed him an envelope. Frank opened the tab and poured out the contents. There were two pictures of a man. Vincent Street. Twenty-six years old. Dark hair. Darker eyes. Mediterranean looking. Maybe Middle Eastern. Medium build. Handsome. The photos had been taken with a telephoto lens. One was a close up, the other mid-range in front of a brownstone building. There was also a worn envelope with the address in the upper left hand corner. No name. Just the address. The handwriting was small and neat. Frank picked up the envelope and felt the indentions on the outside. The envelope was addressed to Jenny. It was empty.

There was a recent photo of Jenny. Probably a school picture. You could see the nervousness in the eyes, wanting desperately for the picture to be good. The smile was sincere. The eyes were large and brown and deep and quiet, as he had remembered. Her brown hair was shoulder length and parted on the side. She had on a pretty green dress. She looked everyday of fifteen.

There was also a report from Burt Wilson, a private investigator in Atlanta. His detective agency was Ace Detective Services. Probably the first one in the Atlanta yellow pages, Frank thought. His report was three typed pages, double spaced, covering what he had done to try to find Jenny. It was very precise and contained a lot of law enforcement jargon. Ultimately, he had been unable to find her. There was also a receipt for ten thousand dollars.

"Ten thousand? Is that what he charged you?"

"Yes, but we would have paid anything to find her. He said he had exhausted every avenue."

"But?" Frank asked.

"But?"

"But, he said if he had more money, he could do more."

"Yeah, he said he could check through some underworld informants he knew, but that would cost more money, and he still couldn't promise if it would lead to her or not. The fellow tried real hard. Didn't make much sense to make him keep looking. Not around those kind of folks. So Sybil said to come talk with you. She hoped you might be willin' to help."

Frank looked at the information. It was all pretty clear to him. If you were going to look into the belly of the beast, better to send someone who had lived there. Someone like Frank.

"Alright," Frank said simply.

"I was hopin' you would help us. You're our last hope."

"Sybil always says everything happens for a reason."

"That she does."

"Can I have this?" Frank said, indicating the contents of the manila envelope.

"Sure."

"I want you to call this private detective, this Burt Wilson. Tell him I will be down to talk with him tomorrow. Tell him I have your authorization to discuss this case in detail with him, that I represent you on this matter from now on."

"I'll call him right now. I got one of his cards in my billfold."

THE LAST SPARTAN

"Lamar, one more thing."

"What's that?"

"When I find her, what do you want me to do with her?"

Lamar was silent for a moment. He twirled his hat through his fingers. "Well, son, just make sure she's okay. That's the main thing. If she'll come home, we want her. We love her and miss her something fierce. But if she don't want to come home. Well, then that's that. You don't make her. She would just run off again. Just let her know she's welcome and Sybil's sorry for the way she acted."

"And this boy, Vincent. He doesn't look like your typical farm boy."

"No. His daddy's people owned the farm, but his dad worked on the oil refineries out in Kuwait. Over there in the Middle East where they're always fightin'. He met this pretty local girl and up and married her. When the boy was about twelve, the dad got killed in some kind of accident. He and his mother moved out here to the farm. Her people wouldn't take her in because she married an American."

"I can see how Vincent would stand out to a fifteen-year-old girl."

"I think all the attention just went to her head. She never had anybody older act that way toward her before. Treat her like she weren't just a kid."

"When are you heading back, Lamar?"

"I got a plane this evening. Didn't see no reason to stay the night."

Frank reached into his pocket and took out his cell phone. "Call Wilson and tell him I'm coming. I'll go tell my boss I need a few days off. Then I'll take us to get some food before you have to catch your flight."

Lamar smiled, and Frank could see the tears in his eyes.

Frank left Lamar in the office and went to find his boss. Elliot Burns was busy in his office working on some kind of paperwork. When he saw Frank, he stopped and stood up.

"Frank. What can I do for you?"

"If you got a minute, Elliot."

Elliot glanced at his paper-covered desk. "This stuff can wait. Just trying to balance the old books. I'm no good at book work. You know that. Don't have the brain for all those figures."

"I need some time off. A few days, maybe ten days tops."

"Fine," Elliot said.

"I need to be off the clock for the first forty-eight, but I want you to punch my card after that until I get back."

"You think there might be trouble?"

Frank's forced smile sent a shiver through Elliot.

"I always think there's going to be trouble. That's what kept me alive in the old days. Can you do it?"

"Absolutely. I'll even add a little overtime to make it look legit."

"You do it personally, Elliot. I don't want it fucked up. Something goes wrong, I'll know where to come."

Elliot nodded. "I'll take care of it, Frank. You know you can count on me."

Frank turned and left. He knew Elliot would agree. What else could he do? When the Spartans had first started, they had used Elliot to repair their bikes. Later, Elliot started fencing hot parts and bikes. Elliot was an entrepreneur, so his business kept growing. They washed money through his bike shop for years. He was kept off the list. He was known only to the inner Spartan circle. They had kept him clean. Since the fall of the Spartans, Elliot had been strictly legit.

When Frank had been released from prison he needed a job. A straight job. A square job. One where he could work and pay taxes and become a citizen. He called Elliot and asked for work. He knew Elliot wouldn't refuse him. He couldn't. He knew the kind of man Frank had been. Frank Kane only asked once. God help you if you didn't give him the right answer.

THE LAST SPARTAN

Chapter 2

Frank took Lamar and waited at the airport with him until his flight home departed. They didn't speak much. There wasn't much more to be said. After the plane took off, Frank drove home in his old Chevy truck.

Frank owned a small, two-bedroom house in a working class neighborhood. He parked in the gravel driveway and took off his work shirt. He tossed it onto the front seat. He didn't bother locking the truck as a matter of pride. His neighbors knew him by sight, if not by name. Who would dare to steal from him?

Dressed in his skin tight, red nylon t-shirt and his work pants, Frank took off on a leisurely five-mile run. He ran the same route every night after work. It was more than just exercise. It was an announcement to the neighborhood that he was still there, still to be reckoned with.

Usually his neighbors would wave greetings as he ran past. Often the young men would congregate as he passed. They would look and point and whisper among themselves. Occasionally, a local girl would make a point of being busy in her front yard as he passed. She would try hard to catch his eye. Frank just ran.

A little over an hour later he was back at his truck. He took the shirt off the seat and went to his front door. He unlocked it and went inside. The house was spartan by design. Others would have called it barren. There was a small television in the living room and an old sofa in front of it. In one bedroom was a single cloth-covered chair. There was a good lamp positioned behind it. Along the walls were several book cases filled with books. Most were histories by Kagan and Halberstam and Keegan or classic Greek authors like Thucydides and Herodotus and Xenophon and Plutarch.

The second smaller bedroom contained a small dresser and a mattress on the floor. A cheap alarm clock rested on the floor near the head of the mattress. A free standing full length mirror stood watch against one wall.

There was one bathroom with a full bath. There was a small linen closet. Towels hung from a cheap rack on the wall.

The house contained a small kitchen with a simple round table and three uncomfortable wooden chairs. There were the usual kitchen appliances. The shelves contained a hodgepodge of plates and glasses. There was no sign of a woman's civilizing touch.

Frank took off his work boots and socks. He dropped to the hardwood floor and began his regime of exercises. He did two-hundred-and-fifty push-ups and two-hundred-and-fifty sit-ups. Then he went to a doorway with a chin-up bar and did three sets of twenty-five pull-ups. He no longer lifted free weights. They made him feel bulky and slowed his reactions. His workout was based on primitive concepts: using the body as its own resistance, repetition, discipline, and pain. They called it calisthenics after the Greek words *kallos* for beauty and *sthenos* for strength. Beautiful strength.

Perfect.

Frank stripped off the rest of his clothes and walked into the bathroom. He took a cold shower. It hurt. The cold water stung his skin, and his body cried out in protest. But the pain made him feel good. That was one of the things Cyrus had taught him. To get beyond the fear of pain. He didn't love it the way a masochist loves pain, but he enjoyed his dominion over it. For many men the only way to be free of fear was to seek death. Recklessness is not the same as mastery. In prison he had placed pieces of gravel in his shoes, so as they cut into him, he would be forced to concentrate not to let it weaken him. Another small test. Forging the will.

He stood in front of the mirror. He studied his body with detached interest, like a man studying a sculpture. He ran a calloused hand over his stubbly scalp. He missed his long hair and beard. Unlike most Greeks, Spartan warriors grew their hair long. They wore beards to make them seem more fierce to their opponents. The Spartans had a saying that a beard made a handsome man ugly and an ugly man terrifying.

He was six feet four inches tall. He still weighed two hundred and twenty odd pounds. When he had joined the Spartans he had been a big, strong country boy. Over the years he had transformed his body, perfecting its strength and shape. He had virtually no body fat now. His diet had changed from alcohol, drugs, and fatty foods to fresh vegetables, protein, and water. His skin stretched like Saran wrap over an endless swell of muscles and tendons.

He stared at the scars from the twin bullet holes. They still held a bluish tinge around the edges, classic .9 millimeter wounds. In an arch across his stomach was the tattoo of a single word—SPARTAN. The letters were three inches tall. It was a mark reserved for those promoted to the position of First Citizen or Peer, much like the Mafia rank of "Made Man." A First Citizen had total rights over other Spartans. He could take whatever he wanted from them. His word was unquestioned. It was the law.

On his right forearm just above the wrist was a ritual scar. It was the Greek letter *L*, *lambda*, for Lacedaemonians. It looked like an inverted-*V*. Sparta was the city-state, but Lacedaemonia was the entire territory the Spartans controlled. The lambda was the sign of Spartan power. It was the insignia the ancient Spartan warriors wore on their great bronze shields. The scar was placed just above the wrist so that when two men met and clasped each other by the wrists, they could feel the scar and know you were a brother. All who were Spartans, or their associates, were required to wear the mark. On some it was more subtle. Women who worked as strippers and whores and drug runners also wore the mark. But on them it was ring size and burned into the flesh of their right buttock.

A varied array of tattoos ran the length of his left arm from his shoulder to his wrist. On his left shoulder was another ritual scar. This one was the size of a fifty-cent piece. It was the Greek symbol *pi*, for the letter *P*. This scarring was reserved for the most elite members of the Spartan Peers. The mark of the nucleus of the inner circle. The letter was chosen by Cyrus. It was attached to the first letter of a Greek God whose qualities the wearer represented. Only seventeen had ever been given this special distinction.

The letter pi was for Poseidon. Poseidon was the younger brother of Zeus, lord of the sea, great shoulders, earth shaker. Poseidon, the famed nemesis of Odysseus on his many travels.

Frank walked to the refrigerator and took out a liter of water. He walked naked out onto his back porch. A small washer/dryer unit sat on one side of the screened porch. Here was Frank's one indulgence. It was a two-man, Hot Springs tub/spa. It was self-contained and only needed a 110 plug to run it. There was a large plastic container with various spa chemicals inside. The spa was barely big enough for Frank alone. He slipped his body into the 105-degree water that sloshed over the sides. He unscrewed the cap on the liter water bottle and began to drink. He closed his eyes and thought about what he would have to do next. The path seemed clear. The only question was whether he could do it the easy way or if it had to be the hard way.

* * * *

Frank awoke a six o'clock. He climbed out of bed and did his routine of push-ups and sit-ups, then he ate a breakfast of fresh fruit and a chicken breast, washed down with a bottle of water. He dressed in fresh khaki pants and his Timberland work boots. He pulled on one of his sleeveless red t-shirts and covered it with a long sleeved, dark black, checked shirt. He found his gym bag and packed another pair of pants, blue jeans, and a couple of shirts and t-shirts. He opened his dresser and took out a thin beanie and put it inside. He stared for a few minutes into the drawer, then he removed three pairs of thin, brown leather gloves. Less chance of leaving trace evidence. Just in case he had to do it the hard way.

Frank went into the bathroom. He tossed in his electric shaver and his spare toothbrush from the bathroom. Under the sink behind the spare rolls of toilet paper was a manila envelope. Frank took it out and counted out three thousand dollars in hundreds and five hundred in twenties from the thick stacks. A small ruby ring fell out of the envelope into his hand. He stared at the woman's ring for a long minute, turning it over in his thick fingers. The tiny stone was flawless. He slipped it back into the envelope, then put the envelope back into its hiding place.

It was the last place anyone would look if they broke into his house. Frank knew, he had robbed enough homes. The envelope represented only a fraction of Frank's wealth. He had amassed a fortune with the Spartans. The money was secreted away under various aliases in safe-deposit boxes all over the country. Some money waited in checking accounts. He had a private attorney who activated the accounts every two years with small withdrawals to keep them from being closed. When Frank had been arrested he had been allowed one telephone call. He had called his private attorney. Someone kept clean from the rest of the Spartans' associates and informers. All he had said was that he was going away for a while and that the attorney should take care of things as they had discussed. That was all that was needed. Frank smiled slightly at the memory.

He added an electric screwdriver from his tool kit and a small leather case that held his lock-picking tools.

He glanced up into the mirror in front of him. There were other men who were larger, others who were stronger, others who were smarter, and still others who were more schooled in the ways of combat and brutality. There were even a few his size who were faster than he was. Not many, but a few. He saw the spark in his cold, blue eyes. What made him different from other men, what had made him feared, was what he had inside. It was his will. The iron discipline of a true Spartan warrior. The ability to commit to an outcome, no matter the obstacles, no matter the risks, no matter the cost. He was like some mythic supernatural beast. He would not quit, and he could not be stopped.

How many men had he killed as a Spartan? He couldn't remember. Fifty? A hundred? More? There had been so many. He did not see their faces in his dreams. They did not haunt his waking hours. They were only shadows. They had not deserved much better than they had gotten from him. They had all been corrupt and vicious. But still. . .

During his first year in prison he had only been allowed out of his cell for one hour a day. One day a week he was allowed to shower. He stood under the hot water that particular day and waited. The shower was empty. It had never been before. Something was going to happen. It didn't take long. Two young black men materialized at the entrance to the shower. One held a homemade shiv fashioned from a metal spoon. They stared at Frank. The older one encouraged the one with the shiv to do it.

Frank had not run or attacked them or done anything. He looked at them for a minute. They were probably not assassins sent to take him out. More likely they were trying to get respect to be allowed to join one of the black prison gangs. You had to show you were worthy before you were allowed to join. You had to establish your street cred or you might get turned out, made into somebody's prison bitch.

Frank had done the one thing they did not expect. He turned his back on them and continued to wash. In his deep voice he had said only, "Don't. Not if you want to live."

The two men stood rooted where they were. Their plan had seemed good. They weren't sure how good it was now. They didn't know who was predator and who was prey.

"Get on out of here. I won't ask a second time," Frank added moments later.

He had listened for their approach. None came. When he glanced over his shoulder they were gone. The shiv was on the floor. In the old days, before he had been reborn, he would have killed the two of them without a second thought. He never doubted he could have that day. But now he was a changed man.

He grabbed one of his fleece-lined corduroy jackets off the hook near the door. He walked out to his truck and tossed his bag onto the front seat, the jacket on top of it. He cranked the old engine up. It would take six hours to reach Atlanta from Greensboro. He would kill a couple more hours to give the detective time to do his job before he arrived. Time for war. A Spartan lived for it.

THE LAST SPARTAN

Chapter 3

He drove straight through, only stopping twice for gas and to buy a map of Georgia and a city map of Atlanta. He also bought three large bottles of water and an Atlanta Braves baseball cap. He rode in silence. His truck had no radio. It made it less appealing to thieves. A radio was one more unnecessary comfort that Frank didn't need.

Atlanta had not changed much since he had ridden there as the Spartans' enforcer. It was still a big, sprawling city and a transportation hub for the entire country. It was held up as an example of the "new south," but half of the residents of the new Atlanta were not even from the south. They came from up north and overseas. Since the days of the Spartans, Atlanta had grown to nearly four and a half million inhabitants. He hoped that would make it easier for him to stay invisible while he found Jenny.

He spotted a Comfort Inn off the highway. There were few cars in the parking lot. He drove past and stopped to get lunch. He chose an Applebee's restaurant and ordered a large chicken salad. He ate in the air-conditioned anonymity. Afterward he drove to the hotel. He registered under his own name. He paid cash and the old man at the register gave him a key to a first floor room as he had requested. He went inside and tossed his bag on the desk near the bed. He stretched out on the bed and turned on the television. He switched the channels to an all cartoon network and fell asleep.

At three o'clock he got up and went into the bathroom. He brushed his teeth and splashed cold water on his face. He opened the small individually wrapped bar of soap. He unscrewed the cap on the shampoo and poured some into the tub. He turned the shower on and let it run, then got a couple of the plain white towels and passed them through the stream of water. He cutoff the shower and tossed the towels onto the floor beside the tub.

Frank went back into the room. He pulled the comforter and sheets down on the bed and stirred them around. He propped the two pillows up facing the television and left the television on. He opened the curtains a couple of inches. He took the telephone book from the drawer under the telephone and put it into his gym bag. He took out one of his old denim shirts and hung it on one of the metal hangers. Anyone glancing through the curtains or checking the room would be

19

confident someone was there. Someone who would eventually be back.

He grabbed his bag and went outside. He climbed back into his truck and cranked the engine. He spread his maps out on the seat and checked his route. Satisfied, he refolded them and crammed them into the glove compartment. Frank had two problems to solve. He decided to solve the easiest first. He checked the parking lot again and drove to the office of Burt Wilson.

* * * *

Burt Wilson, owner and operator of Ace Detective Services, had an office located on the fourth floor of an old brick building. Frank parked in the paved lot outside. He took off his dark shirt and left it in the truck. He put his sunglasses behind the visor. He locked the truck and went into the lobby. A glass-covered roster showed who was in the building. Wilson shared the same floor with two other small businesses, AAA Pest Control and Falcon Carpet Cleaning. Perfect. Those offices would hold little more than answering machines and spare chemicals. He walked to the elevator and pushed the button for the fourth floor.

Despite what many modern people think, the Spartans were the most religious of all the Greeks. They constantly consulted oracles as to the gods' wishes. They made daily sacrifices. And they always watched for omens. Above the elevator door the symbol for the "up" arrow was actually shaped like the Spartan lambda. Frank smiled. It was a good omen. He slipped a pair of thin, leather gloves out of his pocket and put them on.

He knocked on the door labeled "Ace Detective Services." It was unlocked.

"Come in," a voice called from inside.

Frank opened the door and stepped inside. He quickly surveyed the office. It smelled of sweat and cheap cigars. The office consisted of one large room. A row of filing cabinets covered one wall. Across from it was a small table with a coffee pot and condiments. A radio sat quietly beside it. A small refrigerator crouched beneath the table. A second table filled the rest of the wall with a fax machine, answering machine, telephone, and various business supplies neatly arranged on the top. An expensive looking camera and camera bag also rested there. There was a large, old post office safe standing sentry in the far corner. There was an empty coat rack along the near wall with a large waste basket below it. There was a black garbage bag lining it, but it was empty. A sickly yellow plant struggled for light near the only window. In the center of the room was a large executive desk. Except for a computer monitor and keyboard, the desk was bare. Burt Wilson had apparently straightened things up in anticipation of having a visitor.

The man behind the desk stood up as Frank entered. He was in his late fifties. Most of his hair was gone, but he had tried to comb what was left of it over the top. He was medium height with a body that had once been strong but had since slipped into softness. He wore a cheap blue suit with a striped tie. Frank could see coffee stains on the tie. The jacket was hung over the back of the chair. The top right drawer of the desk was slightly open. That could mean only one of three things. It made Frank's decision easier.

The man stuck his hand out. "You must be, Frank. Lamar told me you were going to drop by."

Frank just stared at him. He didn't take the hand. After a few awkward seconds Burt let his hand drop. Frank turned to the framed pictures on the wall. He walked up and stared at the photos. It gave him an unobtrusive excuse to finish examining the room. He saw no hidden cameras. He walked from one picture to the next. They showed a younger version of Burt Wilson in various important days of his life. There was a picture of a uniformed Burt graduating from the police academy. A frumpy woman and two round-faced kids stood beside him.

Another picture showed Burt decked out in camouflage posed beside a dead boar. The Spartans had been great hunters in ancient Greece. They had hunted wild boar as well. Burt had used a large caliber rifle. The Spartans had used spears and nets and dogs.

There was a picture of Burt shaking hands with someone. A politician probably. There was a picture of Burt standing in front of a large black limo, his eyes squinted like Clint Eastwood.

"That one was when I guarded the president when he was down here for a speech," Burt volunteered.

Frank didn't say anything.

Another picture of Burt shaking someone's hand, this time in civilian clothes. The last picture was Burt, smiling big, giving the thumbs-up as he stood beside Michael Vick outside some restaurant. Vick was not smiling.

"You know Michael Vick?" Frank asked.

"You better know it. Best damn quarterback ever to play in the NFL. I still do some security work for him."

Frank turned back toward the desk. He forced his smiled. It was a chilling smile. "You were a police officer?"

"Fifteen years. Then I went private. Have a seat."

Frank continued to stand. "Did you have enough time, Burt?"

"Enough time for what?" Burt asked, perplexed.

"Enough time to check me out. I didn't want to press you. I wanted you to have plenty of time."

"Why would I check you out?"

"Burt, you're an ex-cop. You still got contacts. You can still access federal databases."

"Why would I want to do that?"

Frank looked into those dead cop eyes. All cops had the same tired, seen-it-all-before, flat eyes. They were dull. Lifeless. Frank didn't say anything. Burt tried the silent routine but couldn't hold it. The Spartans were famous for their long silences.

Burt glanced at the tattoos and scar on Frank's arms. "Yeah. I checked you out. So what?"

"What did you learn?"

"That you're an ex-con with a thick file, but not much ever stuck. Supposed to be real scary. But you don't scare me."

"I read your report on Jenny. Very detailed."

"I'm glad you liked it." The friendly, good old boy lilt was gone from the voice.

"Very professional looking. It really convinced Lamar and his wife. Of course, it was all bullshit."

"Don't come in here. . ."

"Burt, I read it all. It was a complete fabrication. You got to know your job better than I do. All your hard work was a smoke screen. You know as well as I do, Jenny came here on a bus. There was an outline of a bus ticket in the envelope Lamar brought you."

"It could have been anything," Burt answered defensively.

"Maybe. But you said you checked all the Greyhound manifests to make sure Jenny hadn't come by bus. You know buses don't keep passenger lists. They don't ask for ID. That told me you were lying."

"Since 9/11 they started."

"Look, I don't have a lot of time to waste, so I'm going to ask you a couple of questions, and then I'm out of here."

"Ask away."

"I'll only ask you one time."

"Fuck you. Ask me or don't. What the fuck you want to know, convict?"

"Do you know where Jenny is?"

"No. I told you already. I looked, but she's vanished if she was ever here."

"Vincent Street didn't tell you?"

"It's all in the report. He hadn't seen her since he came back. He was on the level."

"How much did he pay you to buy into that story?'

Burt's cheeks flushed red. A vein in his neck started to throb. Then he smiled. He sighed loudly and sat back down at his desk. He put his feet up on the top and leaned back. The soles of his shoes were wearing thin.

"I don't want to get into an argument with you. I'm a legitimate private detective. I do good work for a fair fee. I don't know where she is, but she's not here in Atlanta as far as I know."

Frank walked past Burt and looked out the window. The parking lot was just about empty.

Frank continued for him. "I understand what you are saying, Burt. Teenagers run away for lots of reasons, to lots of places."

"Now you're talking sense," Burt said, a little of the old bluster returning.

"So how do you want to do this?" Frank asked.

"Do what?" Burt said, swiveling in his chair a little to look at Frank.

Frank turned back and smiled. "Refund their money, of course."

Burt's right hand shot out toward the open drawer. Frank swept the back legs of the chair, tumbling Burt to the floor. Burt tried to scramble to his feet, but Frank grabbed his right hand and spun it around behind his back. He applied pressure to the wrist and turned the hand sharply inward. It was an old police move. He hoped Burt appreciated the irony. With Burt's arm locked behind him, he drove Burt onto the desk. Burt's large belly cushioned the impact, but it still drove the wind out of him.

Frank used one hand to keep Burt immobile while he opened the drawer the rest of the way. There was a large pistol inside. Frank pulled it out.

"Colt Python. Six-and-one-half-inch barrel. That's a mighty big gun. What were you expecting, an army?"

"Fuck you," Burt hissed.

Frank flipped the chamber open with his thumb and spun the cylinder to let the bullets fall to the floor. He tossed the gun across the room. He started to frisk Burt. Burt tried to wriggle free, so Frank applied more pressure. Burt held still. He found a hideaway piece in an ankle holster. It was a snub nosed .38 with a rubber grip. It held five rounds.

"You cops and your back-up pieces." He flipped the cylinder open and dumped the bullets on the floor with the others.

"I think it's time we open your safe and see what you got for a rainy day fund."

"Go fuck yourself," Burt snarled.

Frank gently pried Burt's right index finger back and broke it.

Burt started to scream, but Frank punched him in the kidney, and the sound died in his throat.

Frank didn't ask again. Once Burt's breathing had returned to normal Frank broke the second finger. Burt thrashed wildly to get free. Frank let him struggle, then slammed him back face-down on the desk. He broke the third finger.

Burt began to sob. Frank let him cry. When he was once again under control he took hold of his thumb and paused.

"Stop. Stop. I'll do it. You can have it."

Frank spun Burt around and pushed him toward the safe. Burt scrabbled on his knees and began working the combination. He had trouble working the knob with his left hand, but he managed. He swung the heavy door open and lunged his hand inside. He was too slow by ten years. Frank kicked him in the ribs, and Burt rolled against the table. Frank squatted down and looked inside the safe. An Austrian-made .40 caliber Glock 22 rested on the top shelf.

"You are a persistent little fucker, aren't you, Burt?"

Frank took the gun out and slipped it into the waistband of his pants.

"Now stay still, Burt. If you make a break for the door, I will shoot you through the back of your head, then I'll go to your house and kill your wife and your kids."

Burt lay where he was. He cradled his broken-fingered right hand with his left.

Frank found a leather money bag with a bank's logo stenciled on the outside. Inside was eight thousand dollars. Frank smiled.

"Close. But they paid you ten." He pulled out some files and began flipping through them.

"Hey, that's got nothing to do with you," Burt protested. "Those are other cases I'm working."

There were nude photos of a older man and a young blonde woman at a motel. There was also a list of payments on a piece of paper. There were three other similar files. And one with two men together.

"Blackmail, Burt? I'm proud of you. It takes a smart man to maximize his business opportunities."

He found two small bottles of white powder in the back. "You continue to impress me. Not all payments have to be in cash, I see." He dumped the powder into the safe. "A word of warning, Burt, just in case you try to burn me. You know a decent forensics man will find traces of this shit no matter how hard you try to clean it up. They'll take your license for sure. Maybe throw in a little jail time. Maybe reacquaint you with some of your old friends you put away when you were still on the force."

Burt sulked quietly.

There was a videotape in the back. The cover was blank. Frank just shook his head.

"No wonder everyone hates cops. You're as bad as I ever was. Now back up to your desk."

Burt got to his feet. His eyes slipped toward the office door.

Frank clicked the safety off and chambered a round. "Burt. Do like I tell you, and you'll come out of this alive."

Frank uprighted the chair, and Burt set down. "Now boot up your computer. Good. Pull up your business letterhead. Now write a little note to Lamar. Say something about how sorry you are you couldn't find his daughter. That you are a man of integrity. That you guarantee your work. And that you are refunding most of his payment. Thank him for allowing you to work for him, etc., etc. Good. Good. That's fine. Print it. Excellent."

"I can't sign it. You broke my fucking hand."

"That's alright, Burt. This will do just fine."

Frank picked the letter up from the printer. He folded it into thirds and slipped it into one of Burt's pre-stamped envelopes. Ace Detective Services was written in the upper left-hand corner along with the address. There was even a little logo of a magnifying glass next to his name. Frank slipped the envelope into his back pocket.

"Now go sit back in the corner by the window."

Frank went through the desk quickly. He found the tape recorder in the top center drawer. Cops were so predictable. He tossed it on top of the desk. There was nothing else of interest in the other drawers except spare ammo and blank computer disks.

Frank picked up the garbage can by the door and started stuffing it with the tape recorder, files, guns, money, and videotape. Burt said nothing. Frank walked over to the filing cabinet and found the copy of Jenny's file. He tossed it inside as well.

"Are there anymore files on what you did for Lamar?"

Burt just scowled.

"Don't make me start on your other hand."

"No," Burt said quickly. "That's everything."

Frank believed him. He unhooked the telephone and tossed the cable into the can. He tossed a phone book in and then knelt beside the computer. It was in a tower under the desk. He carefully disconnected the wires and tossed it inside the garbage can. He patted down Burt's coat and found his wallet and cell phone. He rifled through the wallet. Thirty nine dollars. Not much, but better than nothing. He turned the cell phone on.

"Come on, man. Don't take my cell."

"Tell you what. I don't want to be unreasonable. I'll drop it outside by the dumpster. You can get it after I'm gone. I just want a little head start."

He pushed the Glock's safety on. He ejected the round from the Glock's chamber and released the magazine. He thumbed the rounds out onto the desk then tossed the pistol into the garbage can.

"I'm leaving," Frank said.

"What about the refrigerator? You don't want to take it with you?"

Frank turned toward Burt. "Open the refrigerator."

"You got to be kidding."

"Open it."

Burt stumbled over to it and opened it. There were a few cans of Coke and a lunch bag.

"Toss the brown bag in here with everything else. I might get hungry."

Burt did as he was told, grumbling under his breath. "I would hate for you to leave me anything."

"I'm leaving you alive. That's more than I planned on doing. I'll tell you what, Burt. You think of something that will help me out, and I'll give you back your junk. That sound fair?"

There was a tiny flash behind Burt's cunning little eyes. "Sure. If I think of something, where can I find you?"

"I'm staying at the Comfort Inn off the Interstate, exit 42 B. But I'll only be there a day or so before I take off. If I haven't heard from you by then, I'll start burning this shit."

"Sure. Sure. If I think of something, I'll call."

"Great. Remember, you looked me up. You know what they say I've done in the past. You fuck with me, you'll end up in a box. You got that?"

"Yeah. Sure. I'm not stupid."

"You get a flash and remember how to contact Lamar and his wife, give them some trouble. . .well, you know what I'll do."

Burt nodded.

"Good." Frank backed out the door carrying the stuff of wicked dreams.

He walked to his truck and wedged the garbage can inside on the passenger's side. He walked over to the dumpster. He could see Burt in the window. He waved the cell phone in the air then tossed it into the green dumpster. He got in his truck and drove away.

* * * *

The flight from New York always seemed long to Yusef. Even in first class the seats seemed small and tight. He did not like to be cramped up. Sometimes airplanes felt like steel coffins to him. He could admit, to himself at least, that he had a touch of claustrophobia. He could manage it. He was a professional. He still missed the open deserts of his homeland.

Yusef took the crowded airport shuttle to his terminal then went down the long corridors to baggage claim. He did not like the crowds. He scanned them constantly for threats. He knew, given the opportunity, the Israelis would kill him. They had placed a bounty on his head years ago. So far, no one who had tried to claim it was still alive.

Yusef found his two dark leather suitcases. They were a deep, rich burgundy, the color of old blood. He walked outside, beyond the line of taxis, and checked his watch. It was a gift from the Ambassador. It was a Cabaret watch in white gold made by A. Lange and Sˆhne. The black rectangular face sparkled with inset diamonds. It retailed for sixty-five thousand dollars. He knew. He had had it appraised. On the back was an inscription in Arabic. It was simple. It read, "My brother." The watch kept very good time, but so did all watches. The watch was a sign of his importance to the Ambassador.

Yusef's eyes swept the bobbing signs until he saw the one with his name printed in Arabic on it. It was a small precaution he insisted upon. He approached the man holding the sign. The man had probably been waiting for some time. He knew better than to be late. They spoke in Arabic briefly. The man indicated a Lincoln Town Car with deeply tinted windows, then he opened the trunk and placed Yusef's bags inside. The car was kept ready at their disposal. A telephone call was all it took. No one else was allowed to use this vehicle. He took the keys from the man and drove away. Someone else would pick the man up and return him to his job. He drove to the Four Seasons hotel. They always stayed at the Four Seasons. The Ambassador loved it for all of its amenities. Yusef pulled up front and popped the trunk on the car. A bellman hurried to take his bags. The valet took the car keys and drove away.

Yusef went inside. The manager was beaming.

"It is so good of you to come. I hope your stay will be another pleasant one."

Yusef did not answer.

"If there is anything we can do for you or the Ambassador, do not hesitate to call," the manager continued. "We are here to serve."

Yusef drew a Montblanc pen from his suit pocket.

The man slid a registration card out for him to sign. Yusef signed in a flourish of Arabic that the manager could not read.

The manager smiled. "We have a case of the Ambassador's favorite champagne like he instructed, as well as the spiced lamb and other dishes he prefers."

Yusef nodded and extended his hand.

The manager passed him two keycards. One was for the elevator to the penthouse, the other was for the outer door of the presidential suite on the nineteenth floor.

Yusef turned and went to the elevator. A hotel employee hurried behind him with his luggage. They took the elevator to the penthouse and went inside.

The hotel man started to go into his usual spiel about the suites many luxuries. Yusef stopped him with a raised hand.

"I have stayed here many times. You do not need to explain it to me."

"Yes, sir. Sorry, sir. I forgot."

Yusef dismissed the apology with a wave of his hand. "Place my bags there in the hallway."

The man did as he was told.

Yusef held out a hundred dollar bill. "For you and the valet. See that the car is ready for me out front at eight o'clock."

"Yes, sir. Thank you, sir."

Yusef hated Americans. They were spoiled, lazy, and greedy. They were a morally bankrupt people. They had no control over their desires. They let their desires consume them. They and this entire country sickened him. How dare they act so arrogant? By the will of Allah, one day they would be humbled.

The man left, and Yusef walked to the draperies and pulled them back. The skyline of Atlanta was not as beautiful as his homeland, but it was beautiful in its own cold way. He went to his suitcase and opened the smaller of the two. He removed a rolled object tied with string.

Yusef unfurled his prayer rug. Inside was a worn copy of the Quran and a pistol nestled in its holster. He placed these to the side. He removed his socks and shoes and knelt on the rug facing toward Mecca. He began his prayers. He prayed at least five times a day.

The pistol was a cynical reminder of what was in store for him. He was a soldier for Allah. He would have to call Vincent soon to find out where the new girl was.

THE LAST SPARTAN

Chapter 4

Frank drove until he found a bank. He put on his dark checked shirt, sunglasses and ball cap before he went in. Never underestimate, he thought. He went in and quickly converted the eight thousand and thirty-nine dollars into a cashier's check for the same amount made out to Lamar. He put it into the envelope with the letter. The helpful cashier offered to add it to the bank's mail for him. Frank accepted, thanked her for her kindness, and left.

It was approaching five o'clock. He drove around Atlanta until he found a construction site. It didn't take long. On most job sites, the five o'clock whistle blew at four. Sometimes three. There was a flimsy chainlink fence around the building site. There was a new padlock on the gate holding an old chain. Nothing moved around the site. He shook the gate. Nothing. He slipped his lock-pick kit out of the truck and popped the lock. He drove his pickup truck inside and relocked the gate. He looked like ten thousand other redneck construction workers.

He drove around and parked near a fifty-gallon drum they used for burning. He climbed out of the truck and carried Burt's garbage can with him. He set the can down and squatted by it as he pulled out the files.

He tore the pictures in half and tossed them into the barrel. He started to ball up the printed pages when he heard noise behind him. Frank turned very slowly.

The guard dog was a Doberman Pinsccer. It was a deep chocolate brown with a surprisingly thick chest and a big head. The dog began a deep, throaty growl. Its head was down. The hair along its back stood at attention. Its ears were back and flat against the side of its head. The dog sniffed the air with deep breaths through its long nose. It was trying to identify the intruder. It was searching for a clue. It was trying to detect the rich scent of fear.

Frank had always been told to never look a strange dog directly in the eyes. To kneel and offer your hand so it could smell you. That was bullshit. He had faced many dogs in his life, and lowering yourself into a better target was never a good idea. Dogs were pack animals. They sought order and hierarchy. There was no fear scent. Frank wasn't afraid. He had killed guard dogs before with his bare hands.

The Doberman's weakness was its thin neck. He would hate to have to kill it. He stared hard at the animal before him.

"Sit," he ordered.

The dog hesitated.

"Sit," he commanded again, firmly.

The Doberman's ears popped up. It whimpered and began wagging its nub of a tail. It started to sit, then slunk forward with its rump inches from the ground. It whimpered again. Frank reached under its chin to pet it. He knew you never petted a strange dog from above. They might misinterpret that as an attack.

The dog rolled over onto its back. Frank knelt and rubbed the pale stomach. After a few minutes, Frank walked back to the garbage can and got out the brown bag lunch. Burt must have a healthy appetite. There were two empty tinfoil wrappers inside, but also two more sandwiches. He unwrapped them. They looked like ham and cheese in one and pastrami on rye in the other. He tossed the food to the dog. It was good policy to leave a hungry dog on watch.

The dog grabbed the food and wolfed it down. Frank went back to shredding the contents of the files. He lit one file and used it to light the paper already in the barrel. He continued shredding the files until they were all in the flames. He looked through Jenny's file to be sure there was nothing different from the copy Burt had sent Lamar. There wasn't. It too went into the flames. He threw the telephone cord in as well. No sense keeping it. The videotape was the final chaser. He was tempted to see what was on it, but decided it didn't matter. If Burt kept it in his safe, it had to be bad. He lifted the computer tower out and carried it back over to his truck.

He took his electric screwdriver out of his gym bag and took the shell off of the tower. He didn't know much about computers. When he had gone away, they weren't as popular as they were now. He removed the hard drive and used a brick to beat it into metal mush. He threw it into the fire as well. He took out all the insides, the memory chips and the motherboard. He smashed each with the brick before tossing them into the barrel. He took the two halves of the shell and threw each one a different direction. He did the same with Burt's garbage can after dumping the guns out onto the ground. He scrounged around the building site and found a few small pieces of wood and added them to the flames to help cover any evidence.

THE LAST SPARTAN

Another layer of ash and debris would help obliterate what he had been up to.

He opened the phone book and flipped through the yellow pages. He tore out all the pages having to do with adult services—strip clubs, genlemen's clubs, escort services, massage parlors, and juice bars. He patted the dog on his head and waited for the fire to die down. He wasn't in a hurry now. The bank had been a little risky, but now that that was done, he needed to stay out of sight until dark. Sitting by a low fire with a good dog seemed as nice a way as any.

Frank thought back to when he had died. It was a strange turn of events. He had wrecked Spanish Johnny's motorcycle on the dirt road leading to Lamar's farm. Frank had been propped against a tree. Lamar and his family just happened to be passing when his heart finally stopped. When they found him, Frank had no pulse. They were sure he was dead, but Sybil would have none of that. She performed CPR just as she had been taught back when she was a nurse for twenty years. She was relentless, and it kick-started his heart. Lamar had hoisted him into the back of their pick up. Sybil had kept a check on Frank's vital signs as they drove toward their farm. It was closer than the hospital. Little Jenny had pushed his intestines back inside him where they were spilling out. She had used her sweatshirt to apply pressure to the ghastly wound.

Somehow they had managed to get him into the house and into a bed. They called the doctor, but he was away. They could only leave a message. Sybil stitched up the wound in his belly. Both of the .9 millimeter bullets were still lodged in his chest. By all rights either one should have killed him, but for some reason they hadn't hit with their usual force. While Frank drifted in and out of consciousness, she removed the bullets. She cleaned the bits of his clothing from the wounds and soaked the holes with peroxide and iodine.

It was on the start of the second day before the doctor finally arrived. He checked Sybil's work, announced that it was excellent, and pumped Frank full of antibiotics. He hooked up an IV and left several bags of saline and dextrose. He promised to return with more soon. The doctor didn't think it was safe to try and move Frank. It could kill him. The third day thesSheriff arrived to see the injured man. It was obvious even to him that someone had tried to kill Frank.

Frank was in a coma. He had no identification on him. The

sheriff fingerprinted him and had the motorcycle carried into town. The highway patrol had arrived the next morning. The fingerprints had told them who Frank was. The highway patrol had insisted he be moved to a secure hospital location. Sybil and the doctor stood firm. Eventually the highway patrol men left.

Frank regained consciousness after a week. Lamar told him what had happened. When the police learned Frank was conscious, they sent a man out to stand guard. Lamar, Sybil, and Jenny took turns watching over Frank.

One night, Sybil was sitting vigil when she got up suddenly and moved her chair close to his bedside.

"You awake?" she asked. She didn't bother to whisper.

Frank nodded.

"Everything happens for a reason," she said. "With God's help, I was able to reach into hell's heart and bring you back to life."

Frank stared at the old woman but didn't speak.

"Either you're a man or you ain't. There's a debt that needs paying. You got your second chance. You'll use it or you won't."

"Do you know who I am?" Frank asked, his voice raw.

"The police were quick to tell us once they learned. That don't mean a hill of beans now."

"They told you the things I've done?"

"Enough."

"I was a bad man."

"Don't matter now. That man died back under that tree out yonder. You been reborn. Resurrected from the grave, boy. You got a chance most men don't get. Make amends. Do good while you still can."

"And I will find forgiveness?" Frank asked. There was a clear tone of mockery in his voice.

"Don't know about that. God don't forget past deeds."

"I thought you were trying to inspire me. Your god seems awfully harsh."

"Life's hard, boy. And you chose to live it that way."

"Thanks."

"Don't go soft on me. The world is in balance. Sounds like you did a heap of bad. That tilted the scale. Now you have a chance to right the scale. Do the right things. Forgiveness is between you and

God. When you're ready to ask, he'll forgive you. But until then, make amends."

"I don't know if I can."

"That name you got for your gang, Spartans, I know a thing or two about them real fellas. They lived for honor. Courage. Loyalty. Those were the things that mattered to them. You live that way, you'll be alright, I reckon."

She got up to leave.

"I'll try," Frank said.

She turned back and smiled. It took twenty years off the lined, leather-like face. At one time she might have looked like a passably attractive woman. "You'll do a sight more than try. I can tell. You got the will in you. Else you woulda been gone for good."

Her words struck a chord in Frank. They reminded him of an ancient Spartan maxim: Look to the end. It meant that you should never judge a man's life until you saw how he died. He owed her his life. He would do as she asked.

On the twelfth day they had moved him to the hospital. Eventually he was charged with illegal possession of a firearm, carrying a concealed weapon, and possession of a stolen motorcycle. Frank refused legal counsel or to speak at his trial. Rebirth had to include punishment. The ancient Spartans loved punishment. He would take his. They were petty charges, but the DA had pushed hard. They had sentenced Frank to four years.

He served three years active and was on parole for a year. During that time, Lamar, Sybil, and Jenny all came to see him every third Sunday. He got to look forward to their visits more and more. It kept him strong. After prison he had moved away, and their contact had settled on occasional telephone calls. He had forgotten how much they had meant to him. How much he missed them.

Chapter 5

Frank left the dog at the construction site and drove back into the city. He found a nice steak place and ordered the twelve ounce filet mignon with a side of asparagus and squash. He left a little after eight o'clock. He walked through the parking lot looking for the right vehicle but didn't find what he wanted. He checked his map and drove to Vincent Street's address. He knew if Burt had planned on trying to catch him there he would have already given up by now. Burt didn't seem like a patient man.

He drove around the building a few times to see if it was watched. He didn't spot anyone. To be on the safe side, he parked three blocks away. He turned his gym bag upside down on the floorboard so the black bottom pointed upward. To a casual observer, the floor of the truck's cab would appear empty. He locked the truck and walked back to Vincent's building. He pulled the baseball cap down low over his eyes. He checked the mailboxes and saw a listing for a V. Street. He picked the lock but only found a foreign newspaper and a bunch of discount flyers. He walked across the street to a small park directly opposite from Vincent's apartment.

Not a bad building. Decent view. The guy obviously had some money. Frank buttoned his shirt all the way up. He checked under the nearest tree to be sure no dog had left him a present. He stretched out under the tree with his back resting against it. For a second he flashed back to his ambush five years before. But the image faded. In the shadows, he knew he was practically invisible to anyone walking past on the street. From the lighted apartment building he was totally invisible. He placed the stolen newspaper over his lap. He could be a workman who had fallen asleep after a few too many rounds at the local bar. He could be a poor homeless guy down on his luck. Whatever he was, he was harmless.

The building was big with four large apartments. He watched the light in Vincent's apartment but saw no movement inside. He could be patient. This was just the first night. Time for a little recon.

Three hours later it was creeping up on eleven o'clock. He stretched his cramped muscles and walked back to his truck. There was a flyer on the window about an escort service, but otherwise no one had bothered it.

He drove back toward the Comfort Inn. He drove past to the next large motel he found. He casually cruised the parking lot and parked beside a big black Cadillac from Florida. It had seen some long miles. He locked the truck and walked back to the Comfort Inn.

He slipped around the building through the surrounding darkness. There were a few more cars in the parking lot, but not many. He worked his way to where he could see his room. The light filtered out from inside, and the curtains were still cracked. He watched for twenty minutes but saw nothing suspicious. He worked his way back around to the main entrance and slipped into the lobby. It was empty except for the clerk. The desk clerk was new. He was young, about twenty-two, with long greasy black hair and quick ferret eyes.

Frank walked up to him wearing a small smile. "I'm Frank Kane. Any messages for me?"

Something slid across the man's face. "No. Sorry."

"Anybody come to visit? Leave a note?"

"No. Not while I was on duty."

"What time is your shift?"

"Six to six."

"And no one came by?"

"Nope." Ferret-boy went back to staring down at the registration book on his desk.

Frank pulled a hundred dollar bill out of his pants. He slide it across the counter to the boy. One big hand still rested on it.

"Think hard, now. You're sure? No one?"

The boy smiled. He reached out for the bill. "Well, now that I think about it, three guys did come by about seven."

Frank didn't release the bill. "And?"

"Like I said. They might have been cops. Asked for your room number."

"They show you a badge?"

"It wasn't necessary. You can always spot a cop. It's the way they walk. Look everything over. Pushy assholes, like the world should bow down to them."

Frank released the money. The boy scooped it up and slipped it into his pants pocket.

"You give them a key to my room?"

"Like I said, they were cops. What was I supposed to do? They went down, came back ten minutes later. Said not to tell you they had been by."

"They tip you like I did?"

"Hell no. They said they'd be back before morning, and if I saw them to stay quiet."

"Do you remember what they looked like? One of them have a hand that was fucked up?"

"He sure did. It was all bandaged up. The other guys all looked like him. Old guys in bad suits. Beer bellies, bad breath, bad hair. Middle-aged shit."

"Thanks. I thought I might have some company."

"There was one thing odd. The more I think about it, I'm not sure they were real cops."

"Why's that?"

"They were driving a white car—"

"Cops love white. Easy to touch up the paint."

"Sure. But this was a Honda Accord. I never seen a cop in a Honda Accord. And never three together in one."

"You may be right. Well, good night."

"You going back to your room?"

"Sure. Why not? I paid for it. I ain't afraid of three old cops."

The boy bobbed his head in agreement. "Fucking-a, man."

Frank walked out of the lobby toward his room. Once out of sight of the desk clerk, he angled away into the darkness. The three guys in the Accord would be back around four in the morning, he figured. It was the perfect time for a surprise attack. The late nighters would be asleep, and the early risers wouldn't be up yet. It caught everyone at their most vulnerable time.

There were some things Frank was sure of now. He knew Burt had talked with Vincent. That was his job. He knew Vincent had bought or scared Burt off. A payoff was the more logical of the two. He knew Burt liked to play both ends of a deal.

Frank had told Burt where he was staying for a reason. His response would tell Frank a lot. Burt only had so many options. If he did nothing, he was a coward. Cops, even ex-cops, never liked to think of themselves that way. If Vincent Street was a serious player with serious muscle behind him, Burt would tell him about Frank's visit. Vincent would probably put a bullet in Burt's head to show his thanks, then Vincent would send professional muscle to take care of Frank. That Burt showed up at the motel with a couple of his former cop buddies told Frank something different. The deal with Vincent was over. There was no more profit in it for Burt. There were thousands of runaway girls. Jenny was just one more. A lone man in a strange city, even as tough a guy as Frank, seemed a pretty safe target. Real cops would have identified themselves as police officers and shown the clerk their IDs, even if they had been working off the clock.

These guys wouldn't have killed Frank. That would have been too much. Burt just wanted his files and hard drive and money. A severe beating should do the trick. He was pretty sure Burt had gotten a glimpse of his plates. He didn't doubt for a second that Burt had pulled up his license number and had his friends on the force looking for Frank's car.

Frank worked his way back to his truck. He took the electric screwdriver out of his bag, quickly removed the license plate from the Cadillac he had parked next to earlier and put it on his truck. He didn't bother putting his license plate on the Cadillac. He would need it later.

He felt below the cushion on the passenger's side until his fingers found the razor thin slit. He carefully worked his license plate into the slot. He had done it before.

He started the truck and eased out of the parking lot. The Caddy's owner probably wouldn't even notice it was gone and would be on his way home soon enough. If anyone spotted Frank's old pickup truck and checked the plate, they would probably stop when they saw it had a Florida tag, not North Carolina. The Cadillac had some road wear, so the owner was probably a traveling salesman of some kind. If he had any brains, he would list his car as a business car, or it might even be a company car. Either way it would come up as a commercial vehicle. If someone checked a little deeper on Frank's new license plate, it would show it was a commercial vehicle. If they saw Cadillac, they might think it was a mistake or a joke. He felt pretty safe. He planned to be out of Atlanta in a few days anyway. Let them try to find him.

His home loan and deed were under his nephew's name. The car tag under one of his aliases at a different address. They could never track him through that. Frank wasn't a fool.

It was a nice night. The October nights were quickly moving from warm to cool. He rolled his window down to help keep him awake. He was starting to wear down a little. He thought he might find a convenience store, get a few things, find a new motel room. Get some real sleep. He wasn't stupid enough to ever go back to the Comfort Inn.

THE LAST SPARTAN

Chapter 6

The Handy Mart's parking lot was empty except for an old rusted out Ford Taurus. Frank pulled up to the pumps and filled his tank. He liked to keep a full tank whenever he could. You never knew when you might need to cover some serious distance, and you didn't want to be stopping to find gas. An old Chevy Nova eased into the parking lot and parked beside the dumpster. It sat silent. Could be anything. Kids hot boxing. Maybe something worse. He went inside the convenience store.

The man behind the counter was Indian or Pakistani. He nodded by way of greeting. Frank did the same, then wandered back to where the bottled water was kept. He chose a large bottle and a package of beef jerky. He slowly made his way toward the cash register. He paid for the gas and supplies. He pocketed his change and the beef jerky, then did a slow examination of the magazine rack. He pretended to be studying the various men's magazines while keeping an eye on the car. He might be paranoid. Probably was nothing.

A dark gray Acura pulled up in front of the store. Frank immediately noticed the Acura symbol looked like the Spartan lambda. It was an omen. Had to be. A guy got out. He was young, maybe early twenties with medium-length brown hair and a slight build. He was wearing baggy cargo pants and a white pullover shirt. He hurried inside.

"Yo, Sayed. How's it going tonight, dude?"

The clerk shrugged. "Always slow this late, DC."

The young man walked up to the register. "I need a couple packs of Monarchs and one of Marlboro Lights."

The clerk turned to the rack of cigarettes behind the counter.

Frank saw the doors open on the Nova. Four black teenagers got out. They were still hanging back from the store, still loitering in the shadows. They had a bag with a bottle inside and passed it around. They each kept shifting their eyes toward the store. Sayed was occupied behind the counter and hadn't noticed them yet.

"How many packs you want, DC?"

"Three."

"Three each. Three of Monarch and three of Marlboro Lights?"

"No, man. I told you. Three all together. Two of Monarch and one of Marlboro Lights."

Sayed turned back to the display and got the cigarettes down. He was still confused. "Did you say two of Marlboro Lights or one?"

"One."

Sayed picked up the extra pack and turned to replace it. DC rolled his eyes at Frank and smiled. It was a pleasant smile.

The four black men had moved outside the main door. They were getting their courage up. Frank had seen it before. It was classic pack mentality.

DC paid and headed out the door. He was busy opening a pack of the Monarch and had his head down. Frank winced as DC ran directly into the four teens. Their bottle crashed to the ground.

"Oh, shit. Sorry, dudes. My bad," DC quickly apologized. "I'll get you another one. What're you drinking?"

One of the men wearing a white t-shirt shoved DC hard in the chest. DC stumbled to the ground.

"Better watch your step, mother fucker," White T-shirt growled.

DC stayed calm. He picked up his cigarette packets. "Stay cool, brother. There's no need for that."

DC got back to his feet. Another of the four, this one wearing a black do-rag, struck DC across the mouth with a hard backhanded blow, knocking him off his feet again. DC wisely stayed down.

"I ain't your fucking brother. Better watch who you disrespecting, fool." Do-Rag said. "I don't take to no white beeeach gettin' all up in my grill."

Sayed reached for the telephone. He had seen what was happening. Frank reached a hand out and touched Sayed's wrist.

"Cops will never make it in time. Stay tight, let me see if I can straighten things out."

"You are not going out there?" Sayed asked rather than said.

"Seems like the best plan. Stay off the phone until I get back."

Sayed let his hand fall away from the receiver. He stood with his mouth open as Frank stepped outside.

Frank took a long drink from the water bottle and screwed the cap back on.

"We got a problem here?"

Frank's size didn't intimidate them. There were four of them. Do-Rag turned his anger at Frank.

"This ain't your 'biness, red neck. You know what's good for you,

you be gettin' your cracker ass out of here."

"And if I don't?"

Do-Rag smiled and lifted up the front of his shirt. The black handle of a pistol protruded from his pants' waistband. "Then I be bustin' a cap in your big motherfuckin' country ass."

The other teens all grinned in support. Pack mentality. The two rules for taking on multiple enemies were simple. Always go after the leader first. Break him hard, and the others are less likely to fight. The other rule was don't follow any other rules.

Frank hit Do Rag across the face with the water bottle. It was a good blow that combined the weight of the bottle with the power of Frank's massive arm. Frank's speed left no time for reaction.

Even as Do-Rag's nose exploded and he fell, Frank delivered second blow across the left shoulder, breaking the clavicle. Do-Rag was tough, he tried to draw his gun from his pants. Frank smashed a big booted foot down on his right elbow, breaking it. Do Rag rolled on the ground screaming. Frank knelt and retrieved the pistol from his pants. It was a Beretta, one of the 92 models. It was a nice gun. Brand new. The others hadn't moved. Frank glanced over his shoulder. Sayed was still standing, watching, frozen by the action. Frank had to be quick.

Do-Rag rolled in agony on the ground. Frank placed a foot against his neck and held him still. The moans grew quieter.

"Shhh," Frank said. He looked at the faces around him. There was no fight in them with their leader down. He held Do-Rag's gun loosely, but the threat was there. "Hand over your guns," he said.

The teenagers glanced at each other. No one moved.

"I won't ask again," Frank said.

White T-shirt took a .38 out of the back of his pants and handed it to Frank. Frank stuck it into his back pocket.

"And yours," he said to the one in the FUBU longsleeve.

A small .32 appeared from a front pocket. Frank stuck it into his other back pocket.

"And yours."

The last teen was trembling. "I ain't got no piece, man."

"Then let me have the blade. It a switch or butterfly?"

"Butterfly," the teen said and took the knife out of pocket and handed it to Frank.

Frank reached a hand down to help DC back to his feet. Blood trickled from his nose and mouth.

"Get their driver's licenses. Start with the pile of shit at my feet."

DC knelt over Do Rag and took out his wallet. Docilely the teens took out their driver's licenses and passed them to DC.

Now, you gentlemen would be wise to take your friend to a hospital. The guy inside will have your IDs, so I don't want you ever coming back, or the cops will put you away. Now get the fuck out of here."

The three teens lifted their friend and carried him over to the car. Moments later, they went screeching out of the parking lot.

"Let's get you cleaned up," Frank said, guiding DC back inside the store. DC smiled weakly and hustled back to the bathroom in the rear of the store.

Frank saw Sayed's hand was on the telephone.

"No need," Frank said. Frank laid the pistol on the counter. He handed the four driver's licenses to Sayed.

"Lock these away somewhere. I don't think those thugs will ever come back here, but if they do, you got insurance."

"Thank you, sir. They meant to rob me, did they not?"

"They were sizing you up alright. Might have been a straight stickup. Might have offed you as the only witness. It's a dangerous job you got. Ever been robbed before?"

"Once. But it was long ago when I first bought this store."

"This your business?"

"Yes, it is."

"You got cameras for surveillance, right?"

"Yes. Everything is taped. And the tapes are locked away."

"I got a favor to ask of you, Sayed. I need you to erase those tapes. You got positive ID on the guys, so you don't need the tapes. And I'm not exactly in the best standing with the local cops. It would put me in a bad way if they saw those tapes."

Sayed held up one hand. "Say no more." He turned to a cabinet behind him and unlocked it. Three VCR recorders were inside. He ejected all three tapes. He handed the tapes to Frank.

"For what you have done, this is a small thing. If you are ever needing anything, you come and see me."

"Thanks, Sayed. I appreciate it."

DC came out of the bathroom. He had wiped away the blood and was holding a wet paper towel against his lip. He stuck his hand out.

"I'm Donny Chaplain. Everyone calls me DC."

"Nice to meet you, Donny."

"No, its DC."

"Like Washington, D.C.?"

"No. Like the skateboard company. You know, they make shirts and shoes and shit."

Frank looked blank.

DC shrugged. "You saved my ass back there."

"No problem, Donny."

"Whew. I could use a drink. How about you?"

Everything happens for a reason. That was what Sybil had told him when she saved his life. Look for divine guidance in everything that happens.

Maybe she was right. It sure seemed like it a lot of the time. The ancient Spartans were like that, too. Except when they got a bad omen. They would refuse to accept it, thus nullifying the interpretation. At the battle of Plataea, the Spartan king had taken four sacrifices before he found one favorable for battle. Good news or no news.

"Sure," Frank said.

"Killer. I know a great place to get this negative shit out of our heads."

"Lead on. I'll follow you," Frank said. "Good night, Sayed."

They headed outside.

"How did you know that one kid had a blade?" DC asked.

"Got to have something if you're running with a hard crowd. It had to be a blade."

"But why a switchblade or a butterfly knife?"

"Only two knives with the proper image for a young tough."

DC nodded as if it made perfect sense once it was explained. "What's your name?"

"Frank."

"Got a last name?"

"Everybody's got one."

"Mind telling me what it is?"

"You don't need to know me that well."

DC laughed. "Come on, Just Frank. I owe you a drink. Maybe even get a smile out of you if you're not careful. People say I'm a very funny guy."

Frank got into his truck and followed DC into the city. Wonder what DC meant about the smile? Frank smiled. He smiled a lot. Frank had a good sense of humor. Just like the ancient Spartans. Everybody just assumed the Spartans didn't. They were just serious about the art of warfare. They fought silently. That didn't mean they couldn't laugh. Dumb ass. Frank unspooled the surveillance tapes as he rode and tossed them out the window.

THE LAST SPARTAN

Chapter 7

Burondo Geisha, The Blonde Geisha, was a very exclusive men's club. It wasn't listed in any telephone directory. That was because it was a fetish club. Its membership requirements were very strict. Each member had to be referred by a current member; the members had to be wealthy; only Japanese men were allowed to become members.

The entrance to the Blonde Geisha was on street level, but you had to take a flight of stairs up to reach the club. There was a Japanese doorman at the street entrance to prevent uninvited visitors.

The club interior was art deco, all done in black and white. There were fifteen large booths facing a central stage. The stage was lighted from beneath and gave the women who performed there the appearance of being lighted statues. On the stage, women dressed in various costumes, ranging from latex and leather to feather wings and gossamer thin panties, writhed in stylized simulated sex acts. The women never actually touched. In fact, they made it clear they were not touching, only mimicking the erotic actions. They never came closer than inches from the areas of their erotic focus.

The Japanese gentlemen sat rigidly at the tables watching the tableau unfold before them. All the tables were bare except for a small lamp. When a member wished for service, he would turn on the small lamp. Madame Yung would approach, and the gentleman would request a drink and certain waitress. Madame Yung would place the drink order and have the desired girl deliver it. Behind her, on the table, Madame Yung would leave a large silk napkin.

The waitresses were all young American girls with their hair dyed blonde. No natural blondes were hired. No Asians were hired. The waitresses were all dressed in identical outfits. They wore very short, pleated, black-and-white plaid Catholic schoolgirl skirts. The ones never worn at any Catholic school, but in every man's fantasy. The girls wore white, sheer tops. Dark bras were worn beneath the tops so they would be visible. The girls were allowed to choose the color of their bras. The girls also wore white knee-high socks and black patent leather shoes.

The chosen girl would approach the gentleman's table and place the drink down. The charge and appropriate tip were charged directly to the member's account. The member, if he so desired, would raise the edge of the napkin for the girl to see. If there was money beneath it and the girl wished to, she would kneel beside the table. Without making eye contact with the member, she would reach beneath the table. The member's zipper would be drawn downward. She would hold the napkin with one hand and masturbate the Japanese gentleman with her other hand until he had an orgasm. The member would never look at her, speak to her, or acknowledge her presence in any way. He would stare at the women performing on the stage only. As far as the sex trade went, this was mild stuff. Japanese men were desirable customers because they were very polite, very clean, and came very fast.

This was where Jenny and her roommate Caron worked. Caron's actual name was Karen, but she felt the new spelling seemed more mature and exotic. In the Blonde Geisha, Jenny was called Kochou Chiisai, which meant Little Butterfly. Caron had worked at the club for four months. This was the start of Jenny's second week.

A small lamp flicked to life on table five. Madame Yung approached. Her head was down. Her hands were clasped before her. She wore a typical geisha costume. She bowed slightly.

"Sukocchi," the man said. "Kochou Chiisai."

Madame Young bowed. She placed the napkin on the table and moved away slowly, respectfully. She spoke the order to the bar man. He grunted understanding. Madame Yung hurried over to Jenny. She called her only by her Japanese name, Kochou Chiisai.

"Kochou Chiisai, table five has requested you to serve him his Lagavulin."

Jenny nodded.

"He is a very good customer," Madame Yung continued. "Very influential. Very wealthy." She rubbed her fingers together to add emphasis to the last part.

"I know," Jenny said without much enthusiasm.

"He does not feel welcome. You do not make him feel welcome."

"I'm sorry. Maybe he should request another girl."

"He does not want another girl. He wants you. He has been in every night this week. Each time he request Kochou Chiisai, Little Butterfly. Yet, you dishonor him. You only bring him his drink."

"I'm sorry."

Caron walked up and put an arm around Jenny's shoulders. "Leave her to me. Trust me, Jenny girl, it's not that bad."

"I don't know. The first time I tried I gagged so bad I thought Madame Yung would fire me."

"She won't fire you. Everybody loves Little Butterfly," she mocked.

"You too?"

"Relax. Here, take this." Caron offered her a small white pill.

"What is it?"

"Trust me. It'll make it easier. I know."

Jenny took the pill. She went to get the Scotch for table five. Within minutes, she felt the warm glow inside. She felt good. For the first time in weeks, she felt good, really good. Life seemed alright. In fact, life was pretty damn good. She got the drink and carried it over to the man's table. He lifted the edge of the napkin. There was a fifty dollar bill beneath it. President Grant watched her with the hooded eyes of an alcoholic. Jenny didn't know if she had ever seen a fifty dollar bill before. She took a deep breath. She scooped the money up and tucked it into her front shirt pocket. She picked up the napkin and knelt down beside the table.

Chapter 8

Donny led Frank to Pandora's Box, a gentlemen's club. Frank liked the Greek allusion. It was probably some kind of omen. He backed his truck into a open space near the building. No reason to give someone an easy look at his new license plate.

He met Donny beside the front door of his truck.

"Button your shirt up, man. This is a high-class place. They got a dress code."

Frank buttoned up. Donny nodded his approval.

"That's better. Now you don't look quite so scary."

Frank forced a smile.

They walked up to the door. A doorman dressed all in black opened the door to let three businessmen out. The men were all wearing expensive coats and ties. They were laughing and high-fiving each other as they stumbled off into the parking lot. The doorman was no bigger than a small mountain. He eyed Frank with a mixture of curiosity and latent menace. Frank did not challenge the other man and followed DC inside.

A hostess in a faux Greek tunic met them. It was all white and very sheer. Gold cords crisscrossed the front, separating and accentuating her breasts. She wore sandals that laced up to just below her knees. She was young, extremely pretty, and definitely not Greek.

"DC. It's good to see you, baby." She gave DC a hug and a small kiss on his cheek. She smiled at Frank. "Ten to get you in," she purred.

Frank looked blankly at her.

"Come on, Connie. He's with me. It's late, cut him some slack."

Connie smiled. "Okay. Anything for you, DC."

They walked into the main room of the club. It was very large. One of the largest Frank had ever seen. There were three main stages with tables and chairs set up all around them. Behind the chairs was a section of small sofas. The club was divided into two floors. The VIP rooms were probably up the wide set of stairs. A long ebony bar stretched halfway across the far wall.

"Come on," DC said.

The bar area was nearly deserted. Most of the patrons favored being closer to the action, so Frank and DC had no touble finding seats at the bar. They took seats at the far end. A thin Hispanic man came over to take their orders.

"I want a Vodka, naked. The good stuff you keep in the back. The French one. Grey Goose. And don't water it down, just one cube of ice."

The man nodded as if insults were routine. "And you, sir?"

"What will you have, Frank?"

"It's been a long time. I guess I'll have a beer."

"What kind?"

"Any kind. A longneck." Frank liked the long neck bottles because they could easily be transformed into weapons if things turned bad. Always be prepared. That was the Spartan way.

The bar man went off to get their drinks.

"You like this place?" DC asked.

"It's a little ritzy for me. Most of the strip clubs I've been to are rougher."

"Not any more. Biker bars are a thing of the past. Now they're all gentlemen's clubs. Makes them more appealing."

"Whatever."

"Cool name, though. You know the story of Pandora's box?"

"Not exactly," Frank lied. He had read a great deal about Greek myths, but he wanted to hear DC's version.

"Pandora was the first beautiful woman. Zeus sent her down to earth as a gift. But she carried a box with her that she was supposed to keep closed. When her curiosity made her open it, all the evils of the world came out. That's when men started lying, cheating, and stealing. All because of what was in Pandora's box. You get it?"

"I think so."

"I mean the sexual metaphor of the story, dude. They say you can pull a battleship across the ocean with a cunt hair."

Frank looked blank.

"She opens her box, and men go crazy. Just like they're doing here. Men come in hoping for a glimpse of Pandora's box."

"Then it is a cool name."

DC nodded to himself over the thumping of the techno music playing through the loud speakers. "Listen, Frank. That was awesome the way you handled those black dudes back at the store."

Frank shrugged.

"I'm serious. Are you former military? Special forces? Delta? Some shit like that?"

"No. I'm nobody."

"It ain't a nobody handles something like that so coolly. You looking for work?"

"Why?"

"I mean a man of your talents. I got connections in Atlanta. I could find you work."

Frank didn't ask what kind of work. He knew what kind. Instead he asked, "What's in it for you, Donny?"

"Nothing. Just paying you back for helping me out back there at the store. I mean if you're looking for work."

The bar man brought their drinks. DC toyed with the swizzle stick in his drink before tasting it. He grimaced and then smiled. "Sweet."

Frank stared hard at him. "What's in it for you, Donny?"

Donny couldn't hold his stare. He looked away, then back at his drink. His eyes danced about the room. Finally, they returned to Frank.

Frank took a slow drink of his beer. It tasted so familiar. It had been five years since he had taken a drink of alcohol. The sensation was as natural as slipping on your favorite pair of boots. It fit, perfectly.

"What's your end, Donny?"

DC looked away again. "I make a little something if you get hired. That's all. Not a big cut. Just a little thank you if I find somebody reliable."

Frank smiled. "You play the middle. That it, Donny?"

"Yeah. Sometimes."

Frank patted him hard on the back. "Good. I got no problem with a man making some coin. I just don't care to be lied to. I take that as a personal insult."

DC smiled back. "I would never do that to you, Frank. We're friends, aren't we? Friends don't do friends. Isn't that right?"

"That's how it's supposed to work." Another drink of cold beer. Liquid gold.

"That reminds me, Frank. About those guns. What are you going to do with them?"

"Why?"

"Do you always answer a question with a question?"

"Why?"

"Never mind. Anyway, they could bring a good piece of change if you fenced them to the right people."

"And that would be you?"

"Sure. Like I said. I know some people who know some people. How many did you get back there? Three? I could probably get you three hundred for all three. If you're interested."

Frank smiled and took another drink. "Donny, what about that bullshit about friendship?"

"What do you mean?"

"Three hundred. The Beretta itself is worth eight from a gun store. It hasn't even been fired."

"You can't get eight on the street."

"I'll tell you what I'll do, Donny, since we are such good friends. You help me move 'em, I'll split the money with you. In return, you let me crash at your place while I'm in town."

"How long you planning on staying?"

"Two, three days tops. I got some business to take care of and I need a quiet place to crash."

"I take it you don't like hotels?"

"Exactly."

"Don't like all that registering and ID shit?"

"Exactly."

DC thought for a few moments. "Shit. Why not? You got yourself a deal, dude. Hell, you saved my ass." He raised his glass and clinked it against Frank's bottle. "Done deal."

DC waved the hovering Hispanic bartender back over. "Hey, man. Tyronne working tonight?"

"He's pouring the champagne in the VIP room upstairs. He should be back down in a few minutes."

"Tyronne?"

"He's my connection for the guns. Why did you think I chose this place?"

"Shrewd."

DC tapped his temple. "Always thinking, dude. Always thinking."

Tyronne materialized a few minutes later. He was a larger version of the doorman, a medium-sized mountain with a shaved head and one large gold hoop earring. The gold glistened against his black skin.

"You got something for me, DC?" Tyronne said. The base in his voice rumbled like an approaching train.

DC made a pistol out of his hand.

"How many?"

DC held out three fingers.

Frank shook his head, no. He held up six fingers.

"Six?" DC asked.

"It's been a busy day."

"Where they at?"

"In the parking lot," Frank answered.

"Show me."

Frank stood up, and DC got to his feet. "You stay here. It'll draw less attention."

DC sat back down.

Tyronne followed Frank out to the parking lot, pausing to nod to the doorman. Maybe they were brothers, Frank thought. He went straight to his truck, opened the door, and pulled the gym bag toward him. He laid the six guns out on the seat.

"Three got full loads. Three are empty."

Tyronne picked up each gun and examined it with a practiced eye. He was quick but thorough.

"Nice," Tyronne said. "How much you askin'?"

"What's your top offer?"

"Normally, I'd bullshit somebody like you. Intimidate you a little. Jam you up. But I see that wouldn't work on a hard case like yourself. I give you seven hundred for the lot." He said it like it was a favor.

Frank smiled. "Look. I don't want trouble. I'll take an even nine, and that'll still leave you a lot of room to make a good profit."

Tyronne looked from Frank to the guns and back again. Then he smiled. It was a smile as big as his biceps. He laughed a deep baritone laugh. "Had to try. You know that. No offense."

"None taken."

Tyronne scooped up three of the pistols and dumped them into the outside pockets of his coat. "Grab those other three, and help me offload these motherfuckers."

Frank slipped two of the pistols into the waistband of his pants, covering them with his shirt. They walked around toward the back of the building to where presumably Tyronne's car was parked. Frank hoped it was. He had palmed the little .32. It was still loaded just in case. He truly hoped it wasn't a set up. If the doorman suddenly appeared or someone else tried to take him out, he would have to kill all of them.

Tyronne stopped at the trunk of a black BMW. He popped the trunk lid, and the interior light came on. He lifted the interior carpet and placed the three guns inside. He reached back, and Frank passed him the other two, then the third, the little .32. If he had to, he knew he could kill Tyronne with his hands. Tyronne opened a brief case and counted out nine crisp one hundred dollar bills.

He passed them to Frank.

"Nice doing business with you."

"Same here," Tyronne said, reaching his arm out. Frank shook the large hand.

"You some kind of biker?" Tyronne asked. "You give off a biker vibe."

"Not me," Frank said. "I'm just a poser."

Tyronne laughed again. "You was a little tense back there. Thought I might try to jack you out of those guns?"

"It crossed my mind."

"Always pays to be careful. Not my style. But you never know."

Tyronne laughed again, and they walked back inside.

Tyronne went past DC, chuckling to himself. DC said something to him, and Tyronne whispered a reply while watching Frank. Then he smiled again and went to his station at the foot of the stairs. Bouncer, waiter, gun smuggler, Tyronne was a jack of all trades.

"How did it go?"

"I'm alive."

He slipped DC five bills. DC did a quick count as he scooped up the money. Frank smiled to himself. Frank hadn't needed the money any more than he needed the guns. The sale was all image. He had to not look like a square. You were inside, or you were outside. That was all. The deal made him look like he knew his way around. He might come back tomorrow night and buy a little information from Tyronne about Vincent Street. He would have to see how it played out. He could always do it the hard way if he had to.

Frank chuckled to himself again. It was such second-class bullshit. DC had asked Tyronne how much he had paid for the guns. DC wanted to be sure he could trust Frank to deal him fair. It was the obvious move. Frank wondered what DC would have done if Frank had shorted him.

THE LAST SPARTAN

Chapter 9

After turning down the persistent requests for lap dances, shower dances, table dances, and to buy them drinks, the strippers finally left them alone. Frank drank two more beers. He had to be careful. He wasn't afraid of getting drunk. His weight required a good deal of alcohol to affect him, but he wanted to stay alert. Things were starting to happen fast around him, and he wanted to be ready when whatever opportunity presented itself. He was sure it would.

A young girl came in. She looked barely seventeen. Her hair was pulled back into a thick ponytail. She wore straight leg white jeans that were so tight you could read her lips. Her long-sleeved, baby blue blouse had a ruffled front. It was unlaced enough to show a hint of cleavage. No, more than a hint. It was a clear suggestion of what lay hidden beneath her thin blouse and lacy black bra. They were not the breasts she was born with. Even without looking at her six-inch heels, Frank recognized her as a stripper immediately. They carried themselves differently. They moved like show animals, which, he guessed, in a way they were.

She walked over and kissed DC on the cheek. "Hey, baby. You get my cigs?"

DC pulled the unopened pack of Marlboro Lights from his cargo pants and slipped them to her. "How could I forget?"

She kissed him lightly. "You are such a lamb. You spoil me."

"I try, baby."

She turned toward Frank. "Who's your scary friend?"

"Bren, this is Frank. Frank's an old friend of mine who's passing through town. He's going to be crashing with us on the couch for a few days. If that's all right."

"Sure, DC. Any friend of yours. What kind of business are you here on, Frank?"

"Personal stuff."

"Ooh. The mysterious type."

Frank tried a smile. He really wasn't good at smiling, and it worried him.

"I just got off work, and I'm totally wired, DC."

"You're always wired. I still don't get it. You dance your ass off all night, and you still got energy to burn."

She moved behind DC, and a long finger drifted lazily across his shoulders. Her nails were the same blue as her top. She spoke to DC, but she looked at Frank.

"You know how turned on I get dancing. All those strangers seeing me naked. Wanting me. Hoping they can come home with me. But all the time I know I'm saving myself for my man."

She leaned down and kissed DC hard on the mouth, her eyes still open and on Frank. She broke the kiss. "I've got to pee," she said. "Hey, Frank, you want to go party with us? I have a girlfriend that would just eat you up."

"Some other time."

"Your loss," Bren said as she walked away with an exaggerated swing of her thin hips.

DC turned quickly to Frank. "Thanks, man. I'll just tell her we met when I was at Georgia Tech. Some bar. Partied together, shit like that."

"You afraid she might want a cut of the rent money?"

"Absolutely. That girl is all about the dough." He grabbed a napkin and hurriedly wrote out his address on the front. "It's on the third floor. Apartment 3-C. 237 Old Stateside Road. It's off Johnson Street behind the big grocery store."

Frank stared hard at him.

DC blushed. "It's legit. I swear. Only been there a couple of months. I'm not stupid enough to fuck you over, dude. Not when you could probably find me."

"Could and would, DC. I take things like that personally."

DC slipped the napkin over to Frank. Frank scanned it and slipped it into his pocket. They were still nursing their drinks when Bren returned.

"Did you convince him to come with us and party?" Bren asked.

"He's bushed. Maybe tomorrow night."

"That a promise?" Bren asked.

"I never make promises," Frank said.

"Not even for me?" Bren cooed in her sexiest voice. It was a pretty sexy voice.

"Not even for you," Frank answered, while a smaller brain lower down in his pants shouted for him to say yes to anything she asked.

DC dug out his keys and worked a key off the ring. "You can have my key. I got a spare back at the apartment, and we can use Bren's tonight."

Frank looked at the key. It was a copy of a copy of a copy from something carved out by trolls in the mines beneath Moria. It was as nondescript as any apartment key he had ever seen. Bren was watching him. Listening with dancer's ears.

"You still at the new place off Johnson street, behind the grocery store? 237 Old Stateside Road?" Frank asked.

"Yeah, apartment 3-C."

Bren leaned over and snuggled into DC's arms. She kissed him lightly a couple of times. "How come you never mentioned Frank before?"

"A man has to have secrets, baby."

"You ready to go?" she purred.

"Just a sec—"

She began slowly moving against him in a dancer's grind. "I can't wait much longer to get you alone."

"Is she something else or what? You know what her stage name is, Frank?"

Frank looked blank.

"No. Don't tell him," Bren said. "It's embarrassing." Bren didn't look like a girl who was easily embarrassed.

"Please. Let me, baby."

Bren grinned her smile of practiced innocence. "Alright. If you want to."

"Aphrodite. You get it? The most beautiful woman in the world. The goddess of love. My baby doll."

Bren made a little dip with her knees like she was taking a bow. "The squares love it. It feeds their dirty little fantasies."

"An appropriate choice," Frank said. "I'm sure it works wonders."

"See. I told you he would appreciate it, baby."

"Thank you," she said.

Bren seemed satisfied. For now. Grifters were always curious, always looking for an edge.

"Sorry about tonight, kids," Frank said. "I got a long day tomorrow. I'll make it up to you before I leave."

"Is that a promise?" Bren cooed.

Frank laughed. "Hardly. You get the tab, Donny. I'm out of here."

With DC settling up the tab, Frank had enough head start to reach his truck and pull out of the parking lot before Bren could see which way he was going. If she was clever enough, the direction might be a give away. Frank drove aimlessly looking for a good spot to check his maps and figure out how to get to DC's apartment.

He thought about the Greek legend of Pandora. DC didn't have the whole story. Pandora had been carved from stone by the gods to punish mankind. She was beautiful and curious and cruel. Hephaestus had used the perfect image of his own wife, Aphrodite, as her model. Aphrodite. He hadn't heard that name since just before he died. Everything for a reason, he thought again.

THE LAST SPARTAN

Chapter 10

He found DC and Bren's apartment. Frank locked the picklock set and the electric screwdriver in the glove compartment, as well as a thousand dollars of his money. Spread the money, spread the risk.

The key worked, and he went inside. It was a two-bedroom apartment. One bedroom contained a king size bed, some mismatched pieces of bedroom furniture, and a small television. The other bedroom had been converted into some kind of office. There was a computer desk and an impressive array of electrical gadgets arranged on it. There was a tall bookcase with what appeared to be technical journals. There was a big screen television in the main room and a decent sofa and two chairs.

He liked the idea of staying here. There was no way anyone could have predicted it, so he should be safe. He did a thorough search anyway. He found their hideaway places without much effort. There was about an ounce of marijuana, a tiny trace of cocaine, and an assortment of pills. The pills looked like ecstasy, but Frank didn't recognize the brand. He had been out of the business too long. They were marked with the Nike swoosh. To the Greeks, the goddess Nike represented the spirit of victory. She hung out with Athena a lot of the time. Could be they were more than just friends, he thought. There was a time when he was into that lesbian stuff.

There were no weapons. No cryptic notes. No strange clothing, unless you counted the leather outfits that Bren had. They may have been for her act or just as easily for play time at home.

Frank decided he better take a quick inventory of what he had in his bag. He wasn't worried about DC. He was a goof. He knew Bren would search his stuff the first chance she had. She was that kind of girl. Probably do it tonight when they came in or early tomorrow while he was still asleep. It would be too suspicious to leave his bag in the truck if he really was an old friend of DC's.

He put a couple hundred into the front pocket of his jeans and distributed the rest among the other pockets. He didn't want the cash to be too tempting for her, and it would be. Nothing else was incriminating or offered any clue to who or what he was. He got a pillow and a spare blanket out of the bedroom closet and carried them to the sofa.

In the quiet of the apartment he looked over the yellow pages.

Jenny didn't have a lot of options open to her. If she had simply run away from home, she would have been turning tricks on the street by now. She would have to if she couldn't find a job. She would have to eat and find a place to sleep. Something that seemed so precious when you were a teenager soon became your only commodity of value when you were on the street. He would never find her if that was the case.

But Jenny had not just run away from home. She had come to Atlanta at the urging of Vincent Street. That much he was sure of. Vincent had only sent her a single bus ticket, which would lock her in with no way back. The bus ticket also showed either he wasn't sure she would come or that he was a second-rate sleaze.

Frank could guess the drill. The Spartans had worked it themselves. You placed a guy at the bus station and watched the prey unload. At first there would be other predators there—pimps, perverts, and hustlers of all types with all kinds of schemes. When the Spartans arrived, those would drift away and disappear. No one but a fool stood up to the Spartans.

The runaways were easy to pick out. Alone with big suit cases and bigger eyes, they came to the big cities from everywhere. They were looking for something better. Something they had seen in a movie or read in a magazine or heard in a song. They never suspected what was waiting for them prowling the streets as hungry as any shark.

After Jenny got to Atlanta she would have gone straight to Vincent's apartment. That was a given. Where else could she go? It was too late to go home. So that shit about not hearing from her was a lie. She was a good girl at heart. Even if she had bailed on coming to Atlanta once she hit the road, she would have called Vincent and told him. It was the right thing to do. But she would come. Vincent would greet her like a lost sister. She would be nervous, shy. He would put no moves on her. He would calm her fears. She would have her own bedroom. He would show her around Atlanta. Show her the big city. Make her feel special and safe.

He would snap some shots of her for her modeling portfolio or acting career or whatever he had promised her. The photographs would all be what Jenny would think of as artistic. No nudity. Nothing topless. All very tasteful. Lots of make-up and different hair styles.

Vincent would promise to get them to all his contacts. That would take a week, ten days tops if he didn't want to rush it.

Vincent would get her her own place. A small apartment to share with another girl. Someone who had been there a little while. Someone to help break her in. Someone to keep an eye on the fresh meat.

Then the big letdown. No one was interested, Vincent would say. But he still believed in her. He wouldn't give up until she was a star. Some crap like that. By the end of the second week he would let the other shoe fall. It would take some time, so she would have to get work to help cover expenses. Food and rent weren't free, you know. There were not that many places for her to get a legitimate job even just shy of sixteen.

Jenny had grown up in a small town on a farm. Vincent knew that. It wasn't a scam on her part. He would take baby steps with her. Probably let her new roommate get her a job as a hostess somewhere. Somewhere meant a gentlemen's club. It would be too big a jump to have her go to work for a massage parlor or escort service or out on the street. A strip club was the best choice.

It would have to be some place that didn't pay too much attention to IDs. He might even make her a fake one so the club could pretend not to know how old she was. It couldn't be one of the big fancy ones, like Pandora's Box. Too much exposure. Too much risk. It would have to be small. A second-rate strip club or juice bar. They were the most likely.

She would start out just greeting customers or serving drinks or working the bar. She would get to know the other girls. They would seem nice. Not unlike her. She would hear about the money they were making.

By the end of the third week one of the girls would call in sick or twist an ankle. They would ask Jenny if she would take her place. Come on. You'll be great. No one will know. It's no big deal. And there is so much money. And it's so easy to make. You don't have to do anything but dance. That's all. Nothing but dance. She would agree. But she would be nervous. Smoke a little of this. Snort a little of that. Pop one of these. There, isn't that better? You can really feel the music now, can't you? Go on, girl, show them what you got.

Each time it would get easier. Each time it would be harder to go home. Locked between the lure of the cash and the guilt over what she was doing to earn it.

By the end of the month it would be easy to move her another step. It could be anything. Nude photos. Escort service. Private parties. Porno. Prostitution. Just this one time. If you don't like it you don't ever have to do it again. Maybe Frank would get lucky and she would just keep dancing. There was plenty of money in that. Maybe Vincent would be happy to bleed her a little at a time.

It would be tougher to find her once she left dancing and entered the other life. It would take longer to penetrate that world and drag her out. Every day she lived in that world the harder it would be to ever go home again.

Frank studied the pages again. He would start tomorrow trying to run Jenny down. He folded the pages up and put them in his pocket. He hung his long-sleeved shirt over the back of the couch. He left his short-sleeved nylon shirt on. He took off his pants and rolled them up into a crude pillow. He figured if he had been an old friend of Donny's' he would watch his money.

He turned the television on with sound down low. He found the cartoon network. He liked that channel. He didn't know why. If Bren wanted to search his bag, he might as well give her some light to do it with.

He stuffed his pants in the pillow, pulled the blanket up, and closed his eyes.

THE LAST SPARTAN

Chapter 11

Jenny and Caron came out of the Blonde Geisha laughing.

"So? How was it? Did he have a little dick?"

"It was so gross," Jenny said.

"Ah, it's not that bad."

"Yes, it is. It's so pathetic. What kind of freak gets off like that?"

"Looks like a lot of Japs do," Caron laughed.

They both giggled. Jenny shoved Caron playfully.

"How many did you do tonight?" Caron asked.

"Just two. I was starting to think I was going to puke if I had to do it again."

"How about you?"

Caron held up eight fingers. Then she mimicked stroking up and down. "A regular hand full and a half."

"Gross."

"How did you make out?"

"I got fifty from one and sixty from the old guy," Jenny said.

"Sixty," Caron said amazed. "It must be because you're new. I only got twenty each for mine."

"Maybe you aren't any good," Jenny joked.

"Like you are. Just wait. Your price will start to drop now."

"It is so humiliating. Don't you think so?"

"I've done worse to survive. At least it's not blow jobs. That's nasty business. Bastards always trying to pull out at the last second like they do in porn movies."

"Ewww," Jenny said. "No way I could do that."

"You do what you got to do."

They waved a cab down and rode back to their apartment. It was a rundown building on the edge of the bad part of Atlanta. They paid the cab driver. He made a request as to what he would like for a tip. Caron flicked her tongue snake-like in the air, then laughed. She tossed him two dollars instead. They turned to go into their apartment when a man stumbled out of the dark alleyway.

He was a homeless man. He stunk of body odor, urine, and cheap booze. He was clutching at them.

"Have you got some spare change for a man down on his luck?"

Jenny backed away from him. "You scared us."

"Can't you help a fellow traveler?" the man begged.

"What do we look like, the fucking Red Cross?" Caron snapped. "We aren't exactly living the good life either."

"Anything would help," the man persisted.

"I bet it would. Try taking a bath." She grabbed Jenny and pushed her ahead into the building.

The bum stood outside staring up at the building.

* * * *

Yusef was parked with his lights out across the street from the Blonde Geisha. He saw the two girls come out. They were both blondes. He had seen the photos Vincent had sent. The girl had been a brunette then. It was still easy to pick out Jenny. She had a coltish gait and an air of innocence the other girl did not possess. They were laughing and giggling, although he could not hear what they said. He watched them hail a taxi and followed it at a discreet distance.

When the girls reached their apartment, he watched as a man stumbled at them from the darkness. The girls were startled. The man, apparently harmless, was left outside as they went inside the building.

"Pathetic," he said outloud. Vincent was a fool. He risked this girl's most valuable treasure by letting her wander around unprotected. The Ambassador would not understand if she were attacked and violated.

He pulled his pistol from his shoulder holster. It was a .22 Beretta Model 71. It was the weapon of choice of Mossad assassins. Yusef smiled at the thought. For a time as a youth he had fought with the PLO in Gaza. He was a ruthless soldier and a remorseless leader. His successes were many. He had been marked for assassination by the Israelis. He had taken this weapon from the body of the Mossad assassin that had come to execute him. That was ten years ago. He had killed a score of men since. He removed the suppressor from his pocket. He carefully twisted it into place.

When he began working for the security forces in Kuwait he had the special silencer machined for his pistol. The added weight helped stabilize the weapon. When he had been promoted to the Ambassador's chief of security, he instructed the other members of his entourage to carry the same weapon.

THE LAST SPARTAN

Yusef waited until the girls had had plenty of time to get to their apartment. He pulled across the street. The homeless man was returning to his shopping cart. He turned when he saw Yusef.

"Can you help a traveler out?" he asked.

Yusef got out of the car. He took the man by the back of his shirt and pushed him toward the car.

"Hey, what're you doing? Where are you taking me?"

Yusef didn't answer. He forced the man into the back seat. Yusef got back behind the wheel and drove off.

"What's this about? I wasn't hurting no one."

"Silence," Yusef shouted.

The old man fell silent. Yusef drove for fifteen minutes until he found a deserted industrial section. He parked between two old buildings. He went back and opened the rear door of the car. The old man protested, but Yusef dragged him outside and pushed him to the ground.

"There's no need for that. I was coming."

Yusef stared at the pitiful man kneeling before him. He was the epitome of America.

"Are you at peace with your god?" Yusef asked.

"What? What're you talking about?"

"I am a religious man. It is time you made peace with your god."

The old man started to cry. "I never hurt no one," he blubbered. "This ain't right."

Yusef raised the pistol. "Use your time to make peace or, by Allah, I will kill you now."

The old man folded his hands and began to mumble a prayer. Yusef watched silently. Suddenly, the old man smiled. He opened his eyes and looked up at Yusef.

"I spoke to God like you asked. You want to know what he said?"

"What did your god tell you, old man?"

The old man smiled. "He said you were all going to die."

The sound of the pistol was swallowed by the dark night.

Chapter 12

Frank awoke Saturday before dawn. He had always been an early riser. His gym bag had been moved slightly. Bren must be very good, or he must have been very tired not to have woken up. He could hear DC and Bren in the bedroom through the closed door. They were laughing and whispering, then her voice got husky and filled with passion. He could hear their moans. He could hear Bren urging DC on over the creaking of the bed. Finally, there was silence.

Frank thought back to when he had first met another girl who came to be called Aphrodite. That had been eight, no, nine years ago. Back then she had called herself Helen.

The Spartans were expanding their presence in Florida. It was the Fourth of July. Frank and Spanish Johnny were doing a final check on one of their newest affiliates. It was a biker gang called the Ghost Riders. The Ghost Riders had a first-class connection to the Colombian drug lanes. One of their brothers was dialed into a large cartel through his sister. Although she was not particularly close to him, using her contacts did ensure less risk of double-crosses, which the Colombians were known for. Cyrus wanted that connection. His plan was to expand the size and scope of the Ghost Riders' cocaine shipments. If Cyrus could establish a guaranteed source, he could plug it into the Spartans' established distribution pipeline.

Spanish Johnny, called that because of his Latin good looks and fluency in Spanish, had accompanied Frank to the final meeting. Sending two elite members of the Spartans' inner circle was both a tribute and a warning. Every rider on the East Coast knew the reputation of Frank "The Hammer."

Everything had been agreed upon. The deal was set. The Ghost Riders would continue to act as intermediaries and funnel the cocaine into the Spartan distribution network. In return the Ghost Riders would be given a percentage of the profits. They would be allowed to keep their club colors and not become Spartans by name. However, they would have the privileges and rights of other Spartans. Foremost was the protection offered by the Spartan organization. The Ghost Riders would be allowed to send representatives to meetings when appropriate and have a say in how the Spartans expanded throughout Florida. A final concession was that the leader of the Ghost Riders would become a full Spartan First Citizen, a Peer. It would grant him access to the highest levels of the organization. It was a position of prestige and power.

It was one of the most generous deals the Spartans had ever agreed to. Cyrus wanted to expand their drug revenues that much.

Frank and Spanish Johnny had arrived at an isolated house north of Miami. The house was located at the end of a short dead-end road. The Ghost Riders owned all the property, six odd buildings, along the road. The buildings were supposedly being used as ad hoc shops for repairing their own motorcycles and a small car repair business. In reality, it was for chopping stolen cars and distributing the cocaine they got into secondhand cars that were "sold" to dealers and then broken down.

The club's central house was a two-story Spanish-style building surrounded by a high, wrought iron fence. Security cameras swept the perimeter. Motion sensitive lights and alarms further added to the security. All information was funneled inside the house to a central security room. A Ghost Rider monitored the screens twenty-four hours a day.

The large concrete parking area held not only a couple dozen motorcycles, but several expensive cars as well. The Ghost Riders had learned that sometimes the vehicle of choice was not a motorcycle. They wanted options to fit the occasion.

Inside, the club house looked like any upper middle-class home. Maybe a little messier. There were five bedrooms, one downstairs and four upstairs. There was a large living room that connected directly to the modern kitchen. There were also a number of smaller rooms that the Ghost Riders used as offices and arsenals.

The leader of the Ghost Riders called himself El Diablo. It was not a very original moniker, but he seemed to love the title. His fellow riders seemed unimpressed but used it when addressing him. As a mark of his authority, he wore a large silver skull ring on his right index finger. He was said to have subordinates kiss the ring as a sign of respect, a la the *Godfather* movies. Like El Diablo, the ring was gaudy and clichÈd, as were many things in the outlaw biker world. Image was everything.

As was the custom, the Ghost Riders offered to provide women from their stable of prostitutes for Frank and Spanish Johnny's pleasure. Spanish Johnny had thought it a good idea. Frank had declined for both of them. He was always suspicious of prostitutes run by other groups. Spanish Johnny was not so discerning, but had agreed to Frank's position. Only women who were full members of the Ghost Riders would be there. And if the two Spartans changed their minds and wished to indulge, well, something could always be arranged.

Frank and Spanish Johnny arrived wearing their Spartan colors, which consisted of red t-shirts under black leather vests. The leather vests had a lambda branded into the back. They both came strong. Coming armed was for practical as well as symbolic reasons. Spanish Johnny wore an inconspicuous Smith and Wesson .40 caliber strapped to his right ankle. It was the 99 model with the short barrel. The entire gun measured just over six and a half inches. His Spanish style jeans had silver studs from calf to ankle. The snaps were more than decorative. It allowed Spanish Johnny quick access to his weapon if he needed. His weapon of choice, a large knife, hung by a sheath from his waist. Spanish Johnny was known as a knife man. It was a well-deserved honor. Frank wore his double rig of twin .9 millimeter Sig Sauers in the underarm position, under his vest. They were the pro models reserved for law enforcement and the military.

They both wore jeans jackets over their vests to hide their colors and weapons until they reached the Ghost Riders' club. They left their jackets draped over their motorcycles. Frank stuffed his thin leather gloves into his back pocket. There were several Ghost Riders standing in the parking area waiting for them.

Frank pulled a half empty bottle of Jack Daniels Black from his saddle bag. He tossed the bottle to Spanish Johnny, who took a deep drink and drained half of the remaining contents. He grimaced and shivered and tossed the bottle back to Frank. Frank saluted the Ghost Riders standing nearby and finished the bottle. With a dramatic flourish, he threw the bottle high over the encircling fence. The Ghost Riders nodded their approval. These were men.

Frank was not averse to clichÈs either. As a member of a perceived redneck outlaw gang, it would be assumed that his drink of choice would be Jack Daniels, straight out of the bottle. Frank liked Jack. They had spent many a good night together, but Frank liked to sip it and enjoy its smoky flavor. He could nurse a few ounces of Jack by a fire and appreciate the nuances of caramel and vanilla it left in your mouth. Yet, Frank knew the Ghost Riders would be watching them tonight. Evaluating. Judging. The bottle of Jack that he had shared with Spanish Johnny had showed that these two men were brothers. It showed that they were tough. It showed they were outlaws. In reality the bottle had been filled with sweet ice tea. It was a trick Frank had picked up watching a television show about metal rockers. It was all about the image.

El Diablo had them brought upstairs to his private study. El Diablo professed to speak no English, so Spanish Johnny acted as interpreter for the meeting. The few minor points of contention in their deal were smoothed away. In fact, they weren't points of contention at all. They were just a final opportunity for El Diablo to gain respect from his outlaw brothers. Hands were clasped. Backs were slapped. There was even a high-five tossed out. The agreement was finalized. Now was the time for the ritual celebration party. A night to party. Independence day.

Spanish Johnny was a handsome man, with thick black hair and a rogue's brilliant white smile. He kept a perpetual tan and a ready charm that women seemed unable to resist. Women were drawn to him. Old women or young, educated or illiterate, shy or wild, they all heard his call. There was something they found both equally dangerous and innocent about him. Spanish Johnny was drawn to them as well. He indulged women with a fervor. He was insatiable. Tonight should have been a good night for debauchery.

El Diablo offered them a sample of the cocaine the Ghost Riders had access to. Frank and Spanish Johnny sampled it. Spanish Johnny snorted cocaine like he did everything else in his life, with unrestrained passion. Frank was more controlled. He was not opposed to drugs in any way, but he was the enforcer. It paid for him to be vigilant. Drugs were often the precursors to trouble among bikers. A little cocaine would help keep him awake and vigilant. It would lessen the effects of the alcohol he would consume. Too much cocaine would quickly release his rage. Those were demons that Frank wanted to keep in check. When the mirror was passed a second time, Frank waved it away.

El Diablo provided an endless supply of expensive liquors and ethnic beers. The drink of choice for the Ghost Riders was tequila. They were not immune to the dictates of image either.

The men talked and joked. They told stories about epic rides and fierce battles. This night was to lay the first stones in the slow road to bonding for men. It was a crucial step in the relationship of the Spartans and the Ghost Riders. Neither wanted the Spartans to seem like conquerors. As a special treat El Diablo brought out his newest possession.

She was a girl named Helen. She was tall and thin with blonde hair that needed to be touched up. She had long dancer's legs and small breasts. Her neck was slender and impossibly long. But her real magic was her face. Frank felt it immediately. It was like being struck with lightning. Her face had been designed by the gods. The high cheekbones and small nose were perfect. But her eyes were what set the face off. They were huge and bright and green. They seemed filled with an inner fire of excitement, like a child on Christmas morning. She smiled at Frank. It was a young girl's mischievous smile. Like the Helen that sent a thousand ships to bring her home from Troy, she was the most beautiful woman Frank had ever seen.

She came over almost shyly and stood before Frank. She did a self-conscious little flutter wave, and Frank noticed a small red ring on her left hand. Her fingernails were painted deep red, Spartan red. El Diablo spoke in Spanish. Spanish Johnny translated in a whisper for Frank.

"This girl, she is my gift to you tonight. Take her and do with her whatever you desire. She thinks she is being initiated into the Ghost Riders tonight. She will refuse you nothing. Make her your whore," El Diablo said and laughed.

"Are you not going to initiate her?" Frank asked.

El Diablo smiled. He spoke loudly and again Spanish Johnny whispered the translation. "Ghost Riders are for Latinos only. Tomorrow I will sell her to the Colombians. They will put her on the street."

Frank said nothing.

El Diablo continued with Spanish Johnny translating. "This whore is my personal gift to the great enforcer of the Spartans. It is a sign of my respect. Do not insult me by refusing."

Frank made a small mock bow. "How could any man refuse the great El Diablo." There was the slightest hint of challenge in his voice.

Perhaps Spanish Johnny felt the tension between the two men. Maybe he just wanted to dance. He grabbed Helen's hand and pulled her to the middle of the room. There were three other couples already dancing there. The surround sound was belting out some hot Latin sounds. There were heavy organs playing and a deep drum bass for rhythm. Over it all a Spanish woman yelled gibberish that Frank couldn't understand. Frank sat down on one of the sofas to watch.

Spanish Johnny swayed and moved with practiced assurance. Frank was envious of that. He couldn't dance. He just wasn't built for it. The music changed, and the dance took on a more sensual rhythm. He watched Helen move against Spanish Johnny, and he felt a spark of jealousy. He crushed it. She was a good dancer too. Her body moved with an effortless grace. Her hips swung in fluid harmony with the dictates of the music. Frank found it very erotic. She tilted her head back and laughed. A female Ghost Rider grabbed Spanish Johnny as the music changed once more and began to grind against him. Helen skipped back to where Frank was.

She was laughing, and her face was flushed. He noticed a tiny collar of freckles on the upper part of her chest just below the nape of her long neck. She was perfect.

She extended her hand toward Frank. "Would you like to dance?" she asked.

"I don't dance," Frank said.

Without a word, she crawled into Frank's lap as smoothly as a kitten. El Diablo laughed and wandered off to find more cocaine. Helen snuggled close to Frank's neck and kissed his hairy cheek. Frank wrapped a massive arm around her tiny waist. He had not felt this strong of a desire for a woman in a long time. As she nuzzled him she whispered.

"They are going to double-cross you tonight."

Frank leaned back to look into her eyes. The green was as rich as jade. His face was blank.

"They didn't know I spoke Spanish," Helen said. "They've cut a deal to ally with the Lucky Sevens and Dragons. They think they will be too strong for the Spartans to retaliate then. They want Florida for themselves."

Frank turned and kissed her. The kiss was more passionate than a diversion needed to be. Helen returned it.

He whispered, "How?"

"They'll send me off with you to take you off guard."

Frank kissed her again. Divide and distract, not a bad plan.

Helen broke their kiss. She looked into his cruel, blue eyes. "They'll burn you while you're in bed with me, then the other one."

Frank laughed and pushed her from his lap. He slapped her butt playfully. "Johnny, I need another beer," he yelled.

Spanish Johnny left the dance floor and danced his way into the kitchen. He opened the refrigerator door and rummaged around.

"Modelo or Corona?"

"Corona."

Spanish Johnny got out two bottles of Corona. He popped the top on both using a metal hook near the base of his knife. He carried them to Frank.

"Here you go, brother. You going to be tapping that ass any time soon? I might want a taste myself."

Frank laughed.

They clinked bottles and took long drinks of the amber beer.

El Diablo stood up and said something in Spanish.

Spanish Johnny nodded to him. "He says it is time for you to accept your present. He said enjoy her in that bedroom." Spanish Johnny pointed toward a door down a short narrow hallway.

Some of the Ghost Riders cheered. Others continued to dance to the loud boom of the music.

Frank gave El Diablo the thumbs up and turned toward Spanish Johnny. They shook hands and leaned together in a manly hug. When his face passed Spanish Johnny's ear he said, "Double-cross. Go on the first hammer fall."

Spanish Johnny gave no sign of what he had just heard. He stepped back from Frank and pointed at him, "Save some for me."

Helen giggled like a typical slut. "There's plenty. You'll get your turn."

Frank saluted El Diablo with his beer and turned to usher Helen toward the bedroom. He gave her another playful pop on her round bottom as they went inside. He turned back at the doorway.

"Don't come bothering me. I don't need no fuckin audience." Then he winked at Spanish Johnny.

Once inside the room, he locked the door behind him. There was another door along the right side. He checked the handle. It was locked from the other side. Helen pointed toward the door and nodded her head, yes.

"Slow down, baby," Frank ad-libbed. "Let me get my damn boots off."

Helen caught on quickly. "Oh, baby, I can't wait much longer. I'm on fire."

He motioned her toward the far side of the room beside the bed. He signed for her to keep talking.

"Yeah, baby. That's it. That's it. Hurry. I'm dripping," she said.

She climbed onto the bed. Frank mimicked unbuttoning a shirt. She took her top off. She wasn't wearing a bra. Her small perfect breasts stood out high and firm. It was hard to pull his eyes away from the pale pink tips. Frank put his thin leather gloves on.

"Please, baby. Please. Give it to me. That's it. You're so big. Oh, god. All the way. Yes...Yes... Yes..."

Helen was a good actress. She was really getting into her role. Frank smiled. He was getting an erection. He heard a tiny click of the lock being released on the inside of the other door. He saw the handle start to turn. Helen was still playing it up on the bed. She was bouncing up and down so the bed would squeak. The door started to inch open.

Spanish Johnny was back in the kitchen. He had his knife out and was showing one of the Ghost Riders the best way to cut limes for the Coronas. He would toss the lime in the air and catch it on the tip of his knife. He would roll the knife up his hand and stab the blade down through the lime. A few quick flicks of the wrists, and the lime was neatly sliced.

The door edged open an inch, then stopped. Frank yanked it all the way open. A Ghost Rider stumbled forward. He was staring at Helen's breasts. He was holding a pump shotgun in one hand. Frank smashed him across the face with his forearm and tore the shotgun from the man's hands as he crumpled to the floor.

The man lay stunned, staring up at Frank. He was the Ghost Riders' enforcer. The butt of a pistol protruded from his pants. He started to rise, but Frank pressed a boot onto his chest. Frank recognized the shotgun. It was an exceptional weapon, the Benelli model M1 tactical assault shotgun, a semiautomatic twelve gauge. It carried up to eight rounds, including the one in the pipe. He raised the shotgun.

"Don't, please," the enforcer said. "Let's talk about this. There are two dozen of us. You pull that trigger, you won't get out of here alive."

"Never go against the Spartans or you'll lose," Frank said and pulled the trigger.

The shotgun blast was still echoing when Spanish Johnny sliced the nearest Ghost Rider across the throat. He spun and buried his blade in the chest of the man next to him. His hand flew to the pistol at his ankle.

Frank used the shotgun to blow the bedroom door open and strode into the living room. Ghost Riders were scrambling to their feet. Some had weapons drawn. Apollo had said the key to the SEALs success was that they used surprise and overwhelming firepower to overcome superior forces. Advance and fire, that had been their maxim. Frank racked and fired six quick blasts, sweeping the room. He dropped the shotgun and drew his twin Sigs from beneath his arms. He methodically fired as more Ghost Riders rushed into the room.

Spanish Johnny was crouched behind the bar in a firefight with some Ghost Rider women on the landing above them. Frank spun to help him.

Frank felt something slap his left leg from behind and cut his legs out from under him. He looked over his shoulder as a second Ghost Rider appeared in the bedroom behind him. He must have been the backup, Frank thought as he fell. He tried to roll, to bring his right gun arm into play, but he knew he was too late. The man's gun was already zeroed on Frank's head.

Then the man's head exploded in a pink mist. His body slumped to the ground. Helen was standing behind him holding a pistol. Smoke still swirled from the barrel. She must have taken it from the dead enforcer.

Frank managed to roll and swing his fire to the women on the stairs. Helen ran beside him and emptied her pistol at the women. Frank didn't know who had hit them, but the two women fell. Helen helped Frank to his feet.

A naked Ghost Rider charged from an upper floor bedroom. Frank shot him twice in the chest. Spanish Johnny hurried down the hallway. Frank heard him kick in a door and fire.

THE LAST SPARTAN

The stench of gunpowder and the thick haze of smoke filled the room. He heard a groan and limped over to the couches. El Diablo lay on his back. The Benelli shotgun had nearly cut him in two. He was trying to talk. He pointed at Helen.

"Puta," he gasped.

Frank shot him in the forehead.

"How bad are you hit?" Helen asked.

Frank looked down at his left thigh. The bullet had passed clean through. He could stand, so he didn't think any bones were broken. The blood was flowing, but there was no urgency to it. Unless it had nicked an artery, he should survive.

Chapter 13

Yusef called Vincent on his cell phone. Yusef was courteous and polite. He requested a meeting at the hotel before the Ambassador arrived. Whatever time was convenient for Vincent would be fine with Yusef. After sending the penthouse key down to the desk for Vincent, Yusef knelt and said his morning prayers. He ate a light breakfast of fruit and eggs. Vincent arrived in the late morning. He was jubilant.

"Have you seen her, Yusef?"

"I have seen her."

"Is she not as I have said? An untouched child, as he likes."

Yusef slapped Vincent hard across the face. The blow staggered Vincent. Yusef fought to control his anger.

"Never speak of his Excellency in that way. His weakness is not a source for your mockery."

"I meant no disrespect, Yusef. Forgive me."

"You are a fool, Vincent. You have always been a fool. By Allah, you will always be a fool."

"What do you mean? I've only done as I was asked."

"Fool," Yusef said once more, almost as if challenging Vincent to deny it.

"How?" Vincent whined. "How have I been a fool?"

"You spend a great deal of time finding this girl, this Jenny. You make sure she is brought here for my master. You make certain she is still a virgin. You bind her to you. Yet, you leave her without protection. You leave her alone at the mercy of this world."

"She's not alone. She's with Caron. Caron looks after her and makes sure nothing happens to her, that she stays a virgin."

"So she is Caron's responsibility?"

"Yes."

"A young girl to watch a child. It is a fool's plan. And so close to the Ambassador's arrival. You risk much with your laziness. You are becoming too American."

"A thousand pardons, Yusef. I will make sure the girl stays at home until the Ambassador calls for her. Nothing will happen to her. I swear it."

"She is aware of the Ambassador coming?"

"Only what I have told her. A very important man from the Middle East saw her pictures. He is interested in using her in some promotional campaign for his country. The same story I always tell. He is rich, powerful, older. He would like to meet with her to discuss these things."

"She is a fool to believe these lies."

"Of course. She is young. She still is full of hope."

"Very well, Vincent. See to it that she comes to no harm before tomorrow night. This is your responsibility."

Vincent fidgeted from foot to foot, uneasy about what he was going to say next. "There is one other thing."

"Yes."

"We may have a small problem. After the girl, Jenny, came here, her parents hired a detective to try to locate her. They knew about me, and he came to see me."

"What did you tell him?"

"Nothing."

"Are you sure?"

"Well, he requested a bribe to leave me alone. He implied he could make life difficult for me if I didn't make a contribution, as he called it, to his retirement fund."

"Did you?"

"Yes. Five hundred. I thought more would be suspicious."

"True. But you were always cheap. What is this man's name?"

Vincent handed Yusef one of Burt Wilson's business cards. Yusef studied it and slipped it into his coat pocket. "Worry no more about this. I will see this man. He will not be a problem. Is there anything else?"

"No."

"See to this Jenny. If something were to happen to her chastity the Ambassador would be most unhappy."

Vincent nodded.

Then Yusef added. "He would ask me if you were at peace with Allah."

Vincent's eyes betrayed the terror he felt. He knew what those words meant. He bowed his respect to Yusef and hurried out of the penthouse, intoning a silent prayer that Caron had done as he had instructed her.

Chapter 14

"Not bad. I'll live." Those were Frank's exact words. Just like something from an old Bruce Willis movie.

"Good. I would hate to have to go through all that and have you die on me," Helen said and smiled a tender smile. "Put pressure on it, and I'll get something to use for a bandage."

"Get something dark-colored if you can find it."

Helen didn't question his reasoning. "The sheets in our little love nest were black silk. That should work fine."

Helen grabbed a knife from the kitchen and hurried into the bedroom. Frank heard another gunshot off somewhere in the house.

She came back with long strips of cloth. She wrapped them around Frank's leg. She watched his face to see if she was hurting him. She tied the strips of bedding tight.

Spanish Johnny came in. He was filthy from the gun battle.

"Shit. You are the fucking Earth Shaker," he said to Frank. "They're all done. We better motor."

"We got some things to do to set it right first."

"What things? We did it all, brother. They're all toast."

"No. This is an example. We have to use it." Frank turned to Helen. "Pack whatever you need. You're coming with us."

She hesitated, then she smiled her heartbreaking smile. She kissed him quickly and ran off upstairs. When she was out of hearing, Spanish Johnny spoke.

"Coming with us? Are you fucked up, Frank? Fuck her if you want before we go, then let's burn the bitch. Tie up the loose fucking ends."

"She's not a loose end."

"She's a witness."

"She saved my life."

"Fuck that. I say she dies. If you can't do it, I will."

Frank pointed a Sig Sauer at Spanish Johnny's face. He fought the urge to pull the trigger.

"Don't ever contradict me, Johnny. She saved me. She's a Spartan now. A First Citizen. She's one of us. By my word, she's a Peer."

"You can't just decide that. It's up to Cyrus. The council has to vote. You're not the law for the Spartans."

Spanish Johnny watched Frank's face, trying to gauge Frank's commitment.

"I am tonight."

"Her over me? Is that it?"

"If needs be," Frank said, the barrel still pointing at Spanish Johnny.

"Cyrus will never stand for it. Not even from you."

Frank thumbed the hammer back. "So be it. For now, you will do as I tell you or suffer the consequences."

"For this bitch? It don't make any sense. You don't even know her."

"I know all I need to," Frank answered.

Spanish Johnny sighed. "Fuck it. Chill out, Frank. Shit. You want the bitch, keep her. But just so you know, from where I'm sitting, I think you're wrong about her. She could have been in on the set up. I think she might have put the first round into you, and the Ghost Rider stepped in front of the second one by chance."

"She backed us up out here."

"What other option did she have then? You were still alive. One false move and you would have capped her pretty, tight ass."

"She doesn't concern you, Johnny. It's my call."

"You got that right. You want me to sanitize this joint?"

"Yeah. A nice big fire would be perfect. Use the gas from their bikes and the cars outside to soak everything good. To pull off what I have planned, I'll need some time. Say an hour and a half, maybe two."

"You want me to just chill out in this slaughterhouse for an hour and a half?"

"Yes. If the cops show, go ahead and light it and split. But if everything stays cool, wait it out. Take a shower. Watch the tube."

"What about swag, man?"

"Spoils of war. Search the house and take whatever you want. Leave the guns, dope, and jewelry, anything that can be traced or might be hot. Once you pop the fire, get back to Cyrus as quick as you can. Tell him what has happened. Tell him the Ghost Riders were planning a double-cross. They had allied with the Dragons and the Lucky Sevens to try and stand up to us."

"Got it. What about you?"

"I'm going to pay a little visit to the Dragons."

"That's your plan? Are you nuts? They'll do you when they see El Diablo failed."

"No, they won't. I'm going to scare some sense into them. Turn them back into good Spartan allies."

Frank limped over to El Diablo's body. He pulled a lock back knife from his back pocket and cut off El Diablo's right index finger, the one with the large skull ring on it. He waved the severed finger at Spanish Johnny.

"Proof," he said.

Frank pulled off his leather vest and laid it down on the sofa. He pointed his twin Sig Sauers at it and emptied the remaining three rounds into the vest. He tossed the pistols aside. He was unarmed. Spanish Johnny could do something if he wanted to. If he was man enough. He didn't. Frank picked up the vest. There were ragged holes where the bullets had penetrated the leather. He put the vest back on.

"Proof that El Diablo is dead. Proof that I can't be killed." He slipped the finger into his vest pocket.

Helen came back into the room. She was carrying a large, old black suitcase. She seemed nervous. It was probably the sound of the gunfire. Frank waved her down.

"It was all I could find," she said as way of explanation.

"An hour and a half. Two if you can stand the stench."

"I got it," Spanish Johnny said. "I've killed time in worse spots than this."

Frank limped outside. Helen followed him. He grabbed his jean jacket from the bike he had rode in on. He fumbled through the saddle bags. There was nothing to identify him in them. The bike itself was stolen.

"That black Lexus out front, whose is it?"

"El Diablo's, I think," Helen said. "I've seen him driving it sometimes."

"Are the keys in it?"

"Probably. Who would have the balls to steal it from in front of their clubhouse?"

"Good point." Frank used his knife to remove the screws holding the bike's license plate. He wrapped it in his jacket and handed it to Helen. "Take this with you. It's the only part of the bike that's legit.

The cops can't trace the rest back to me."

"Aren't I going with you?" There was obvious disappointment in her voice.

"Yeah. You follow me in the Lexus. They won't be looking for the Lexus yet, so it should be fine. We're heading down route 1 to the Dragons' main house. Stay close. When I signal, you pull over and park."

"You're going in alone?"

"Exactly. You wait for me to come out. If something goes wrong on the way there or once I'm inside, cut me loose."

"I couldn't leave you."

"You would have to. There's nothing you could do to help. But nothing is going to happen. You can trust me. The gods look after me. They always have."

Helen leaned over and kissed him. The kiss held for a long time.

"What was that for?" Frank asked.

"Luck," she said. "And because I like you."

"Go get in the car before I change my mind."

Helen ran over to the black Lexus and threw her suitcase into the back. She climbed into the front and started the engine. Frank looked over the bikes parked out front. It was easy to tell which one belonged to El Diablo. It had his name painted on one side of the gas tank. There was a fierce devil painted on the other side. The devil held a pitchfork. To Frank the pitchfork looked like the trident used by Poseidon. It was a good omen. He climbed onto the bike. His left leg hurt like a bitch. The bike turned over on the first try. He rolled out of the compound into the night. Clouds were building in the blackening sky. It would rain soon.

It took forty minutes to reach the Dragons' lair. He signaled Helen. He pulled to the side of the road. The Dragons were having a Fourth of July party, too. Celebrating their own independence day. Celebrating their new alliance. Celebrating his death or their life. It didn't matter. Any excuse to party. He rode the bike inside. The deep rumble of the engine seemed to hang above the music blaring from inside. He parked in the center of the courtyard but didn't get off the bike. He revved the engine. Louder and louder.

A handful of bikers loitered outside watching him. The sky rumbled dramatically. Fat drops of water splashed onto the ground. Frank didn't speak. One of the bikers drifted inside. A minute later the music died. The porch filled with Dragons. Other Dragons stared out of the windows and doorways of the main house. Some wandered across the yard to Frank's other side, trying to flank him. Some carried guns. Some carried pool cues. Probably close to twenty members and that many more hangers-on, whores and pushers and pimps.

The bikers parted, and a tall, lean man stepped outside. He wore no shirt or shoes. He had long white hair combed straight back. He held a bottle of Jack Daniels in one hand and a large bore pistol in the other. For an instant, Frank wondered if the bottle really contained whiskey or not.

The man was cautious but unafraid. What was there to fear from one lone man on a motorcycle?

"Do I know you?" he asked without inflection.

Frank cut the engine and stood up. He spread his arms and turned in a tight half circle. He made eye contact with all of them before he spoke.

"Bronze, do you not recognize your old comrade?"

"Is that you, Frank?"

"Alive and well."

Murmurs ran through the crowd.

Bronze seemed unsurprised. He tucked the pistol into the back of his pants. "I didn't expect to see you here. I heard you were visiting with the Ghost Riders tonight."

"Been there and gone."

Bronze motioned with the bottle toward Frank. "Come in out of the rain. Party with us. We'll show you proper hospitality."

Some of the Dragons laughed. More mumblings.

"I cannot. I have come on Spartan business."

Bronze was more wary now. "What business is that?" His eyes swept the entrance to their yard looking for signs of other Spartans.

Frank smiled a wolfish smile. "I am alone. It seems my negotiations with the Ghost Riders did not go as expected."

"In what way?"

"They tried to ambush me. They claimed they were in accord with you and the Lucky Sevens."

Fear flashed on some of the Dragons' faces.

"You didn't believe them, did you, Frank?" Bronze asked.

"No, of course not. The Dragons have always been friends to the Spartans. That is why you have been allowed to maintain your independence."

"What happened then? With the Ghost Riders?"

"You know me, Bronze. I cannot tolerate such things. They were fools. They thought they would kill me and escape Spartan wrath."

"How did you escape?"

"Escape? I did not escape," Frank paused for effect.

"What then?" Bronze asked.

"I am a Spartan. I did what Spartan warriors do. I killed them. I killed them all. They and all they possessed are wiped from this earth."

"All of them? There are thirty or forty riders there."

"Their numbers did not matter. I cannot be killed."

Frank heard the murmurs now.

"Look at his vest. Look at his vest," someone said.

"That's El Diablo's bike. He never lets anyone ride it," another voice.

"No man could have survived that."

"It can't be true," a voice inside said.

"There are holes in his vest. I can see them. He should be dead."

Frank reached into his vest pocket and took out El Diablo's severed finger. He tossed it up onto the porch at the feet of Bronze.

"Here is my proof. Tell me El Diablo lied."

Bronze glanced down at the finger and up again at Frank. He recognized the ring and did not hesitate.

"As you say, Frank. El Diablo lied."

"Good. Tell the Lucky Sevens what has happened tonight. I would not want them to hear of the lies of the Ghost Riders and think the Spartans believed them."

"Whatever you say, Frank. Would you like to come inside?" The voice had taken on a tone of respect it had not held earlier.

"No. I apologize for disrupting your party. As compensation, I leave you this bike that once belonged to that finger. Do with them as you will."

"That is very kind. It is a very nice bike."

"Do not forget this night, Bronze. The Spartans cannot always be merciful."

Bronze made a small bow in Frank's direction. Frank turned and strode toward the entrance to the yard. He felt their eyes on him. He fought the screaming agony of his leg. He felt their guns pointing at him. Still circled by the spotlights in the yard, he kept walking until he reached the darkness.

Once beyond their view, he stumbled to his knees. Suddenly, Helen was there helping him up.

"Come on," she urged.

The music cranked up again.

She held him up and opened the car door. She had turned the interior light off. Frank collapsed in the front seat. She backed the car up with the lights off until she was well down the road. It would make a better story if they didn't know how Frank had left.

"Where to now?" she asked.

"Head south down I-95. Drive steady for the next thirty minutes, and then start looking for a good hotel."

"Like a Holiday Inn or something."

"Think Marriott or Westin or nicer. A big one."

"I can push it a lot longer than that if you want me to."

"No thirty minutes more will put us a good hour from the Ghost Riders' crib. It's too far for cops to look. And they always think you try to get out of the state. If they set road blocks, it will be north."

"What about your friend? They might catch him."

"Not Spanish Johnny. He knows how things work. He'll have a couple of hours head start before the cops figure out what has happened and what to do. He'll get through."

"What about us?"

"I can't make it much longer. We got to disappear for a few days while I heal, but we have to be checked in before the fire is reported."

"So the hotel won't associate us with it, right? I mean how could we be involved with the fire if we are already in our room. Who waits two hours after a gun fight to torch a place?"

Frank smiled at her. She was beautiful, tough, and smart. Spartan women had been like that in ancient Greece. Unlike other Greek women, they went through similar training as the men, and they were renowned for their exceptional beauty. He closed his eyes. Within minutes he fell asleep. His life was in her hands now.

THE LAST SPARTAN

Chapter 15

Frank got dressed. He saw Bren's handbag on the kitchen table. A quick search found her cell phone. He popped it open and jotted down the telephone number. He might need it. He left the apartment quietly. He left his gym bag behind, just in case Bren hadn't had time to go through it. He went down to the street, climbed into his truck, and drove the fifteen minutes to Vincent Street's apartment. He parked and went back to his place under the tree in the park across the street. This time he wore his beanie. It changed his look. The lights in the apartment were out.

At eleven o'clock the lights came on. The shadows indicated there was someone home. He waited patiently. He had found that was one of his virtues, to be able to sit unmoving for long periods of time. Forty minutes after the lights came on, Vincent appeared at his door. He locked the door behind him, checked the street, and went to an underground parking area. A few minutes later, a new white Porsche Carrera 911 eased past with Vincent at the wheel. The car was worth close to one hundred and fifty thousand dollars. Vincent was living very large.

Frank waited ten minutes, then fifteen, to be sure Vincent wasn't on his way back. He slipped to Vincent's door. He was wearing his thin leather gloves. He used the lock pick to pop all three locks and was inside in under fifty seconds. He used to be a whole hell of a lot faster, but he was out of practice.

Vincent's apartment was a converted loft. Vincent had done a lot of upgrading. The floor was oak and waxed to a slick shine. There were Persian rugs placed randomly over it. He couldn't tell if they were originals or cheap knock offs. Frank tried to avoid stepping on the rugs from old habits. It was easy to hide a trip wire or a pressure sensitive device under a rug. The furniture was large and heavy. Probably expensive. Frank started in the back rooms.

There were two separate bedrooms. One obviously for a guest. It was bare of any personal touches. There was no sign of Jenny. There was dust under the bed. Three thick white towels were folded neatly on the foot of the bed awaiting the next visitor.

The master bedroom was large, with more heavy ornate furniture. The bedroom attached to a large walk-in closet. Dozens of suits hung in neat rows. The clothes were hung in precise order. All the pants seemed to be black, as were the half dozen pairs of dress shoes below them. The shoes were all still in their original boxes.

Frank found eight hundred dollars hidden in the toes of the dress shoes. All in hundreds. The shirts were predominately white dress shirts, one hundred percent Egyptian cotton with large pointy collars. Frank figured the pointy collars must be the latest style. There were racks of ties of various bright colors to dress up the shirts. Some casual shirts were hung to the side.

There was, oddly enough, a new black dress in a plastic garment bag. It was long, with faux diamonds in a design around the neck. The material was very soft. It was probably expensive, too. Whose was it? What was it doing here?

Frank found a hidden compartment in the floor behind the shoes. It was very well done. A simple wood slide lock secured it. Inside was a fairly large stash of cocaine and hashish. There were also four small Visine bottles filled with clear liquid. The bottles had small red marks on them. Frank unscrewed the top. It could be Ecstasy. He knew kids used to like to use Visine bottles sometimes to administer their dose because they assumed parents and cops wouldn't realize what it really was inside. Frank doubted parents or cops were still that easy to fool. Frank sniffed it. The liquid was odorless. Probably GHB. The most popular date rape drug, GHB made the victim compliant and induced short-term memory loss, so they didn't even know they had been raped. He put the drugs back. Frank searched the bedroom but found nothing else of interest. There was a well-worn Hustler magazine hidden under the mattress. How mature.

There was a large separate office. It looked like DC's study only more expensive. There was a black enameled desk with a nineteen inch computer monitor. A large computer tower rested in a nook below the desk. The screen saver showed some Arabic women covered in veils dancing. As they danced, they removed the veils, exposing more and more of their voluptuous bodies. Some Middle Eastern music clanged in the background.

Frank didn't like foreign music, especially from the Middle East. Maybe that was why the Arabs were so damn angry, they only had shitty music to listen to. Frank didn't like people from the Middle East in general. It was a Greek thing. The Middle East was where the

Persians had come from. They had been the nemesis of the Greeks more so than even each other.

He used a pencil to click the mouse. The screen asked for a password. On a whim he typed in the word *Xerxes*. The screen asked for the password again. It would have been golden if it had been right. Too bad, that would have been a fucking killer omen. Frank didn't know shit about hacking into computers. There was a high-end copy machine and some kind of laminating equipment. The drawers held nothing of interest. Frank moved back out into the main room.

There were cameras set up around a sofa. There were screens with different backgrounds and large rolls of different fabrics. Lights on adjustable steel poles sat silent vigil. There was a cabinet on wheels that held various cosmetics and costume jewelry. Nothing of any value. They were props for Vincent's models.

A quick search of the kitchen turned up a set of spare keys hidden in the back of the freezer. Frank slipped off his boot and put the keys inside. It was unlikely anyone would find them hidden there unless he was dead and on the coroner's cart, and then it didn't matter. There was nothing else of interest. With a final look, Frank slipped back outside and relocked the apartment.

Chapter 16

Frank used his key to open the door to DC's apartment. It was close to one o'clock. He fumbled around in the kitchen until he heard sounds from the bedroom. He heard mumbled conversation, then the door opened. DC shuffled into the room rubbing his eyes.

"Dude, you missed a hell of a party."

"Sorry, Donny. I brought you all some donuts and coffee from Krispy Kreme," Frank said, opening the two boxes of donuts. "I didn't know what you liked, so I got an assortment."

"Donuts. They are like my favorite thing in the whole world."

"Krispy Kreme makes the best donuts in the universe. Makes Dunkin' Donuts taste like lard," Frank said. The donuts were hot and their fragrance filled the room. Frank handed DC one of the cups of coffee. "I got coffee and milk, too."

"Bren," DC yelled. "You better get that pretty butt out of the bed if you want any hot donuts."

Bren materialized instantly in the doorway. She was wearing tiny thong panties and a short baby doll t-shirt. It said "WICKED" on the front. Very appropriate. She bounced over to the kitchen.

"You just got this for us?"

"Sure. It's the least I can do for crashing here. I don't know how you like your coffee, so I got some little packets of cream and sugar."

"Black is great," she said. "You are so sweet. Most of DC's friends aren't so nice."

DC grinned with his mouth stuffed full of glazed donut. "Very cool, dude. Much appreciated."

DC and Bren each ate the donuts, stopping only to lick the sugar from their fingers and grin at each other. Donuts make children of everybody, Frank thought.

"So what you got planned for today?" DC asked.

"I'm glad you asked. I got a couple of things I have to run down while I'm in town, and I have been doing some thinking. If you guys would be willing to help me out with one of them, I could get things done twice as fast. Of course, I would insist on paying you."

"What do you need done, dude?" DC asked.

"How much?" Bren quickly added.

"It's pretty easy really. Perfect for you, Bren. I'm looking for a girl. She's an old friend. I promised her folks I would look her up when I got to Atlanta."

"If you're just looking for a girl, I can set you up with someone way hotter than your old girlfriend," Bren said, and her smile convinced Frank she was telling the truth.

"It's not like that. She's just an old friend."

"What's her name?"

"Her name's Jenny, but she's probably not using it. She ran away from home. You know, the big city's call and all that."

"What made you think we could help?" Bren asked.

"She's only fifteen. I figure she's dancing in some club around town. Using a fake ID to get by."

"You got a picture?"

"Sure do," Frank said and pulled one of her photos from his shirt pocket. "She's got a little butterfly tattooed on her right wrist. If she's dancing, she's probably calling herself Butterfly or Angel."

Bren studied the picture. "I don't recognize her. How long she been in Atlanta?"

"About three weeks. I thought you might know some other girls, check around, save me a lot of footwork. I'll give you two hundred to look for her. You find her, I'll give you another eight hundred."

"A grand to find some runaway?"

"I promised her folks. They're old friends. Just want to talk with her. Nothing else. I'm not going to force her to go home if she doesn't want to."

"I got to drop my car off to be fixed, but I can go in early and check with the other girls, see if anybody has the 411 on Miss Butterfly."

"That would be great." Frank peeled two hundred dollars off his roll. He wanted them to see he had more and wasn't scamming them. "Payment up front. The rest if you deliver."

"What about me, dude?" DC asked. "What can I do?"

"I was thinking about that, Donny. There is something you can do, and I'll pay you two hundred bucks as well. Another eight more if it leads to results. Just like my deal with Bren."

"What do you need? Want me to check out the massage parlors? I've been feeling a little stiff lately."

Bren punched him in the arm. "You were plenty stiff last night. But I think I took care of that."

DC grinned. "I don't know, Bren. I feel the old stiffness coming back."

Frank cleared his throat to get DC back on topic. "Can you do anything with your computer, or are you just a gamer?"

"Gamer. Dude, I am the king of the gamers. Video poker's master card player. But I can do anything you want. What do you need?"

"You sure?"

"He's telling it straight, Frank. My baby's a whiz with all that computer shit. He's a regular math genius."

"Jenny came here to meet up with a guy. Named Vincent Street. See what you can pull up for me."

"You want general stuff or full-court press?"

"Everything you can get me."

"You got an address?"

"Sure."

"When do you need it?"

"As soon as possible."

"Bren, you go jump in the shower. I'll see what I can find out about Mr. Street, then we'll go see if we can track down the lost Butterfly."

Bren grabbed another donut and skipped toward the bathroom. DC watched her walk.

"Dude, what a perfect ass," he said to Frank. "I'm a lucky boy."

"Yes, you are."

"No, I mean it. I'm lucky to be in love. You ever been in love?"

Frank paused, and for some strange reason, he answered truthfully. "Once. It was a long time ago."

DC smiled knowingly. "Nothing beats it, man. Come on, let's check out your boy."

"You really as good with computers as she says?"

"The dog's nuts. Come on. This won't take long. I got a program I hacked that lets me into all kinds of secure sites. State and federal databases," he said and winked. "All illegal, but what the fuck? I can even slip into some international databases if I have the time. Got to tiptoe very quietly in there not to set off alarms. Nasty security in those places."

"Show me what you got."

DC wiggled his mouse, and the screen saver disappeared. The

screen asked for a password. He looked at Frank. "Do you mind turning around?"

"No problem." Frank did as he was asked.

Donny typed in a series of keys and waited. Then another series. "You can turn around now. Sorry to be so paranoid, but no one knows my password. Except Bren."

"I can understand that."

"I got it booby-trapped, too. If you try to boot it up and type the wrong password three times, it gives you a message that says the password is incorrect, but, and this is the cool part, if you attach it to another hard drive so you can download the files like in binary or something, what it really does is infect the new computer with a real kick ass virus."

"I thought they had protectors to catch viruses."

"Not this bad boy. It's a Trojan horse. You know what that is?"

Frank smiled. "Like the Greeks, it looks like something it isn't."

"Exactly. It's disguised as an operator file. It infects the new computer and attaches itself to all the e-mail addresses in the new host's address book. Sixty seconds later, while the screen still shows files being downloaded, a new screen pops up. It says, 'Fire purify me.' Is that not cool?"

"And it wipes out their hard drive."

"And the hard drives of anyone they have e-mail contact with. It's state of the art. That reminds me, I have to go meet with my hacker friend tonight for some updates. I won't be back until tomorrow afternoon some time. Do you mind picking up Bren from work for me?"

Frank shifted his weight nervously. "I don't know, Donny."

"Come on, be a pal. Help me out."

"Can't she just catch a cab or something. Hasn't she got girlfriends she can bum a ride with?"

"Look, dude, I don't know how to put this, but, I mean I know she loves me and all, but I would feel safer if you picked her up. Her girlfriends can get pretty wild, and she might get in trouble with me gone. All innocent stuff, but sometimes that shit gets out of hand."

"Donny, you don't know me well enough for this."

"I know. I trust you. I don't know why, but I do. Say you'll help me out, Frank. For old times' sake."

"We never had any old times."

"But if we did? Come on, dude, say you will."

"Okay."

"Super. She gets off about one. Now let the master work."

DC's fingers flew over the keys. Screen images flashed and disappeared before Frank's brain had a chance to understand what they were or what they asked. Rows of data typed almost magically across the computer monitor until DC would type in something new, and the screen would change.

"Would you go get my coffee for me, Frank?"

"Sure."

Frank went into the kitchen and found the cup of still warm coffee. He carried it back into DC's study. He handed him the cup as DC leaned back.

"There's some weird shit in here. I work better without you looking over my shoulder. Do you mind waiting in the living room?"

"Not at all."

Frank walked into the living room just as the bathroom door opened. Bren was standing in the steam with a towel wrapped around her. She smiled at Frank and dropped the towel. She let it lay on the floor for about a hundred years. Finally, she bent over and retrieved it. She only stayed bent over in front of him for another fifty years or so. She casually dried herself and then rewrapped the towel. Bren swished into the computer room. Frank heard her whispering to DC. He heard her get a loud kiss and a pop on the butt. She reappeared on her way to their bedroom. Bren didn't bother to close the door behind her. She tossed the towel onto the bed and began slowly dressing. Frank didn't know if it was possible to dress any slower. She was very good. Frank decided he would take his own shower now. He decided he would make it cold,   very cold.

Frank let the cold water beat some sense back into his head. She knew how to push a man's buttons, alright. He dried and redressed in the locked bathroom. He toweled his stubble of hair and hung up the towel.

He walked into the computer room to find Bren already there. She was dressed and glowing. DC was smiling up at her. Vincent Street's picture stared back at him from the screen. It was eerie.

"Did you find anything?"

"Just wait. I downloaded all relevant data I could find into a file, and it should start to print soon."

As if on silent command, the printer started to hum. Pages of crisp black type started to appear, complete with Vincent's photograph. DC scooped the final printed page up and handed them to Frank.

"Remember, this is just the icing. I'll do a more in-depth biography when I get back."

"So there's more?"

"There's always more. You can look this over, but the gist is that Vincent Street is an apparently normal guy. Twenty-six years old. American citizen born in Kuwait. No convictions for any crimes. Freelance photographer. Clears about twenty-nine thousand a year. Lives at this address, etc., etc. But when I pull up his actual police record, he has been arrested a few times. Once for contributing to the delinquency of a minor, four times for speeding, once for possession of narcotics, and once for assault on a female. The odd part is in each case all the charges were dropped by the cops. Your buddy has some influential friends."

"Even the speeding? I mean, that's nothing."

"Even the speeding. The requests seem to have come from the State Department. When I get back tomorrow, I'll dig a little deeper. See where it leads."

"You can't do that now?"

"Sorry, not enough time. Tomorrow. When I can focus on it. If I hurry in these databases, they'll know I'm in their system. They could probably trace my trail back here. That would be bad. Very bad."

Frank patted him on the back. "Thanks, Donny. I'll look this through and see if any of it means anything to me."

"Don't forget about Bren."

"I won't."

"Okay. You hear that, baby? You wait for Frank tonight," DC said, turning back to the monitor.

"I got it. Wait for Frank. I won't forget," Bren said. All the time her eyes were on Frank.

Frank walked back into the living room. If he wasn't careful, he would need another cold shower.

Chapter 17

The Ambassador and his two attachÈs were allowed to deplane before the rest of the passengers as a courtesy. They moved quickly through the airport. The men each carried a single personal suitcase as well as those of the Ambassador. When they exited the airport, Yusef was waiting.

He bowed to the Ambassador.

The Ambassador hugged him and kissed him on either cheek.

"Is everything prepared?" he asked in Arabic. He was excited.

"Yes, Excellency. Everything is as you requested."

"That is fine. Take me to my hotel."

Yusef opened the trunk and helped Jamal and Ali place the bags inside. Ali sat in the front seat beside Jamal. Yusef sat in the back beside the Ambassador.

"Have you seen her?" the Ambassador asked.

"Yes, Excellency. She is an exquisite desert flower. You will be pleased."

The Ambassador smiled. "Today I will go to the consulate as a courtesy call. Tonight I will see my nephew. Tomorrow I will have the girl brought to me."

"As you wish, Excellency."

"Is everything secure?"

"Yes. Vincent has made some errors in judgment. I will correct matters before tomorrow night."

The Ambassador looked hard into Yusef's face. "I cannot allow my reputation to be tarnished. You understand? It is a matter of honor. If the Americans or Israelis knew of this, our country would be embarrassed. I would be ruined."

"Do not fear, Excellency. I will see to everything. Have I ever failed you?"

"No." He patted Yusef on the knee. "You have not. You are as dear to me as my own brother." The Ambassador tapped his own watch. His watch was identical to the one he had given Yusef. "Would that we had ten thousand such as you. We would rule in Saudi Arabia herself, may Allah be praised."

Yusef smiled under the praise. They rode the rest of the way in silence.

THE LAST SPARTAN

* * * *

Frank didn't like being cooped up in the apartment. He wanted a place where he could study the printout without drawing too much attention. It took him a few minutes before he struck on the perfect spot. Frank decided he would go to the Atlanta zoo.

Zoo Atlanta was home to over a thousand animals. It was state of the art with a wide variety of natural habitats. The exhibits held many unique species like pairs of pandas and Komodo dragons. There was a huge gorilla habitat and an area where the primates ran free in a rain forest setting. Frank cared nothing for any of these. He paid his seventeen dollar admission and went inside. He was looking for something else.

Frank strolled the grounds with the other tourists. He was nearly invisible in the large, diverse group. He got no more than second looks. He stopped when he found the lions. Their enclosure was one of the most modern. It was large and open like the savanna they would have roamed. The pen was covered with grass and held a central pool of water. The lions were dozing in the shade of the faux rock kopje. The male was old and tired. The three females lounged. Frank walked to the edge and stared. The old lion seemed to glance in his direction for an instant.

Frank marveled at their purity of form. They were apex predators, but they were also just big cats. Nothing more and nothing less. They didn't aspire to be anything more. They hatched no intricate plans. They dreamed no dreams of conquest beyond their own pride. They felt no remorse. They probably felt no fear. Their lives were often savage and hard and usually short. Yet, lions did not seem to bemoan the cards the gods had dealt them. They lived their time until it was done.

At one time, Greece had been home to thousands of lions. The Greeks had hunted them with spears and bows and dogs. They held the lions in veneration for their perceived courage and fierceness. Frank had just read a book, *Monster of God* by David Quammen. The author had reminded him of something written by the Greek historian, Herodotus. When Xerxes, the King of Persia, had brought his great army to conquer Greece, he had been attacked by lions. The Greek peninsula at that time was said to teem with lions. As the Persian army marched through Greece, the lions would come out at night and attack his baggage train. In a trait peculiar to these Greek lions, they had ignored his men and mules and horses and only attacked his camels. The lions ultimate fate had been cruel. By 100 A.D. the lions of Greece had been wiped out.

These zoo lions were well past their prime as well. The male looked close to the end of his time. The zoo would be looking for a younger male to buy to take over his tiny pride. A young, healthy breeding male. It would be soon.

A mother and small boy walked to Frank's side to see the lions. The boy was eating an ice cream cone wrapped in a thick swath of paper napkins.

"Look, honey. Lions. Aren't they cute?" the mom said.

The boy beamed. Living manifestations of his stuffed toys. Big cats. Nothing else.

The boy was about seven years old. In ancient Sparta, that was the age he would have been taken from his parents' home to the agoge. There he would train for the next thirteen years. It was brutal training that many did not survive. For the rest of his life he would take his meals in a warriors' mess called the syssitia. As a youth he would be underfed so he would learn to steal food, to learn stealth. He would learn iron discipline. He would endure beatings that other nations would call torture. It was called the Spartan fire because it would forge this child into a deadly weapon of the state. He would train to become a warrior, the only occupation available to a man in Sparta. If he survived his training, when he reached manhood at twenty, he would receive his red battle cloak, the insignia of a true Spartan warrior. From that day forth his sole purpose in life would be to fight until he died.

The napkin from the boy's ice cream cone slipped from his hand. A light wind snatched it down into the enclosure. Reflexively the boy's hand darted out to catch the napkin. It was well beyond his reach, yet his response was instinctual.

The old male saw the movement. Without seeming to move, the lion was up and racing toward where they stood. His tail was rigid. His ears were back. In a tawny blur he reached the spot where the tiny white paper landed. The old lion skidded to a stop. He looked up at the mother and child.

The mother gasped and clutched her child's hand. She pulled him away from the lion pit and went in search of tamer sites. The old lion stared at Frank. Frank smiled. Old. Yet, still a lion. Still predator. And we are still his prey.

Frank walked to a nearby bench and sat down. He pulled out the papers on Vincent Street. They didn't make logical sense. If Vincent had powerful friends, why buy off Burt Wilson the detective? It was apparent that Burt wasn't afraid of Vincent, so he couldn't have been braced. It was an angle Frank hadn't thought of. He rolled it around in his mind. How could Vincent be powerful sometimes, but not always? Frank couldn't find an answer.

The charges were suspicious. The major ones fitted well with a man working the runaway scam. Underage runaways and drugs and violence. It was the perfect marriage. On the surface, the speeding tickets were unimportant. If Frank had owned a new Porsche he was sure he would have had some speeding tickets as well. But to have all three pulled? Why? Why not pay the fine and let it go? Your insurance goes up, but so what? If you can afford the car, you can afford the insurance. Unless it was to flex some muscle. DC had said there was evidence of a State Department request to drop the charges. Since when did the State Department give a shit about speeding tickets? Why would they give a shit about Vincent Street? Who the hell was he?

He read and reread the papers. Everything he had found out on his own was confirmed in the Internet search. Name, address, age, all the usual footprints. Frank couldn't quite get a grip on Vincent Street. He had come to Atlanta to live with a nephew or a cousin ten years ago. He had discovered a way to make a living and a way to work his scam. Had his cousin introduced him to this? Had the cousin somehow been a conduit to these scams? Frank had no way of knowing. He didn't even know the cousin's name. Vincent Street. A man can learn a lot in ten years, but a lot of what a man learns is what he wants to learn. A psychiatrist would try to get into Vincent's head. Did he love his mother? Did he hate her? Did he hate his father for dying? Had he been abused as a child? As an adult? Frank didn't care.

He would give the easy way one more day. If nothing turned up, he would go see Mr. Vincent Street himself. He didn't doubt he would find out all Vincent knew about Jenny. He might have to kill Vincent afterward. That would be too bad. He hadn't killed anyone in a long time and didn't relish letting those demons loose again. But he would do whatever was necessary. That was his gift. He would find Jenny. He was sure of that. Twenty-four more hours and then it was back to the old Spartan ways.

THE LAST SPARTAN

Chapter 18

The girls were startled awake by the buzzing at their door. Caron stumbled out of bed first. She pressed the intercom button cautiously.

"Who is it?"

"Vincent."

"Come on up," she said and pressed the button to open the lobby door.

"Get up, Jenny, Vincent's on the way up."

Vincent knocked, and Caron let him in. He was carrying a couple of grocery bags.

"What are you doing here?" Caron asked.

"I just thought I would pay you a little visit. Bring you a few things." He sat the bags down on the countertop. He fought hard not to sneer at the shabby one-bedroom apartment. Caron started going through the bags like a child with her first present at her birthday party.

"Wow. Two bottles of wine. Spaghetti noodles. Paul Newman's special sauce. I love this stuff. Parmesan cheese. French bread. A bag of salad mix. Cokes. Even cookies. Chocolate chip with M&Ms. These are the bomb. This is so great."

"What's the catch?" Jenny asked from the bedroom door. She leaned against the frame. Her eyes were watchful.

"Does there have to be a catch?" Vincent asked.

"With you? Always."

Vincent smiled. "It is a celebration then."

"What are we celebrating?" Caron asked.

"Jenny's first big break."

"The Arab guy?" Caron said.

"Yes. If he hires her as the new face for tourism to his country, it will be worth a fortune."

"To who?" Jenny asked.

"To all of us," Vincent said, appearing to take no offense. "You will get the modeling break you deserve, which we can parlay into more jobs. You will get paid tens of thousands of dollars."

"What's in it for you?"

"I will get a referral fee as well as more future work. If you work out well, they have told me I may be hired to shoot some of the layouts."

Jenny walked into the room. "It just sounds a little too good to be true, if you catch my drift. Like the job at the Blonde Geisha."

"I understand. It is very fortuitous, indeed. You are a very lucky girl."

"I don't know," Jenny mumbled. "He's not expecting anything else is he?"

Vincent tried to look shocked. "Of course not, this is strictly a get acquainted dinner. He will be evaluating you the entire time. Do not forget this. Be very polite. Be respectful. Be professional."

"No sex. I won't do that. I won't fuck him," Jenny snapped.

Vincent looked shocked to hear such language from her. He was. "I would not ask you to."

"That's what you said about the Blonde Geisha."

Vincent made a dismissive humphing noise in his throat. He mimicked stroking in the air. "That? That is nothing. After tomorrow night you will not need to return there again. Your career will be made."

Hope flared unbidden behind Jenny's eyes. "Really? You're telling the truth for once?"

"Yes, really. I already called Madam Yung. And for you, Caron, she has given tonight off."

"Whoopee," Caron said. "I was beginning to get that car pool tunnel thing I heard about."

Jenny laughed. Caron did, too. Even Vincent managed a smile.

"It is a dreary day," Vincent said. "Stay inside. Watch TV. Drink your wine. Relax."

"Vincent, what do you want me to wear tomorrow night?" Jenny asked. "I don't have anything decent."

Vincent paused, as if thinking. "Yes, that is very important. Let me think. Yes. I know a little dress shop. I saw a dress there. It will be perfect for you. It is long and black. Very simple, but very elegant. It has a collar of diamond beads. Very expensive."

"I can't afford something like that," Jenny said.

Vincent smiled again. "Consider it my gift to you."

"Thank you."

"Think nothing of it."

Jenny smiled. Then her smile disappeared.

"Does he know how old I am? That could be a problem."

"No. His country has no such restrictions. All the top models of the world started at your age or younger. Perhaps we will fudge your birth date a little on the contracts." He smiled conspiratorially. "That would not be too bad, I think."

The girls smiled.

"You could handle a little white lie," Caron said. "Every top model I ever read about has a make-up artist who travels with her, right?"

"Absolutely," Vincent lied.

"And you both know I'm good with make-up."

"Of course," Vincent said. "You are an artist."

"That would be so cool," Jenny said. "Then everybody wins."

Caron smiled. It had been a long time since she had won anything. "We could travel the world together."

"It's a deal. If I get a contract, you go with me to do the make-up."

Vincent nodded. "Oh, yes. I brought something else for you to celebrate with."

He fished into his pocket and brought out a little baggy. Inside were a half dozen chunks of hashish. He shook the bag in the air. He opened the bag and started to take some out. He paused and dropped them back into the plastic bag.

"Here. Take them all. It is a special day."

Caron snatched the baggy from his hand. "I haven't had any good hash in weeks. This is just the best high. The landing is so smooth. Thanks, Vincent. You're the best."

Jenny smiled. "I have to go to the bathroom. I'll be right back."

"I must leave as well," Vincent said. "I will bring the dress for you tomorrow evening and take you to your meeting."

Jenny smiled a tight smile. She turned and went into the bathroom. When the door closed, Vincent turned to Caron. All good humor vanished from his face.

"She is your responsibility. Do you understand?"

"Yeah," Caron said.

Vincent grabbed both her wrists and shook her. "Do you understand?"

"I said yes," she whined.

"If anything happens to her, if she does not meet this man, you will have to answer to me."

Caron struggled against his grip. He was surprisingly strong for one so thin. "You're hurting me."

"Listen carefully. If something goes wrong, I will beat you like you have never been beaten before, then I will carve your face so that no man will ever look at you again without being sick."

Caron cringed. "I understand."

"Do not fail me, Caron."

"I won't. I promise."

Vincent released his grip on her wrists. "Tomorrow night is very important for all of us."

Caron nodded. Vincent smiled.

"I am sorry I hurt you."

Caron was massaging her wrists. "It's okay."

Vincent smiled. "One more thing before I go."

Caron looked up into his eyes. Vincent drew his zipper down.

"Quickly. Before she returns."

Caron knelt before him. Vincent couldn't see the tears in her eyes. He wouldn't have cared.

THE LAST SPARTAN

Chapter 19

Frank left the zoo near six o'clock. He found a steak house and got a booth in the back. It was made of fake red leather like all steak house booths. Must be a law somewhere. He ordered a New York strip with garlic mashed potatoes and the vegetable medley. As he was eating he noticed a couple being seated nearby. The man was well-to-do. He had those gray sideburns women found so distinguishing. He was in pretty good shape for an old guy. The girl with him was his daughter's age. She wasn't his daughter. She was beautiful and blonde and in her twenties. She had a gorgeous figure and a drop-dead smile. And when she laughed. . . there was something so familiar in that laugh. She laughed again. It reminded him of Helen. Frank drifted away.

* * * *

Frank awoke with a start. Where was he? Where was Helen? He was lying in a king-size bed. The sheets were tucked in snugly around him. His clothes were gone. Even without lifting the sheets he could tell. He looked around. He was in a large hotel room. Some kind of huge monster suite. There were fresh flowers in a vase across from him. A light breeze drifted from the balcony, stirring the warm air.

He saw Helen on the balcony. She was lying in a lounger reading a magazine. She was wearing a white two piece bikini. He could see her breasts rise and fall with each breath. She was magnificent. His heart seemed to stop beating. She turned her head and saw him watching her. A smile spread across her face. She quickly got to her feet and came inside, closing the sliding glass door to the balcony behind her.

"It's about time you got up, sleepyhead."

"How long have I been asleep?"

"Three days. Almost four. You had lost a lot of blood. But I knew you would make it."

Frank smiled. "Where are we?"

"The Marriott, like you said." She was beaming. She spread her arms and indicated the room. "This is the honeymoon suite."

"Honeymoon suite?"

"I figured it was the best room, and it would guarantee us privacy while you healed. No one disturbs honeymooners. Room service leaves everything in the hall for us."

It was good thinking, but fear nipped at Frank. "You shouldn't have let me sleep so long. There could be problems. We should have dumped the Lexus—"

"I already did," she said as she sat beside him on the bed.

Frank was stunned by her calm. "Start from the top."

"After you took your little nap in the car?"

Frank smiled a sheepish grin. "Yeah, that's a good place to start."

"I checked us in under my real last name. I used my real credit card and driver's license to confirm the room. It was late. I told them we were on our honeymoon and you were passed out drunk in the car. They offered to help, but I told them I didn't need any. They loaned me a wheelchair to help haul your drunk butt up here."

"That was smart."

"Thank you," she smiled again.

She was truly beautiful, Frank thought. Her lips were pink perfection. He wanted to kiss her.

"You weigh a ton," she said. "Did you know that? Eventually, I got you into the wheelchair and up to the room."

"And the car?"

"Not so fast. I'm telling this. I drove to a convenience store and got some supplies. You know, for your leg. I figured the car might be traced, so I drove it down to a Holiday Inn about five blocks away. I wiped down everything I think we touched and left the keys in it."

"You are a clever girl. A car like that with keys in it won't last long. Go on."

That smile again. He would love to kiss that mouth. Feel her body pressed against him again.

"I had left you in the wheelchair, so I got your clothes off," she said.

Frank saw her blush. It was a faint reddening around her neck, then it was gone.

"I had to cut them off. I dumped all the clothes in a garbage bag. I scrubbed your wound as well as I could and bandaged your leg using some Kotex pads and duck tape. Then I wrapped it with another garbage bag. I didn't want you getting blood all over the bed. That would be hard to explain to housekeeping."

"Maybe you were a virgin bride."

"Not likely, stud. Anyway, the next morning I took a cab to a used car lot and bought a Honda Civic. I paid cash. The Honda is faded silver and virtually invisible. I went to a Wal-Mart and got better bandages, towels, antiseptic, over-the-counter meds, and some other things I thought we might need and came back here."

"My nurse."

"You better know it. I watched over you like a mother hen. I was worried the wound would get infected, but it didn't. It's healing nicely."

"Where did you get the cash for the car?"

"I stole it from the Ghost Riders. That's what's in my suitcase. Close to sixty thousand dollars."

Frank grinned. "Nice. I thought that was a big suitcase."

"I figure we might as well spend it. Have a nice little vacation."

"You buy anything else?"

"I had to buy some clothes for me. And this little bikini. Do you like it?" She stood up and did a quick pirouette.

"I love it. You look fantastic in it. But you always look that way."

"Stop it," she said, slapping at him playfully.

"Did you buy me any clothes? Or do I have to go naked?"

"Of course I bought you some clothes. But keeping you naked did cross my mind."

"You are wicked."

"Yes I am. You didn't have anything left. I tossed everything from your jean jacket to your boxers. So I bought you some pants and shirts and new boots. The whole nine yards. I even got you a bathing suit."

"Not a Speedo, I hope."

"It's a thong," Helen deadpanned.

Frank grimaced.

"No. Long boardshorts so they can cover your bandages if you want to sit outside. I even got an Ace bandage for your knee."

"My knee? It's my leg that hurts, not my knee."

"Silly. If you decide to go outside, I can wrap your knee to let that explain your limp."

"You are as clever as you are beautiful."

"How's the leg?"

"Still sore as hell," Frank said, grimacing as he sat up in the bed.

Helen reached to pull back the sheets. Frank stopped her, taking her wrist in one of his massive hands. "I'm naked."

"Of course you are. I cut your clothes off, remember? I've seen everything you got to show."

Frank released her wrist. She pulled the cover back. The bandages looked fresh. There was only a slight stain, more pink than red. His leg looked swollen and discolored. The leg felt stiff, but all in all, not bad for getting shot.

"Have you ever been shot before?" Helen asked.

"No. First time."

"What's it like?"

"Hurts," Frank said. "Burns. But when it first happened, the leg went kind of numb like it was asleep."

She turned away from him. "I never shot anyone before," she said.

"If you hadn't, I would be dead," Frank said.

She nodded. "I know. I didn't want you to die."

"I told you they couldn't kill me."

He could smell her skin. It smelled warm, sprinkled with sweat and suntanning lotion. He had never felt so awkward around a woman before. He felt himself becoming erect.

Helen saw it and laughed out loud. "Well, it seems someone is feeling better than I thought."

Frank reached to pull up the sheet. This time she took his wrist and stopped him. She took him in her hands and began stroking him. Frank saw she was still wearing the small red-jeweled ring. Still wore the red fingernail polish. He moaned and leaned back against the pillows. Helen smiled. She stood up and untied her bikini and let the pieces fall to the floor. She was flawless. She stood there without moving, letting him see her nude for the first time.

Frank remembered a line from a story by Raymond Chandler. His character, Philip Marlowe, was describing an encounter with a woman. "When I turned, she was standing by the bed as naked as Aphrodite, fresh from the Aegean. She stood there proudly and without either shame or enticement." It was like that with Helen.

"Are you sure we should try this with my leg and all? I can wait."

She smiled that perfect smile again. "I can't. I'll be gentle," she said and straddled him. She reached to guide him inside her.

"After all," she said, "it is our honeymoon."

THE LAST SPARTAN

They stayed in the hotel for another ten days. They were the best days of Frank Kane's life. Then the summons from Cyrus came.

* * * *

Frank came back to reality. He drank two cups of coffee. He spread the yellow pages listing all the adult entertainment he could find in Atlanta. He took out an ink pen and used the back of one of the computer sheets to make a list.

He made a list of massage parlors from the yellow pages first. He organized them into rough order to cut down on having to backtrack too much. It wasn't likely that Jenny was working in a stroke joint, but you never knew. She had to be somewhere.

Frank finished his meal and paid the bill. Dessert would have been nice. It was tempting. Frank decided it was time for a little will power. It was time to get back to work.

His routine was simple. He would go to a massage parlor on the list and ask for a massage. When they brought out his masseuse, he would say he preferred an American girl. Most of the massage parlors were run by Asian gangs. Most of the girls who worked there were Asian. If they had any American girls, he would ask for a young one. If they had one, he would ask if they had anyone else, he preferred a certain look. It didn't take long to run through a dozen places. It was good he wouldn't be hanging around too long. It was only a matter of time before the story of the big stranger who wanted a certain type of girl for a massage got around. Someone would be out looking for him to see who he really was. But he had time. It would take days.

He also stopped at a couple of adult bookstores. They all ran peep shows in the back. Some with live girls. Some just sold porno DVDs and sex toys. If he didn't spot Jenny working there, he would run through the same questions. He acted like a redneck with a young girl fetish. Most of the people he talked with seemed scared of him. That was a normal reaction.

He went back to DC's apartment to catch a nap before he had to pick up Bren. Something was about to pop. He could feel it.

Chapter 20

It was just after midnight when he got up. Frank washed his face, brushed his teeth, and locked the apartment up behind him. The club where Bren danced was a thirty-minute drive away. The parking lot was half full. The cars were older here and worn. The juice bar was called Fast Eddy's. The outside had once been painted off-white, now it looked gray. It had a run-down feeling just like the cars.

There was no doorman. He told the girl by the door he was supposed to pick up Bren after she got off. The girl told him to wait by the bar for Bren. The inside was smoky, and the DJ played old school rock-and-roll numbers. There was a blues vibe to the music. Johnny Winter, the Rolling Stones, ZZ Top, and the Allman Brothers all took their turns. The crowd was working men. Their attire casual. Their talk loud. Their appreciation for the full nudity of the dancers was unrestrained. He found he liked this place.

Frank found the bar and took a stool. The bar man was a bald, fat-bellied, sixty-year-old man who looked like nothing surprised him anymore. He seemed supremely bored surrounded by drunks and naked women the age of his granddaughters.

"What'll you have?" the bartender asked.

"You got any water?"

"Tap."

"That would do fine."

The bar man filled him a glass from the bar and handed it to him. "Ice?"

"No. This will be fine. How much I owe you?"

The bar man stared dumbfounded as Frank took a deep drink.

"No charge for the water," the bar man added.

"I thought everything in here had a price."

"It does. Just not the water. First time anybody asked for a glass of water that I can recall. You waiting for one of the girls?"

"Bren."

"Aphrodite," he said, correcting Frank. "We only use their stage names in here."

"Right."

"I thought she was still hooked up with that computer kid, DC."

"She is. I'm just giving her a lift."

"Uh huh."

"Favor for DC. He asked me."

"On the level?"

"On the square," Frank answered.

"Good. I like that kid. She won't let him come here."

"Probably inhibits her."

The bar man smiled. "Nothing inhibits that girl. You a close friend?"

"Nope. Didn't even meet her until yesterday."

"You take my advice. Be careful around her."

"Why?"

"Never mind. It's none of my business."

"Come on. What's the skinny?"

The bar man looked around as if someone could even hear him if they wanted to. "Trouble follows that girl," he said.

Frank fished a ten dollar bill from his pocket. "Here. One more glass of water."

The bar man shook his head. "I said the water was free, son."

"This is for the advice."

The bar man scooped it up and stuffed it into his back pocket. Then he winked. "I appreciate it. Most folks don't pay my fat ass any attention when it comes to tips."

Frank saluted him with the glass of water. "We're all working men, brother. How long until she gets done?"

The bar man leaned in closer. "Her shift is over, but she's got a private party in the back room." He nodded toward a small hallway off to the right. "Picking up a few extra bucks the old-fashioned way. Blow party. But you didn't hear it from me."

The bar man picked up a rag that hadn't been clean in years and went to wiping the faded bar. Frank swiveled toward the hallway. Ten minutes passed. An old AC/DC song began to blare. Frank recognized the tune, but he couldn't distinguish any of the lyrics over the static from the speakers and the singer's snarl. The door in the hallway opened and four guys stumbled out. They were drunk and laughing. High-fives were thrown all around. They walked over to where Frank sat and ordered four beers. A juice bar doesn't sell alcohol, but patrons can sell their alcohol to the bar and have the bar resell it back to the patron. It's a weird law for a weird world.

111

"That was so sweet, man."

"Who you going to believe? I told you, man. I told you."

"Best blow job I ever had," someone said.

"Best any of us ever had," someone else added.

"Best twenty bucks I ever spent."

"No shit."

"I'll be back. I can tell you that."

"But we got to keep it on the low low. Word gets out, that's the last you'll see of those sweet lips."

They all started to laugh. A young dancer tapped Frank on the arm. "Would you like to buy me a drink?"

"No."

"How about a dance?"

"No. I'm here to meet someone."

"Is she prettier than me?"

Frank smiled. She was good. Strippers were relentless. They saw all men as walking ATMs. They just had to push the right buttons, and the money flowed out. "No. She's not prettier."

"Why don't you buy a dance and you can convince me."

Frank shook his head. "Beat it."

Then he saw Bren from the corner of his eye walking out from the private room. She was smiling and talking to the customers. She was fully nude except for a gold belly chain and very high stripper heels. She did a little dance as she moved through the crowd. She walked toward him and leaned over to kiss him. Frank turned his head at the last second, and she kissed his cheek. Bren didn't seem to notice.

"Have you been waiting long?"

"No."

"I'll get changed, and we can go."

"Good."

"Hey, Aphrodite," one of the young men said. "You are the sexiest woman I've ever seen. How about a farewell dance?"

"Sorry, boys. I'm off duty. Come back tomorrow night, and I'll give you an encore."

"Hot damn," the boy said.

She looked at Frank and smiled.

Ten minutes later she was back. She was wearing tight black leather pants and a thin pink blouse. The four young men were gone.

Back to wives or girlfriends or empty apartments. Frank didn't know or care which.

"Eddy," she called to the bar man. "Let me have a Coke on the house."

Eddy shook his head.

Bren pulled out a five and slapped it on the bar. "Fuck you."

Eddy handed her a bottle of Coke and her change. She drank it straight away in one long gulp. She turned to Frank. "You going to say anything to DC?"

"About what?"

"About what you think you know or think you heard."

"No. That's between you and him."

"Damn right. Good answer. Let's roll."

Outside in the parking lot they walked toward Frank's truck. "You got any news for me yet?" Frank asked.

"No. I checked a couple of places before work. The other girls will ask around. I said she owed me a hundred bucks. If I could find her and get it, I promised to split it with the one who found her."

"Good idea. Makes it business, not personal."

"That's what we understand. Come on, I got a friend. Dances at a place over on Canal Street. She knows all the new girls."

"Do I have to tag along?"

"Yeah. The Honey Hole can get rough late at night. I need you for protection."

"You don't need protection."

"Come on, big boy, we're wasting time."

They drove in relative silence, with Bren only bitching once that he had no radio and to give him constant directions. They parked at a run-down building that could have been built at the same time as Fast Eddy's. The brick was painted and refaded so many times it had lost all resemblance to any known color.

"You got a cigarette?" she asked.

"No. I don't smoke anymore."

Bren fished around in her purse until she found a pack and tapped one out.

"Good thing I still do." She lit the cigarette and tossed the match out the window.

"Why did you ask me if you had a fresh pack?"

"Get all you can. That's my motto. Why use one of mine if I can bum one from some guy. Geesh, are you really that naive?"

Frank had been called many things. Many of them colorful combinations of seemingly unrelated curse words. Never naive.

"Let's go," he said.

Bren spoke to the skinny guy working the door, and they slipped inside without paying a cover charge. Frank ranged the room quickly and saw no one he recognized.

"You wait here. My girlfriend, Dawn, might have a lead."

Frank didn't answer. He just leaned against the wall. He put on his fierce face to keep the dancers away. No one bothered him. Although, one old dancer seemed to debate it for some time before wandering off. A few minutes later, two motorcycle riders came in. One was about five-feet-ten and built square. The other was six-one and thin, with long hair and a long nose. They rode for the Jokers, as their colors attested. At one time the Jokers had been under Spartan control. It had not been a particularly happy alliance or a peaceful recruitment. The square-built guy Frank didn't know. He recognized the thin guy as Billy. He made no attempt to avoid eye contact, but he was careful not to stare. To bikers, staring was too much of a challenge, especially if they had you outnumbered. The Hells Angels had a motto, "One for all, and all on one." The Angels didn't fight fair. Nobody did, except in the movies.

The two Jokers found a table and began ordering drinks. Shots of gentleman Jim Beam. They were obviously in a good mood and celebrating something. Bikers were always celebrating something. They each got a lap dance and ignored him.

What finally drew their attention to him was Bren when she returned. They followed her to him.

"Dawn put me onto someone who might know something, but she's off until tomorrow night. I have to go to the little girls' room, and then we can split."

"Then go," Frank said.

Bren skipped away through the tables toward the bathroom in the back.

He noticed the two bikers talking. He tried to watch them in his peripheral vision. It is harder to identify someone from just a profile. A minute later, Billy got up from his chair and came over.

Frank pretended to be watching a short, brown girl do a lap dance. Billy tapped him lightly on the shoulder.

"Excuse me, brother. You look familiar. Do I know you?"

"I don't think so," Frank answered. His voice was neutral.

"You ride hard, or are you independent?"

Frank pretended to be puzzled. He was a pretty good actor. "I don't understand what you mean."

"You wear colors, or you ride independent?"

"I don't ride."

"Bullshit. You're a rider. You look like a rider. Who except cowboys and bikers got these bowed legs?"

"I said, I don't ride."

"Come on, help me out, brother. I know you from somewhere. I just can't place it."

"You don't know me."

Something feral flashed behind Billy's dark eyes. "You calling me a liar?"

"No." Frank's voice was still flat.

"It sounded like you were. The Jokers don't take that shit from nobody. I'll kick your fuckin' punk ass."

Frank's face stayed deadpan. "I don't want to fight you. And I meant no disrespect. I just think you have me confused with someone else. That's all."

"Okay then," Billy said. The fire was settling down. "But I know you. It'll come to me. I never forget a face."

Bren returned. Her face was glowing. Her appearance changed the tense moment immediately.

"Hey, baby," Billy started. "How about a dance?"

"I don't work here. The management wouldn't allow it. Sorry."

It sounded to Frank like she was sincere. She really was sorry she couldn't give him a dance.

"You want to hang around and party with us? Nobody parties like the Jokers, baby. We know how to show a lady like yourself a real good time."

She paused, and again Frank thought she was actually considering his offer. She probably was. Bren shook her head.

"No. I got to split. I got some things I got to do tonight."

"Hey, what's your name, baby doll?"

"Bren."

"I'm Billy. We definitely got to get together. Maybe we can party some other time."

"Absolutely, Billy," Bren answered. "I look forward to it."

Billy bit his lip dramatically. "So do I, baby doll. So do I."

Bren stepped up to Frank and took his arm. They walked outside toward the truck. Once inside, she wiggled in the seat to get comfortable.

"Where to now?"

"One more quick stop, then home."

"Good. Where to?"

She gave him directions to a small twenty-four-hour convenience store.

"I won't be a minute," she said and hurried into the store.

Frank thought it might be another contact until he saw the guy behind the counter slip her a small clear package in exchange for a few bills. She came straight back to the truck.

"Did you find out anything?"

"That? No that wasn't about your little friend. I was just scoring us some blow so we could party a little bit back home."

Frank backed the truck out and headed back toward the apartment. Bren watched him. "What's wrong? You do get high, don't you?"

"I don't do drugs anymore."

"You're kidding me. What about weed? You still smoke weed don't you? I mean, weed isn't even really dope."

"No."

"Come on. Everyone smokes weed. It can't hurt you."

"I don't."

"Not ever?"

"Not for five years."

"Shit. You rarely drink. You don't smoke. You don't do dope. What are you, a priest? You get into AA or something?"

"Or something," he said.

They drove on in silence until Bren said, "You used to wear earrings, didn't you?"

"Yes."

"But you gave that up, too."

"Yes."

"I bet you looked hot with earrings. I think earrings make guys look hot."

Frank didn't answer.

"I guess that means you don't have any piercings, huh?" Bren asked.

"No."

"Too bad. I think piercings are hot, too. Especially on guys down south, if you know what I mean. I use to have my nipples pierced. It kept them real hard. Customers liked that better."

"Sounds reasonable."

"But they kept DC too turned on. He wouldn't leave them alone. He was always messing with them like a little kid. I finally had to take them out."

Frank remained quiet.

"I never got my navel done," Bren said, pulling up the front of her blouse to prove her point. "Everybody does that, so it's kind of boring. That's why I wear the belly chain. That gets guys super hot. The belly chain and stripper heels and nothing else."

Frank grunted.

"That stuff get you hot, Frank?"

"Used to."

"I guess you had to give that up, too."

"I guess. When are you going to talk with Dawn's friend? I'm running out of time," Frank said as he parked the truck.

"Chill out. Tomorrow. Dawn gave me her number, and I'll check her out tomorrow. Eight hundred more if I find her, right?"

"Absolutely. You find her tomorrow, and I'll make it an even thousand."

Bren grinned. "Deal. But don't tell DC. He'll want a cut."

"As you like it."

Bren spoke as she opened her door. He thought he heard her say, "I like it rough and all night long."

Frank acted like he didn't hear. He followed Bren into the apartment. She hung her small purse over the back of one of the kitchen chairs. She fished the cocaine out of her pocket. She opened the packet and began dicing it up with her charge card. When she had some

117

separated into four lines, she fished a piece of a drinking straw from her pocket. She deeply snorted a couple of the lines.

"Are you sure you don't want a taste?"

"Thanks, but no."

"It's pretty good stuff."

"No. Thanks."

Frank flopped down on the sofa and turned the television on. He pretended to be engrossed in some late night sports highlight show. He didn't care much about sports. The Greek word for sports competition was *agonia*. Today the word has been modified to the word *agony*. It was also the Greek word for battle.

"I'm still pretty wired," Bren said. "Do you want to party a little?"

"No. I'm done. Get some sleep."

"We could have a couple of beers and just sit around and talk. Get to know each other better."

"No."

Bren sighed dramatically and went to the bathroom. He heard the shower running. He unlaced his boots and took his socks and shoes off. He hoped she would hurry up. He wanted to hit the bathroom before he went to sleep. His teeth felt like something had died on them. The shower stopped sometime after the ice caps had melted. He heard a hair dryer running. By Zeus, he wondered. How long does it take to get ready for bed? She emerged in a white terry cloth robe. She didn't look at him as she went straight to her bedroom. Thank you, Lord. Frank hustled into the empty bathroom. She had left her tiny thong panties on the floor. He kicked them out of his way.

Frank shaved and brushed his teeth. It felt great. He pissed for an eternity. People really didn't appreciate how good a piss could feel. It wasn't as good as sex, but it was damn fine.

When he came back out, all the lights in the apartment were out. The glow of the television was the only light. He didn't see anyone. He walked toward the sofa. Bren's bedroom door was closed. Good.

He unfastened his jeans and dropped them to the floor. As he stepped out of them, he saw her. She was standing perfectly still in the kitchen. She was still wearing the white bathrobe. She moved toward him. She didn't make any sound.

"Are you alright?" Frank asked. Her eyes had an odd look.

She ignored him. "I was just going to sleep when I started to wonder about something, Frank. You don't hardly drink. You don't smoke. You don't do drugs. You don't party. So I was wondering if you still liked to fuck?"

Frank didn't answer. He knew it was a setup question. Bren moved up until she was almost touching him.

"Do you, Frank? Do you like to fuck?" The way she said it, with the emphasis on *fuck,* was meant to shock and arouse him. Powerful shit.

"Sure. Sometimes. The right times."

"Are you sure? I mean, you haven't looked twice at me. It makes a girl feel unappreciated." She traced a finger down the center of his broad chest.

"Sorry."

"Aren't you attracted to me, Frank?" She lowered her arms and let the robe fall to the floor. She put her tiny hands on her hips. "Don't you want to fuck me? Don't you want to know what it would feel like to be inside me?"

"Shit, Bren. Put your clothes back on. It's not going to happen. So just forget it. I'm too tired." The tiny voice from his other brain started to object to his decision.

"Why not? DC won't be back until tomorrow anyway, and I'm horny. It doesn't have to mean anything."

"It would mean something to me. Now go to bed. I need some sleep."

Bren snatched her robe off the floor. "Fine," she snapped. "Maybe you're gay."

"I'm not gay," Frank said and hated himself for speaking. He wondered why men always had to explain away that charge.

She stopped at her bedroom door. "Prove it," Bren challenged. "If you're not gay, fuck me."

"Go to bed," he answered and turned away from her toward the television.

"Fuck you," she hissed as she stomped off into the bedroom. If the bedroom door had been solid wood instead of hollow particle board, her slamming of the door would have been more impressive.

Gosh, Frank thought. That wasn't predictable. He felt a twinge of sorrow for DC. He was in love with a woman who didn't love him. Hell, she probably had never loved anyone or anything. Maybe money. She definitely had a serious crush on money. She was a fool, Frank thought. She had a chance at love, but she wasn't interested. DC seemed like a decent enough guy, but Bren was using him liked she used everybody else. Frank wondered if she might try again after he fell asleep. Maybe he should lock himself in the bathroom.

THE LAST SPARTAN

Chapter 21

They had spent the day just as Vincent had wanted. Smoking hash, eating cookies, and watching TV. Together they made a big spaghetti dinner with salads and everything. Now they were just watching television. Cruising on the buzz from the wine and hashish.

"Man, wouldn't it be great if I got the job?" Jenny said. She had her stuffed dog, Scampy, in her lap and was petting him like he was a real dog.

"Killer. You would have more money than you've ever had in your life, Jen."

"We could do anything we wanted."

"Everything we wanted," Caron corrected. "An address on easy street. No more hand jobs or blow jobs. Straight jobs."

"Who knows where it could lead."

"Yeah. You might even end up on television or in the movies, Jenny. You're pretty enough."

"No way."

"Way. But then you'd probably get too big a deal to look after your old friends anymore."

"Don't say that, Caron. You know I'll look after you. Just like you've looked after me. We cover each other's backs."

"That's right. Just remember that when you're all rich and famous."

"I'll remember. If it happens."

"It will. Don't worry. I can see it. There's something special about you. Big things are going to happen for you."

"And you, too."

"Yeah, right. I'm a nobody. I'm worthless."

"No, you're not."

"That's what my dad used to say."

"Your dad told you you were worthless?" Jenny was shocked.

"In between beatings. That old son of a bitch sure got mean when he drank. And he drank all the time."

"What did you do?"

"I cried a lot. Locked myself in my room, but he would just bust the door in."

"I mean, did you tell your mom?"

"She didn't care. The old whore. She was as bad as he was. She blamed me for trapping her with my dad. Said she could have been something if she hadn't got knocked up with me. Fat chance of that."

"That's awful."

"I got through it. The beatings weren't that bad. It was not knowing when you were going to get one that was hard."

"Is that why you ran away? Because he beat you?"

"No. My mom stopped sleeping with my dad, and he started to come on to me."

"No way. That's so sick."

"You're telling me. It was like a light came on in his empty head one day, and he thought I might be good for something after all."

"And your mom didn't stop him?"

"She didn't care. She probably gave him the idea in the first place. It kept his fat ass off her."

"Did he . . . you know . . . rape you?"

"He tried to. He was so drunk he couldn't get it up. When he passed out I packed a bag and took off. I was fourteen."

"You've been on your own since fourteen?"

"It's no big deal. You learn to get by with less. Vincent's a piece of shit, but he's helped me land some jobs."

They sat in silence for a few minutes. Each was lost in her own memories of home.

"Did your dad beat you, too?" Caron asked.

"No. My parents are dead. I was raised by my grandparents."

"Did your granddad?"

"No. He's a real old school gentleman."

"Your granny, then?"

"No. She's a tough old bird, but she's fair. She never laid a hand on me."

"Nobody tried to get in your britches or anything?"

"No."

"Didn't get busted for dope, or kicked out of school, or caught drinking?"

Jenny shook her head no.

"Then why did you run away?"

Jenny stared at her hands. "I don't know anymore. I was mad. I wanted to grow up."

"Growing up sucks," Caron said.

"I think sometimes I should go on home."

"Why don't you?"

"I can't now. Not after the things I've done. I can't ever go home again." Jenny started to cry.

Caron came over to the sofa and put her arms around her and held her while she cried. She murmured soothing words and patted her back until Jenny finally stopped crying. Caron used her shirt sleeve to wipe Jenny's face.

"There. Feel better? Nothing like a good cry to set the world right."

"I feel so stupid."

"Get used to it. It's part of life. Now go clean up. You got to look good tomorrow night, or we are both shit out of luck."

Jenny laughed. She handed Scampy to Caron and went into the bathroom. She looked into the mirror. She rubbed her blonde hair. She missed her real hair color. She stared at the deep-set eyes. She once thought her eyes were her best feature. Now they looked hollow. Empty. The fire had gone out inside her. She splashed cold water on her face and dried it with a towel. She stared at the stranger in the mirror once more.

She wished she was brave. If she had courage, at least she could slit her wrists and die without anyone ever knowing what she had done. She was so ashamed. She started to cry again.

Chapter 22

That night as Frank slept, he remembered how he had lost Helen. The call had come ten days into their "honeymoon." It was a text message on Frank's cell phone. It said, "The gods will meet on Olympus. Tuesday at eight o'clock. Bring the girl."

Helen heard his sigh.

"What's wrong?" she asked.

"Message from Cyrus. He wants us to come to Olympus."

"Where's that?"

"He's got an estate in North Carolina. High up in the mountains around Asheville. A thousand acres of remote woods. Well guarded. Heavily patrolled by Spartans."

"Olympus?"

"I told you. The inner circle are treated as gods. Hell, we act like gods. There are sixteen of us. So Cyrus gave us each the names of Greek gods. It's only fitting that his mountaintop home be called Olympus."

"What does it mean?"

"Spanish Johnny ratted me out."

"Why? You saved his life."

"He wanted me to leave you behind. Rape you. Kill you. Whatever."

"But I warned you about the trap. I saved your life."

"He thinks you were trying to kill me and the Ghost Rider got in the way. He didn't want to take the chance on you."

Helen was visibly shaken. "That's crazy. You don't think . . . I mean I never—"

"If I thought that, I would have killed you back there."

"What are they going to do?"

"We'll have to stand before the council and let them decide our fate. I broke the Spartan law. There will have to be consequences."

"By saving me?"

"No. In the inner circle all are equal. When it comes to non-Spartans the law is clear. We cannot oppose another's request. I overruled Spanish Johnny's declaration on you. You weren't a Spartan. You weren't an ally or an associate or even a friend of the Spartans. You were nothing. What's more, I promised what is not in my power

124

to give without council approval. I promised you would become one of us, a Spartan. What's worse to them is I promised to elevate you to the position of Peer. There can only be three hundred full Spartan Peers. That means for me to fulfill my promise, one of them must die."

"That's insane."

"Probably. No Spartan member of the inner circle has ever opposed the desires of another."

"What about your desires? Don't they count?"

"He spoke first. His wishes have precedence. I broke our law. I threatened his life."

"I wish you had killed him."

"So do I," Frank said without any hint of remorse.

"It's all about power, isn't it? Spanish Johnny feels smaller because you kicked his ass, so he runs to Cyrus and poisons him against you. Makes him think somehow this weakens Cyrus."

"Yes. Cyrus will fear he is losing control. He must make an example of me to regain his power. To lead, you must have power. I was his weapon. Now he is afraid I might one day turn against him."

Helen shook her head, unable to comprehend. She managed a weak smile, and the rage in Frank melted a little. You had to play the cards you had, not the ones you wished you had.

"Come on, we have two days to get there and see this thing through," Frank said. "Let's not worry about things we can't control."

"Why don't we just run? We've got money. We could hide."

"They would find us. Anyway, that is not the Spartan way. I am responsible. I will face them."

Helen took his face in her hands and kissed him. "You are as crazy as they are."

Frank laughed. Helen leaned down and kissed him again.

"We still have time for something else before we go," she leered.

Frank pulled her tight against him. His chest felt so tight he thought it might explode.

*****

In the morning they began the drive to North Carolina. Helen drove. On Tuesday at precisely eight o'clock, they pulled up to the huge stone gates of Cyrus' home.

The Spartan guards greeted Frank with almost sorrow in their eyes. They knew what awaited him. She followed the long driveway until they reached Cyrus' estate.

The estate held a huge house where Cyrus lived. It also contained small separate cottages for each of the sixteen members of the inner circle. When the other gods were there, they had their own separate quarters. Helen parked where Frank told her. When they got out of the car, four Spartans approached them carrying MP-5 submachine guns.

"You got any luggage, Frank, you want taken to your place?"

Frank smiled. "No. She's got a bag in the car."

The Spartan shrugged.

"We'll come back for it. Sorry to ask you this, Frank. You know the rules. Are you armed?"

"No."

"I got to frisk you. You understand?"

Frank spread his arms out, and the man did a thorough pat down. Then he used a security wand to be sure he didn't miss anything. Then he repeated the procedure on Helen.

"Satisfied?" Frank asked.

"Yeah. Look, I'm sorry. You want to get anything to eat? Take a rest before you meet with the council?"

"Are they already up there?"

"Yes."

"No. Let's get it over with."

"You know the way. Apollo will meet you at the bottom of the path to escort you."

Frank nodded. He and Helen moved toward the forest. There was a path ahead that would lead them to the council, the entrance was lit with a row of torches. A tall black man stood at the entrance. He beamed a huge smile when he saw Frank. Frank grasped him in a warm bear hug.

"Good to see you, Lord Poseidon."

"Good to see you, Apollo. This is Helen."

"Pleased to meet you. You know this is bullshit, Frank."

"It is the law," Frank said with a shrug.

"It's still bullshit. Anything I can do for you?"

"No."

"This shit turns out bad, Spannish Johnny disappears."

THE LAST SPARTAN

Frank smiled. "I would appreciate that, Apollo. Just don't leave any prints that can lead back to you."

"Who you talking to? But know it's true. Spanish is good as gone."

They followed Apollo up a long winding path. The path itself was unlit. The ancient Spartans had forbidden the use of torches when Spartans moved at night to better accustom them to traveling in the dark. Cyrus had adopted the same policy. He was ever the modern Lycurgus. The walk was hard on Frank's leg, but he hid it well. The path led to a well-lit clearing. Around the outside, forming a semicircle, were carved thrones. Behind each throne was a marble statue of a different god. The Spartan seated before the statue bore the same name. In the center of the seats was a larger throne for Cyrus, their Zeus. They all rose when Frank arrived.

Cyrus smiled a thin smile. He was obviously battling mixed emotions.

"Come forward."

Frank did as he was asked. He nodded recognition to the other gods before him. They all sat down except Cyrus.

"Dark days, brother Poseidon," he began. "You all know the word on the rock at Thermopylae. The rock inscribed to remind the world of how three hundred Spartan warriors had withstood the onslaught of Xerxes' army. 'Go, stranger, and to Lacedaemonia tell that here, obeying her laws, we fell.'"

The other gods nodded. They knew the inscription well.

Cyrus continued. "You know the charges. Know the law has been broken. Your choices are two."

Frank smiled inside. Cyrus liked to use archaic touches in his speech when they played at being gods.

"I know them," Frank said.

Cyrus either didn't hear or felt it necessary to speak them anyways.

"You can recant your actions. Kill the girl, and all is forgiven. The law is satisfied."

Frank made no move.

"Or face the physical challenge as is fitting. How do you choose?"

Frank looked at Helen. Her eyes were wide with fear. The green seemed to have dulled.

"Physical challenge," Frank answered.

127

Cyrus smiled. He had expected no less from his enforcer. The Spartans admired courage above almost all else.

"Very well. Hades, Hephaestus, bring out the weapons."

Two men got up and went to the edge of the clearing. They lifted a table from the side and carried it into the center of the circle. Weapons were covered on the top. They sat the table down and pulled back the covering. On the top of the table lay a pile of a dozen Spartan Lakonians.

Ancient Spartan soldiers, or hoplites as they were called, fought primarily with an eight-foot spear behind a large bronze shield, but when their spear was broken or the fighting was too close, they switched to the Lakonian. The Lakonian was a short sword. The blade was fourteen inches long and leaf-shaped so it could be used for cutting or thrusting. All other Greek city-states of the same time used a longer sword that measured nearly twenty-four inches. The Spartan explanation for the shorter sword was that they liked to get in close. The handle was bronze. It weighed nearly three pounds. Hades and Hephaestus spread the swords into a neat line.

"Your opponent, by law, must be Hermes." Cyrus motioned toward Spanish Johnny who stood up. I also call upon Atlas. Also Ares."

"Your pardon, Zeus, but is that fair?" Apollo asked. "Three against one?"

Cyrus glared. "It is not meant to be fair, Apollo. It is meant to enforce the law. Remember the fate of the great Spartan king Pausanias, the hero of Plataea who destroyed Persia's army. His crime was the same. He offered citizenship to helots and was walled up alive in a temple to die."

"This is different," Apollo added.

"No. It is not," Cyrus said. He faced the men before him. "Your lives belong to Sparta. Prepare yourselves."

Each man chose a sword from the table. Atlas took two. All four men removed their shirts. The men began stretching their limbs. Spanish Johnny was thinner than the others with long, lean muscles. His skin was smooth and clean. His dark eyes seemed to burn with excitement. He handled the short sword like he had been born with it in his hand.

The one called Atlas looked like a Russian or Eastern European. He was huge. Probably a couple of inches taller and a hundred pounds heavier than Frank. His face was expressionless. His eyes dull. He practiced slow powerful swipes. The blades looked child-like in his massive hands.

The one called Ares was a little shorter than Frank but about the same weight. He moved with an athlete's ease of motion. He walked over to Frank and spoke to him.

"Forgive me, brother. I hate this. We have fought many battles together. But I must do what Zeus commands."

"I understand," Frank said, and they shook hands.

Helen hurried to Frank. "What are you going to do? Can you win? Do you have a plan?"

He smiled at her and stroked her face with one thick finger. "I always have a plan. Edged weapons were never my strong suit. Hermes is by far the fastest, but he will try to stay out of the initial clash and dart in when he sees an opening. He is an expert with a blade. Atlas is slow. He fights like an ox, but he will take some killing. Ares is the toughest of the three. He's just this side of me in skill."

"Can you win?"

"At my prime I could take one, probably two. With this leg? No, I can't win."

Tears welled in her eyes. "Then you are going to die."

"Probably. Fate can always play a hand. The gods have always favored me. We shall see."

"If you die, then they will kill me anyway."

"Yes. I am sorry. There is nothing I can do."

"Then you do it. Save yourself. Kill me. I brought all this on. You do what they asked. You kill me."

"I can't. I've done bad things. Terrible things. But I can't do that."

"You have to. If you love me, you have to."

"I do love you. But I can't do that."

"To your places," Cyrus ordered.

Hades and Hephaestus moved the table away. The combatants spread out across from each other. Once more Helen hurried before Frank. She took off her small ruby ring and pressed it into the palm of his hand.

"I will always be with you," she said. "I love you. Do not die for me. I have a plan, too."

Helen turned back toward the gods who were still seated. She was between Frank and his opponents. She faced Cyrus. She knelt and spoke. Her face bowed respectfully.

"Lord Zeus, I beg permission to speak."

Cyrus stared at her. "Very well. Say what you must."

"Lord Zeus, I do not fully understand your laws and ways, but I may have a solution to that which is before you. If you proceed, at the very least one of the inner circle shall die. Probably more. What a tragedy to the gods to lose so many of their own. What would Zeus be without his brother Poseidon?"

"Do not allow her to speak," Spanish Johnny called. "She has no rights here."

It was the wrong thing to say. Cyrus did not like to be challenged. His gaze was cold. "She has whatever rights I say she has, Hermes. What do you propose? Speak."

"If Poseidon will not recant his words, can you not ask the same of Hermes? Without a complaint there is no crime."

Cyrus thought the words over for a minute. He flashed a smile at Frank. "It is a reasonable request. What do you say, Hermes? Will you put aside your charges?"

Hermes face boiled with rage. "I would if I could, but I cannot. My honor and standing has been diminished here among my equals. There must be satisfaction. There can be only three hundred full Spartans. The law cannot be changed to accommodate one man's desires."

Cyrus nodded. "So be it. Step aside now, girl."

Helen started to rise, then dropped once more to her knees. "If there can only be three hundred, then someone would have had to die anyway to make a space for El Diablo."

Cyrus stifled a smile. She was a clever girl. He liked that. He had thought no one else would pick up on that fact. He had already decided which of the full Spartan Peers would suffer an unfortunate accident to make way for El Diablo. However, it was an accident that no longer needed to be arranged.

"Our rules cannot be ignored because of clever words," Spanish Johnny shouted.

"Once more, Lord Zeus, I beg permission to speak."

"You try my patience, girl."

"Once more and then no more. I beg you."

Hermes glared at Cyrus. He silently implored him to silence Helen. Cyrus did not.

"Very well. Proceed."

"I understand something of Greek history and the role of the gods, so please hear me out. The problem that arises is between Peers. One is disgraced because the other has offered that which cannot be given. I see that clearly now. I cannot become a full Spartan. What you call a Peer."

"That is correct. Poseidon cannot offer that which he does not possess."

"I understand that, Lord Zeus. The offering by its nature was an insult to the god Hermes."

Cyrus liked the way she said, "Lord Zeus."

Helen continued. "I do not seek that honor though it is great indeed. What I seek is to be elevated to the inner circle of the Gods."

There was an audible gasp among the men seated and standing.

Cyrus laughed. "I do not think that would be possible."

"Why not? The Spartans honor bravery and courage above all else. My actions stopped an ambush meant to kill two of the inner circle and start a revolt among Spartan allies. By my own hands I saved one, if not both men, in combat. I nursed and protected a god back into the service of Sparta. When the call of the council came, I did not run and hide. I came of my own accord. I have shown the characteristics that the ancient Spartans held most dear."

"But to become a god—"

"Not a god," Helen corrected. "A goddess. Ancient Olympus held many, and I see none before me. Athena, Hera, Diana, all were held in great esteem by the ancients. They saw the wisdom of having females within their inner circle."

"Such a decision—" Cyrus began.

"Could only be made by Zeus himself," Helen said, playing her trump card. "Each here was selected by you and so honored solely on your own accord. Zeus was first among equals. He ruled in the heavens even though other gods were not always happy with his choices. He ruled because he was the strongest. Zeus held the power, that is why the other gods followed him. Show that power now, Lord Zeus. Reunite the inner circle, then there is no crime, no dishonor, no retribution. A great king needs a queen by his side."

"You can't," Hermes shouted. Other heads nodded agreement with him.

Somewhere in the darkness an owl called. Frank heard it clearly.

Cyrus' black stare swept the men. "I can and will do as I please."

Helen looked up into his face. Cyrus looked from Frank to her and then back over the others. The owl called once more.

"I have decided," Cyrus roared. "There are portents that cannot be ignored. Helen shall join us in the inner circle. She has earned that privilege as much as anyone here. From henceforth, she will be known as Aphrodite. My will is law. And I defy anyone here to stand against me."

There was stunned silence. Apollo rose first and walked over to Helen.

"I greet you as an equal, sister Aphrodite. Welcome."

Others moved, some happily, others slowly, to welcome her.

"This calls for celebration," Cyrus shouted. "Dionysus, have the banquet hall prepared. We need wine and women to celebrate."

Cyrus took Helen's hand and led her away toward the house. The others followed, talking among themselves. Ares passed with a nod to Frank. Apollo stood at Frank's side.

"That is fucked up. I've seen some shit when I was with the Navy SEALs, but this beats it all. She's got some balls on her, brother. I see why you fell so hard for her."

Frank pulled his shirt back on. "She is lost to me now. She will be Cyrus' woman."

"Would you have rather fought three guys with swords?"

"Yes."

"Shit. You fell harder than I thought. Look, tomorrow morning I'm taking my plane and flying down to Costa Rica. I got a compound down in Nosara. It's got this big ass swimming pool, right on the fuckin' beach. Come with me. We'll do some swimming, go spear fishing, and those Tico girls, man, they will wear your ass out. Make you forget her."

"I won't forget."

Apollo patted Frank's broad shoulder. "I know you won't, man, but it will dull the pain. Help you live with it."

Frank walked down the path toward the cottage he stayed in. He could hear the sounds of celebration coming from the main house. He stripped and showered and went to bed, alone with his dark red thoughts.

Helen came back to him a final time a few hours before dawn. Frank was waiting for her.

"Does Cyrus know you are here?"

"He sent me to make peace. To heal your wounds."

"They are deep wounds."

"We are still alive," she said.

"I don't think I can stand it," Frank said.

"Of course you can. You are the strongest man I've ever met. In time he will grow weary of me. We will be together again."

"Years."

Helen smiled. "What are years to the gods? Now hold me. It will have to last me for a long time."

They made love throughout the remainder of the night. At dawn, she rose from his bed and crept away. Frank watched her go. He dressed and went to the airfield to meet Apollo. He had lost Helen forever, and he knew it.

* * * *

At five o'clock Frank heard a key in the door. It was DC. He was home early. Frank feigned sleep and heard DC creep into his own bedroom. Bren's screams of surprise and passion were louder than before. She wanted to be sure Frank knew what he had missed. Frank fell back asleep.

Chapter 23

It was after twelve when Frank woke up. DC and Bren were gone. He had no idea where. There was no note. Fuck it. Last day. If Bren didn't turn up something, he would go talk to Vincent himself. Enough of this easy way shit. If it had to be the hard way, it had to be the hard way. He was still confident that Vincent would tell him everything he knew.

He stopped at a fast food restaurant for something called a thick burger. He had seen it advertised on television, and it looked pretty good. It wasn't half bad, so he got another one.

He had the day to kill, so he decided to hit another couple of massage parlors just in case he lucked into something. He didn't like to park right out front in case the business was under police surveillance. He wanted to stay under the radar if possible. He parked his truck at a toy store and walked across the huge parking lot to the massage parlor next door. Now that was creative zoning at its finest.

The massage parlor was named the China Doll. It offered a complete line of oriental massage therapies. Whatever that meant. The odds of finding Jenny there were small, but you could never tell. Unfortunately, the proprietor seemed unable to speak or understand English. So he left.

He was halfway back to his truck when he heard the motorcycles approaching. He lowered his head to hide his face and drifted toward the toy store. He heard the bikes—sounded like three—rumble into the parking lot behind him. They idled, then crept toward him. At least one was, maybe two were, Harleys. He just had to make a few more yards, and he would be safe inside the door. He could duck out a back door.

The white panel van screeched to a halt in front of him. The back door swung open and two men jumped out. They each held a gun. He knew he was fucked.

Frank recognized the first man out of the van. He was called Bear. He was about the same size as Frank but built softer. He had long brown hair parted down the middle and a thick red beard. His beard seemed to grow straight down his neck onto his chest. He was a walking carpet. Bear had been a Joker back in the day. After they had been forced into the Spartan fold he had been promoted to president. The previous president had had an accident. Frank didn't know the other man. He appeared too young to have ridden with the Jokers that long ago.

Bear grinned like an idiot. "Into the van, motherfucker."

Bear was close. The other man was beyond his reach. He couldn't take both of them, and the motorcycles were almost on them. Frank climbed into the van. The other men followed him in. The van started up.

There were no windows in the sides of the van. Tall mirrors stood off the driver's windows to allow vision for backing up. There were two narrow, crude benches bolted to the floor across from each other. Bear moved passed Frank to his other side. Bear leaned over the front seat and slapped the driver on his back.

"Let's roll." Bear turned to Frank. "Stick your hands out."

Frank did, and Bear wrapped several circles of silver duct tape around them. He tore the roll free and tossed it to the floor. He stared at Frank's face.

"Is this the motherfucker?" he asked the driver.

The driver glanced back at Frank. It was Billy from the night before. The biker who thought he recognized Frank.

"That's him. I'm positive."

"I know it's him. But is it 'him'? Let me have your knife, Giggles keep your gun right on his fucking head. He twitches, you blow his head off. Got it?"

"Got it," Giggles said and giggled.

Billy pulled a stiletto from his pocket and passed it back to Bear. Bear stuck his big pistol into the front of his pants. He took the knife from Billy. The handle of Billy's knife was very thin. Bear flipped a switch and a four-inch ceramic blade appeared almost by magic. It didn't flip out like a switchblade. It sprung out of the handle. It was almost silent. It was a mighty fine knife. Bear noticed his gaze.

"It's Japanese. Billy's got a thing for Japs. Now lean back. Stay still. Arms up." He cut the buttons off the front of Frank's shirt. He pulled the sides back. Then he slit the nylon t-shirt down the front. The Spartan tattoo on Frank's stomach stared back at them.

"I told you it was him," Billy shouted.

"Keep your eyes on the fuckin' road, dickwad. That doesn't prove it. Not yet."

He looked into Frank's face again. Frank was emotionless. Bear must not have seen what he was looking for. He slit the right sleeve up to the elbow. There was the lambda scar of the Spartans. Then he pushed Frank over and cut the shirt over his left shoulder. Bear was a little clumsy with the blade, and Frank could feel the trickle of blood start down his back. Bear tore the shirt open wider. On Frank's left shoulder was the pi symbol. Bear smiled and leaned back. He closed the knife and passed it back to Billy.

"Good job, Billy boy. You did real well."

"I told you," Billy said. "I knew I had seen him before, then it came to me. It had to be old Frank."

"It's really him?" Giggles said. "I heard the stories."

"Frank the Hammer," Bear said. "I never thought I would see the day. I've dreamed about this day, motherfucker."

"How did you find me?"

"Billy recognized you. He was talking about it at the clubhouse. Described you. Giggles hear chimed in, said he had been getting his Jimmy waxed yesterday, and some big son of a bitch that sounded like that had come in. He had been asking a lot of questions about some young white chick. Giggles asked the lady who runs the place about it. After a little encouragement, she called around and found out you had been visiting some of the other massage parlors. Asking the same weird questions."

Frank nodded. Bad luck. That explained a lot. Plain bad luck. "I was just curious. I figured someone might have ratted me out."

"Not this time. Billy, signal the boys. It's a-go."

Billy rolled his window down and made an arm gesture Frank couldn't see. One of the motorcyclists moved around the van and positioned himself in front. The other two stayed behind. Bear pulled his large pistol out of his waistband and pointed it at Frank.

"Your day of reckoning has come for what you did to Outlaw."

"He tried to kill me," Frank said

Bear slapped him across the side of the head with the pistol. The blow was short, but it still snapped Frank's head back. Blood trickled down his face in a thin stream.

"Don't you say shit to me. Outlaw brought me into this gang. He veteraned me. Taught me everything I know. And you killed him. Now you got to pay."

THE LAST SPARTAN

Frank remained silent.

"Yeah, we got something planned special for you, Hammer."

"Shut the fuck up, Billy. You just stay calm, Frank. There's nothing you can do anyway. You start any trouble in here, you still got three Jokers outside to deal with." Bear paused to let his words sink in. "Just relax. We got a long ride ahead of us."

* * * *

Carl Ramos sat in his small office. His exterminator business, AAA Pest Control, was doing pretty well. Not as well as he would have liked, but pretty well. Today was a down day. The two jobs he had scheduled both rescheduled. Carl told himself he was in the office to do some paperwork. The truth was he didn't want to go home to Maria and the kids. If he came home early, she would invent a dozen jobs for him to do around the house. Errands he had to run for her. Places the children needed to be taken since he was home. It was harder than working.

He had his small radio turned on to the Falcons' pregame. He kept the door locked and the volume low just in case Maria stopped by unexpectedly to check up on him. He was tempted to open the small cooler at his feet and start on his lunch. No, it was still an hour to game time, and the game would run three hours. He would wait awhile.

He heard the elevator open and then footsteps in the hallway. He turned the radio down a little more. It could be Maria. No. The tread was too heavy, had to be men. The steps walked over to the detective's office next door. He heard the heavy knocking on the door.

Carl's office shared a wall with the detective office. There was a vent on the wall down near the floor. If Carl stayed quiet, he could hear whatever was going on next door. He was not a pervert or anything. He just liked to hear the cases that sometimes came in. Hear the juicy details. He never told anyone what he heard. It was his secret. It was a secret that was pretty easy to keep since the detective business seemed to be pretty slow and most of the stories boring. Find my husband. Find his girlfriend. Find this guy faking an injury.

"Come in," Burt said.

"Are you Burt Wilson?" one of the men asked. He had a Middle Eastern accent.

"Yes. What can I do for you fellas? You looking for a private detective?"

The door closed. Carl leaned closer to the vent. This might be good.

"Are you a Christian, Mr. Wilson?"

"Is that important to you? I mean, does it have anything to do with the job you want me to do?"

"Just answer his question." Another voice, also with that same odd accent.

There was a pause. Burt said, "I'm a Christian. But if that's a problem. . ."

"Are you at peace with your god?" the first voice again.

"What are you talking about?" There was fear in the detective's voice. Something was happening. "What are you going to do?"

"Would you like to pray?" The first voice again.

"Please don't," Burt begged.

"It is time to make peace with your god," the first voice said. "Get down on your knees."

There was a moment of silence. Maybe Carl had misunderstood. He heard two muffled sounds. Another pause and the muffled sound again.

Carl crossed himself. He knew that sound. He had watched enough television. They had shot the detective with a silenced gun. He could hear the two men moving about the detective's office. They were going through his filing cabinets and drawers. They left the office. He heard them lock the door behind them.

Something was said in a language he didn't understand. One set of footsteps moved toward his door. Carl couldn't move. Sweat broke out on his face. He was going to die too.

When the man knocked on the door Carl almost screamed in terror. He couldn't speak. The knock again, and then the hand tried the knob. Carl stared at the handle. It quivered but didn't open. Blessed be the Virgin Mary and all the saints. The knob was tried again. More of the strange language. Some kind of Arabic gibberish. The footsteps receded down the hall. He heard the elevator open and thought he heard the men leave.

He wasn't sure. He was afraid to move. He was afraid to look out his window in case they saw him. He was afraid to crack the door open and peek into the hallway. He wanted to pick up the telephone and call the police. What if they were outside his door? What if they were listening for a sound to give him away?

Carl froze where he was. He listened, straining his ears for any sound that might tell him if they were still there. He stared at his door, willing his eyes to penetrate the cheap wood and see into the hallway. He sat at his desk and waited for death.

An hour passed before he felt he was safe. His legs had fallen asleep, and it took him several long minutes of massaging them before he could stand. He knew in his heart they could not still be waiting for him. Terror still seized him as he opened the door and peered into the hallway. It was empty. He closed his door and slumped to the floor.

What should he do? He should call the police and tell them what he had heard. What if they did not believe him? He was Hispanic. What if they thought he had killed the man, or knowing he did not, still tried to pin it on him? He had seen such a thing many times on the TV. He could just leave and pretend he was never here. Let someone else discover the body. What if they found out he was lying? Would that be a crime? He was a good Catholic. It was wrong not to inform the police. Still he was afraid. His head ached. He got to his feet. He would go home. He would tell Maria. She would know what to do.

His steps were heavy. Now, at the very least, he would be in trouble with his wife for staying in the office to listen to the game. Suddenly, it came to him. Maria didn't have to know why he was in the office. He could have just happened to have come by to get something when the killers arrived. That was it. He was going to come straight home afterward. He felt much better.

Chapter 24

"Something special." That's just what Outlaw had said.

Frank remembered Outlaw. He had been the founder and president of the Jokers. He was a thin, nervous guy with a bad taste for meth. The Spartans had approached him about allying with them. Outlaw had a bad habit of saying what he thought. He declined with some rather harsh words. The Spartans had started applying pressure. Pushing his boys around. Raiding his meth labs. Confiscating his drugs as they tried to wind their way to him. Slowly, they moved into his territory. They didn't want to crush the Jokers. They wanted to absorb them. There was a shootout at a roadhouse that left two Jokers dead. Frank had killed them. Outlaw had contacted the Spartans about a truce.

Outlaw said he wanted to make peace. He asked for a meeting with the Spartans enforcer. Just the two of them, alone. No weapons. A straight up man-to-man discussion about assurances and percentages. No tricks on either part. The Spartans agreed. Outlaw set the time and place.

On the agreed upon day, at the agreed upon hour, Frank drove a black Toyota pickup truck down a deserted road in Gainesville. There was nothing except cleared fields on either side. His destination was an abandoned farmhouse where Outlaw waited.

A lone figure waited in the middle of the road. It was the enforcer for the Jokers. He waved Frank to a stop. He examined the back and underneath the truck.

"Get out of the truck," he ordered

Frank did so. The enforcer patted him down.

"I thought Outlaw was going to be alone."

"Back into the truck."

He climbed into the cab beside Frank.

"Just drive to the house, smart ass."

Frank drove on another five hundred yards to the farmhouse. It was more ruin than farmhouse. The roof had fallen in, and plants fought each other to see who could cover the house first. Only one wall still stood intact, if somewhat tilted. Outlaw sat in a lawn chair in front of the crumbling house.

THE LAST SPARTAN

Frank parked the truck and climbed out. The enforcer followed him. When he saw Outlaw, the enforcer slipped a pistol out from beneath his jacket.

"Is he clean?" Outlaw asked.

"Yeah, so's the truck."

"Good."

Outlaw whistled. Two more Jokers came out from behind the house. They had pistols in their hands.

"I thought no weapons was your rule, Outlaw."

Outlaw grinned like a poker player holding a royal flush. "Guess things aren't the way you thought, tough guy."

"Seems you brought friends, too. That's a no-no," Frank said. Outlaw looked like he was tweaked on meth.

"So, what are you going to do about it?"

"Nothing, I guess. We here to talk business, or is this something else?"

"Get a load of this guy, boys. He ices two of our own, and he thinks we're going to just let it pass."

"That was business."

"That's what this is, too," Outlaw snarled. "Personal business."

"It doesn't have to be this way. The Spartans want to negotiate."

"Who gives a fuck what the Spartans want? They want to own us just like they own everybody else. Make us just another of their biker bitch boys. We don't play that."

Frank could see Outlaw's pupils. The wild gestures of his arms. He was flying for sure. This was going to end badly.

"You sure this is the way you want it?" Frank asked.

"Listen to him. He sounds like he's the one with the guns. Maybe guns don't scare the great Poseidon. Yeah, I know your stupid name. It's a pussy name. You hear me. A pussy name. And the Spartans are all a bunch of pussies. Your time is up. Unless you got some plan to get out of what we got arranged for you. And we got something very special planned for you." The Jokers all laughed. "Now kneel down. I know how to kill a god."

Frank knelt on the ground. He looked up at Outlaw and smiled. "I always have a plan."

Everything seemed to happen in slow motion. There was a distant rumble like thunder, and then the enforcer's head was gone. The other two Jokers turned to stare at his falling body as some huge unseen hand seemed to sweep them from their feet.

"You don't have to die. Lift your hands up," Frank said.

Outlaw pointed his pistol at Frank. The bullet struck him in the center of his chest and blew his back out.

Frank got to his feet. A dark shape moved three hundred yards off in the barren field. As it rose, it became a man. The man walked toward Frank. He was carrying something in his hands. It was a sniper rifle. The man was wearing latex gloves. It was Apollo.

He looked at the bodies of the four dead men. "Dumb ass cracker," Apollo said. "They had to get all country on your ass."

"That was some pretty good shooting."

"That's why Cyrus named me Apollo."

"Far striker."

"One of the best snipers the SEALs ever had. Not that they would admit it. These shots were easy. Like shooting fish in a bucket."

"Loxias," Frank said. "That's the Greek term of respect they had for the god Apollo."

"Whatever you say, Frank. How did you know they would pull the double-cross."

"They had too. Outlaw was too weak. He couldn't compromise."

Apollo nodded. "Makes some kind of twisted cracker sense, I guess."

"I didn't see you out there, Apollo. For a minute I was afraid you had forgotten to show."

"Motion discipline. It's a good thing we did a little recon last night. Gave me a chance to set up."

"Always expect treachery," Frank said.

"What do you want to do with the bodies?"

"They were going to make an example out of me. Something special, they said. It would serve as a warning for the Spartans. Might work the other way, too. Look around. See if you find anything out of place."

Five minutes later, Apollo sang out. "I think I know what they had planned." He showed Frank a brown paper bag he had found hidden in some weeds behind the house. Inside was a heavy mallet and a double handful of large nails. "These crackers play rough."

THE LAST SPARTAN

"Help me drag the bodies over to that wall."

Apollo did as he was asked. They leaned the three dead Jokers against the wall. Frank nailed their outstretched arms to the wall. He used other nails in their shirts to help hold them in place. Outlaw he nailed standing up.

"Don't you think that's a little too horror movie? I mean it is so cliché."

"Sometimes clichÈs are best."

"This will shake them up for sure," Apollo said.

"That's the point. Break your rifle down, and we'll stash it in the truck. Anything else that can be traced?"

"No. Usual protocol. We'll dump the stuff that ties us to this down the road. How long do you think before the Jokers find them?"

"By this afternoon. When they don't hear, they'll come looking. I figure they'll call to renegotiate with the Spartans by tonight."

"They'll go crazy trying to figure out how you killed all four of them by yourself. Your rep will go out the roof."

"I guess."

"They'll be calling you the Hammer from now on."

Chapter 25

The van braked sharply, and it jostled Frank back to reality. A burgundy Sable had tried to slip in front of the van before it saw the biker in front and had to swerve back out of the lane. Sable, that was a car made by Mercury. Mercury was the Roman name for Apollo. It must be a sign, Frank thought. It was a stretch, and he knew it. You took what you were given. He wished Apollo were still alive. On second thought, Mercury was the Roman name for the god Hermes. Frank wasn't sure if the sudden appearance of the Mercury Sable was a good omen or not. He would discard it for now and see if something better appeared.

He looked at the men guarding him, amateurs. Six men was a good start, Frank thought. But they split their force in half. The outside three were out of play. The driver was also out of play. Giggles seemed nervous. He alternately looked at Frank and out the front window. His finger was on the trigger of his automatic, but the hammer wasn't cocked back. Bear was relaxing his watchfulness as well. He was sitting beside Frank with his gun held across his midsection. Bear's gun was heavy. It was a .44 magnum Colt Anaconda. The gun was known for its light, smooth trigger, but it weighed almost sixty ounces. That was a lot of gun to keep trained on a man. The six-and-a-half-inch barrel was already drooping. Worse, they had secured Frank's hands in front of him. That was foolish. It didn't incapacitate a man in the least. Frank decided to wait for the right time. It would come.

The van jostled over a pothole, and Frank let himself rock forward. He righted himself and leaned back against the wall of the van. A few minutes later with another bump, he repeated the maneuver. No response. Perfect.

After forty-five minutes they pulled off the highway onto some back roads. The van went slower now. They turned onto a gravel road. Bear grinned. So did Giggles. It would be soon now.

The lead biker stopped in front of a locked gate. It was a huge iron triangle that crossed the side road in front of them. It was padlocked closed. A sign in the middle of the beam read: "Newton Quarry. Quarry closed. No trespassing." In the center of the beam perched a huge red-tailed hawk.

THE LAST SPARTAN

The hawk did not fly away as the biker approached. It screeched every few seconds with a call that was reminiscent of an old steam whistle. Through the front window, Frank could see its swollen crop, just above its sternum. It had just taken prey. Its long yellow talons were flecked with crimson. This close, Frank could tell that the red-tailed hawk's deck feathers were more brown than red. The hawk eyed them with disdain. The lone biker dismounted and walked toward it waving his arms. Reluctantly, the hawk spread its wings and took flight. Frank watched it catch a thermal and soar up high overhead.

"That's the damnedest thing I ever saw," Billy said. "It didn't want to go. Like it was waiting for us."

Hawks and eagles were messengers for the Greek gods. Zeus often traveled disguised as a bird of prey. Frank saw it as a very good omen.

The biker took a key out of his pocket and unlocked the padlock.

"Abandoned quarry," Giggles said and giggled again.

"Shut up," Bear snapped.

The van pulled through and moved slowly down the old gravel road. The lead biker waited until they were all through before following them and relocking the padlock. They wouldn't want any surprise visitors. The van shook and jerked over the rough road. Frank let himself be tossed forward. Bear and Giggles were both looking out the front window.

Frank struck Bear with a savage right elbow into his throat. In almost the same instant Frank launched a kick as hard as he could into Giggles' chest. He followed it immediately with another kick to Giggles' head. By the time Billy glanced back at the noise Frank had Giggles' gun clutched between his taped hands.

"Steady, Billy, and you can still get out of this alive. You do what I tell you, or I'll splash your brains all over that window."

Billy started to speak.

"Shhh. Just listen. Get your knife out. That's it. Open the blade. Now hold it steady while I cut this tape. You nick me, I'll kill you."

Frank sawed the razor-sharp knife quickly through the duct tape. He took the knife from Billy. It was incredibly light. There was Japanese script on the blade. He had no idea what it meant. He closed it. Man, he liked that knife. He slipped it into his pants pocket. He pulled his gloves out of his back pocket and slipped them on.

"You got a gun up there, Billy? Of course you do. Pass it back."

Billy lifted a revolver from the front seat and passed it back.

"Any hideaway pieces?"

"No."

"Don't lie to me. You draw down on me, I have to kill you. You know that."

"I know that."

"How much farther?'

Bear was making a terrible gurgling sound as he thrashed on the floor of the truck.

"God, he's choking. You got to do something."

"I did. Nothing I can do for him now. His throat's crushed."

Giggles lay motionless. The second kick had struck the side of his head. The human skull has dense bone in the front and back for protection. The sides are thin. The side of his head was crushed inward.

"Is he dead?"

Frank kept one gun against the base of Billy's neck as he felt for a pulse on Giggles. He sat back up. "He's gone."

"My god."

"No. I'm not. How much farther?"

"I don't know exactly."

Frank prodded him with the muzzle of the gun. "Billy?"

"A couple of minutes, I guess. Down by the water."

"You go slow now. I see you try to signal your buddies or you do something crazy, well, it won't be pretty."

"I'm not going to try anything. I swear."

"You just follow the plan you boys had. Park where you were going to park. But you keep your ass in the van. I see you running around, I might forget our deal and shoot you."

"I'll stay in the van. I promise. It's just up ahead."

Frank lifted Bear's gun and slipped it into the front of his pants. He couldn't leave it behind. It would be too much temptation for Billy. The van slowed. It stopped. Frank opened the rear doors before the van had stopped settling on its springs. He had a pistol in each hand. The Jokers on their bikes were stunned to see him leap from the back of the van. They didn't stand a chance. It was over in seconds.

Frank was standing in the haze and smoke looking at the bodies when he heard the van door swing open. He spun low. Billy was stepping out of the door. He was pointing a derringer. Frank shot him through his left knee.

Billy was rolling on the ground when Frank reached him. Frank picked up the pistol and put it into his back pocket. He had always like derringers. He shook his head.

"I told you to stay in the van, Billy."

"Fuck you," Billy said.

Frank knelt down beside him. "Billy. Billy. Listen to me. You can still get out of this alive. I'm going to ask you a couple of questions. You give me the answers I'm looking for, I let you walk. Sorry. I let you limp out of here."

Billy moaned.

Frank prodded him with his foot. "You got it."

Billy nodded yes. "I got it."

"Quit being such a baby. The knee's not that bad. Now listen. You listening?"

"I'm listening. Ask your fucking questions."

"Did Bren or DC have anything to do with this?"

"Who? Hell no. It's like Bear said."

"Alright. Do you know anything about Vincent Street?"

"No. I never heard of him. Who in the fuck is he?"

"Alright. You know anything about the girl I'm looking for. She's a fifteen-year-old kid named Jenny. "

"No. I don't know any Jenny."

"You sure? I'm not going to ask you again. She's got a little butterfly tattoo on her right wrist," Frank said and indicated on his own wrist where it would be.

"No. I never heard of her, man."

"Alright. I believe you." Frank raised the pistol in his left hand and pointed it at Billy.

"Wait, you said if I answered your questions, you'd let me go."

"I didn't like your answers. You're the one who done me on this deal, Billy boy. I told you to stay in the van."

He shot Billy through the right eye.

Amateurs, he thought. Yak, yak, yak. You come to kill a man, you do it. You don't talk about it. You do it. They always want to do something special. Better to have iced Frank in the parking lot.

Frank sat in the back of the open van. He was in no hurry. The Jokers used this place for a reason. It was deserted and isolated. They weren't worried about being heard or seen, so why should he be. His next moves would be critical. The Jokers would snap wise pretty quick. They would come looking for him all over again. He wouldn't have much time. He had to make the right moves. He had to have a plan. Frank wished he still smoked. This would be a good time for a cigarette. Oh, well.

He knew the new Frank should feel bad about the killings. He didn't. Those demons were out, and there was no use pretending otherwise. The Spartans had a saying about warriors without wars. They said, "A blade too long in the sheath tarnishes." He had been tarnishing.

It took him thirty minutes to work his plan out in his head. First, he searched the van. He found the bag with the hammer and the nails under the front seat. He left it there. He meticulously searched each body. He pocketed their cash. It wasn't going to do them any good. He left the small bottles of cocaine he found on two of them. He stripped Bear of his shirt and jacket. The shirt was a little ripe, but it was the only one big enough to fit Frank. The worn leather jacket had the Jokers' colors on the back. He needed that.

He checked out their weapons. There was an assortment of lockback knives, brass knuckles, and a pair of nunchucks. He left all of that. Every one of them was packing a gun. He stacked the unused guns off to the side. All new Berettas. Pretty good quality stuff. Probably stolen from an army depot somewhere.

He pocketed a cell phone from one of the bikers and the quarry keys from another. He found a Zippo lighter on one of the corpses. He checked. It worked. He pocketed it. It had an emblem of a marijuana leaf on one side. Bren was wrong. Smoking weed was bad. It could get you killed, he thought.

He checked out their bikes. He was looking for something special. Something distinctive. Two were Harleys, but one of the Jokers was riding a Kawasaki Ninja ZX-10R. 998cc engine. Aluminum frame. Bright green. A real crotch rocket. Frank had read it would accelerate to sixty faster than a fucking Ferrari.

The sport bike's owner had a nasty knife scar across his face. Frank pulled off his jacket and shirt to reveal some quality prison tats. Perfect. The bright green helmet covered the entire head and face. He took the saddlebags off another bike and strapped them onto the Ninja. It fucked up the look, but so what.

He searched around the rim of the quarry. It was obvious the Jokers also used this as a place to party. There was evidence of numerous large campfires. Bits of bottles littered the ground. It took him a few minutes before he found two unbroken beer bottles. He wrapped one of Bear's big hands around a bottle. Making sure to leave a good set of prints if anyone looked. He used Scarface's hands on the other. He carried the bottles back to the bikes.

He used the gas from one of the bikes to fill both bottles. He cut strips of cloth from one of the bodies. He rolled the cloth into tight wicks. He stuffed one wick in one of the bottles. The other he splashed with gasoline and lit. He held it while it burned for a few seconds before throwing it to the ground. He stomped out the flame leaving the charred margin. He wedged this into the other bottle. He put both gas-filled Molotov cocktails into the right side of the saddle bag. He stashed the unused handguns into the left side.

Frank piled the bodies into the back of the van. He opened the side windows and broke out the front window so the van would sink quickly. The edge of the water covered what had once been a hard-packed road that circled down into the base of the quarry. Frank drove the van to the edge of the drop-off.

There was no dramatic revving of the engine and last second jump to safety. That was for the movies. He left the van in neutral and used brute strength to inch the van over the side. It helped that it was all downhill or he would never have been able to budge it. The van bobbed on the surface for a few seconds until it sank. The other two Harley motorcycles followed suit. Last, he tossed in the guns he had used. Over time, nothing ruined forensics as well as water.

Frank was tempted to keep the derringer. He liked having a back-up. This was only a twenty-two, but it fit neatly in the palm of his big hand. He thought better of it. Follow the plan. He put the derringer in with the other four guns. He needed to kill a little more time for his plan to work. He washed his face in the quarry water. His head had stopped bleeding. He stretched out on the grass to let his pants and boots dry from messing around near the water. The red-tailed hawk still circled overhead, watching him like a forgotten god.

At five o'clock, he stuffed his shredded shirts into the saddlebags over the pistols. He put on Bear's leather jacket and the green helmet. He cranked the Ninja and headed back toward Atlanta. It was time to wrap this puppy up and get home.

THE LAST SPARTAN

Chapter 26

Vincent Street was busy on his computer when he heard the knock on the door. He shut down the computer. He walked to his front window and looked outside to see if he recognized the car. He didn't. He looked through the peephole. He had been expecting Yusef. This was definitely not Yusef. The pretty girl smiled back at him. He returned her smile even though she couldn't see it. He undid the dead bolt and the two other locks on his door.

"What can I do for you?" Vincent asked with as much sincerity as he could manage. It wasn't much.

Bren smiled. "It's what can I do for you. If you got the cash."

"Come in, and we can discuss this."

Bren strolled into his apartment like she belonged there. She glanced around, appreciating what she saw.

"Very nice. I can see you're a man of taste."

"Thank you. I am Vincent. Who might you be?"

"I might be your momma, but I ain't," Bren said and laughed at her own joke. Vincent didn't seem to understand it. She continued, "My name is Bren."

"Pleased to make your acquaintance, Bren."

"Thanks. It's nice to meet you."

They shook hands.

"Can I offer you a drink?"

"Sure. I can see you're a gentleman. What have you got?"

"Whatever you desire."

"I like the way you put that," she said. "Vodka and grapefruit juice."

"Excellent. I'll have the same. Have a seat. I shan't be a moment."

Bren strolled around, peering into the rooms. It was a nice setup. Much better than what she and DC had. Vincent returned with the drinks. He wasn't too bad to look at. Deep eyes. Exotic looks. She like that. Bren took her drink and thanked him. He motioned for her to sit on the couch.

"Now what is it that you can do for me, Bren?" Vincent leered.

Bren laughed. "It's not that sort of thing, baby. Strictly business."

"What kind of business?"

"I got some information to sell. And I think you might be the man to buy it." She sipped her drink and stared at him over the rim like she had seen girls do in the movies.

Vincent did not seem the least bit uncomfortable with their conversation. It was as if he had this kind of discussion every day with beautiful women.

"And why would I wish to buy your information?" he asked.

"Couple of reasons. First, it is valuable, and if I let you have it, then I'll lose the money a second party has offered me for it. Secondly, if somebody bad was looking for me, I think I would want to know all about it."

"Why would anyone bad be searching for me? I'm an easy man to find. I'm right here. I'm not in hiding."

"You ought to be. This is a bad, bad man who is looking for you, baby."

"Why would he want to find me? I do not understand. What do I have of his?"

This was the money shot. She pulled the picture of Jenny out of her purse. She passed it to Vincent. "Her name is Jenny, and he knows you know where she is."

Vincent looked at the picture for only a few seconds, as if it wasn't important to him at all. He passed it back to her. He did not try to pretend he wasn't interested. Vincent nodded a couple of times as he thought about what she had said.

"What is your price? For everything. Why he thinks I know where she is. Who he is. Where I can find him. How you came to be involved in all this."

"He was going to pay me two thousand if I could find her for him," Bren lied. Hey, she thought, this is business. "He gave me a couple hundred up front, the rest on delivery."

Vincent seemed to consider the price before he said, "I will pay you three thousand minimum. And you keep the two hundred you have already been paid. That is a net profit of twelve hundred dollars."

Bren pretended to consider it. She had to trust his calculations. She couldn't do the math in her head without looking like a real idiot.

"Sounds like a fair price. It's a long story. You got a cigarette I could bum?"

"Most assuredly," Vincent said.

THE LAST SPARTAN

He took a pack from his desk and brought them over to her. Bren opened it and tapped a cigarette out. It was filterless with an unusual name on the front.

"Are these American?"

"I am afraid not. I have them sent to me from Kuwait. I hope they will not be too strong for you."

Bren lit one and inhaled deeply. She blew the smoke out in a flashy slow exhale. "Very nice."

"I am glad you approve. You may keep the pack if you like."

"Thanks," she said and slipped the pack into her purse. "I do like your style."

"Now, your story if you do not mind."

Bren told him everything she knew—from meeting Frank, his proposition, DC finding out about Vincent on his computer, coming there. She paused only once for Vincent to freshen her drink.

"Very interesting, Bren. Worth every penny you are charging. There is only one small obstacle to our agreement."

"What's that?"

"It is after banking hours, and I do not have that much cash on hand."

"Are you trying to welsh on me?"

"Nothing of the sort. If you will allow me, I will call my partner. He is the money man, as you Americans say. He can bring the cash over tonight. You do prefer cash, I take it?"

"How soon?"

"Within the hour."

"It'll put me a little late for work, but what the hey. Tell him large bills. Hundreds, if he's got them."

"That will not be a problem. Let me telephone him."

As Vincent went to the phone, Bren was scheming how she could hide the money from DC. He might want a cut. He might be mad that she snitched on his friend, if Frank really was DC's friend. There was something off about their relationship. It seemed odd. Fuck them both.

Vincent punched in the numbers on his cell phone.

"Yes," the voice answered.

"Yusef, this is Vincent."

"I know who it is. What do you want?"

"I need you to come over as soon as you can."

"Why?"

"There's a girl here who knows about Jenny. The girl with the butterfly tattoo I found for you. There is another man searching for her."

"Another loose end."

"Exactly. She wants you to bring her three thousand dollars in hundreds as payment for her information."

Yusef was silent. "Be sure she does not leave. I will be there as soon as I can."

Vincent clicked the phone off. "He will be here shortly."

"That's good news."

"Since you must wait, perhaps I could tempt you with something to accentuate the pleasure of your drink."

"So tempt me," Bren said.

"I have some cocaine and some hashish if you would like."

"Forget the hash. I wouldn't mind doing a little blow while we wait. Is it any good?"

"Excellent," Vincent said and hurried off to his secret stash. When he returned, Bren was lounging on his sofa. Her shoes were off, and she had unbuttoned the top two buttons of her blouse.

"I know we have to wait for your money man, but it's really going to throw me late for work."

"I'm very sorry about the inconvenience, but in these matters I think payment when services are rendered is the rule."

"It's my rule. That's for damn sure."

Vincent laughed. He always found it amusing to hear such vulgar language from women. In his home country, a woman would be stoned for such language.

He diced the cocaine into neat lines. He offered her a silver straw for the first snort. Bren did two lines and smiled. She wiped up the residue with a thin finger and rubbed it on her gums. Vincent did one himself.

They drank a little more before Bren asked, "How much money have you got on you?"

"Why?"

"Just answer. How much?"

"About five hundred, I think."

She leaned forward, and he could see her large breasts sway beneath her thin top.

"Well, since we have to wait for your friend, I was thinking. . . If you are willing to spend your wad we could have our own little party here."

Vincent smiled. "Now. While we wait?"

"Unless you've got a better way to spend your time and money."

"No. It is always wise to invest in one's pleasure."

"That's what I'm talking about," she said. "You got style, Vincent. You get the cash, and I'll slip into something more comfortable."

Vincent led her to the bedroom. He went into his closet and took out the money. He brought it into the bedroom only to find her already nude, lying on top of the sheets.

"Just put it on the nightstand, Vincent. I like to look at it while we fuck."

Chapter 27

The only other motorcycle group of any size in Atlanta was the Jackals. They were a good third the size of the Jokers. They made most of their money doing jobs for the Jokers. Ferrying stolen goods or drugs. Some back up enforcement work. Running whores.

Frank stopped at a rest area off the highway. It was getting difficult to find pay phones anymore. The yellow pages were still hanging there. The Jackals' telephone and address were listed in the business section under the heading "Motorcycle Clubs." They hadn't moved. Frank dumped his ruined shirts into the drainage opening behind the restrooms.

It was after six o'clock when he pulled up outside their club house. It was a run-down brick building they shared with two other businesses, a body shop and a tattoo parlor.

Frank took out the two Molotov cocktails and placed them between his legs. He got out the lighter. He lifted the bottle with the burnt wick and threw it against the clubhouse door. It was a lazy, arching toss. The bottle struck the door and broke into large pieces. He heard a stirring inside the clubhouse like angry bees.

Frank lit the wick on the other bottle and threw it against the side of the building. Close to the door, but not too close to not let them out. The Molotov cocktail exploded in a shower of flames. It was an impressive fire bomb. The murmurs inside rose to shouts. Frank revved the engine on the bike to a roar just as the door burst open and three Jackals stepped outside. Frank dropped the lighter and roared past them down the road. He made sure they saw the colors on his jacket. Behind him there were shouts and curses.

Frank road half a dozen blocks before he started looking for a pay phone. The first one, outside a dry cleaners, was without a handset. The next one didn't even have a call box. The third was near a bakery and appeared fully functional. Frank dialed 911.

"911 police emergency," the voice answered.

Frank raised his voice a few octaves. He tried to sound scared. "I just. . . I just. . . I just saw something."

"What is your name, sir?"

"I just saw some bikers. Hells Angels, I think, throw a fire bomb at a building."

THE LAST SPARTAN

"What is your name, sir?"

"It was over off Belmeade Avenue. The four hundred block."

"Sir, when did this happen?"

"Just now. I wasn't going to stop and call. But I thought. . . you know. . . I better tell someone. Get the fire department. Do something."

"Where are you now, sir."

"I don't know. A phone booth somewhere. I just stopped. I had to tell somebody."

"Stay where you are, sir. I am sending a car out."

"Jokers, that's it. One of the jackets had Jokers written on the back. Are they part of the Hells Angels or something? I've never heard of them. . . I just—"

"Calm down, sir. I will notify the fire department. A patrol car is en route. I have your address. Stay where you are."

"You want me to wait here?"

"Yes, sir, until the patrol car gets there. What is your name?"

"What if the Jokers saw me? What if they come after me?"

"Just wait there, sir. What is your name?"

Frank hung the telephone up. He got back on the bike and rode to find his truck.

The old truck rested quietly among the other cars in the toy store parking lot. Frank parked the motorcycle against the fence near the massage parlor. He left the helmet hanging on the handle bars and the key in the ignition. It had been fun to ride again. A fine bike like that should be gone by morning. It didn't matter if it wasn't. He unhooked the saddlebags and carried them to his truck. He drove for a few minutes until he found a shopping center with a McDonald's. The parking lot was pretty full. He parked away from the other cars, near the dumpster behind the McDonalds. He tossed his leather Jokers jacket and gloves inside. The gunpowder residue might link him to the guns that killed the Jokers.

He used the stolen cell phone to call information. He got the telephone number for Pandora's Box. He punched in the telephone number and asked to speak to Tyronne. He said it was urgent. A minute later a man's voice. He recognized the voice by the single word reply. Deep and smooth like honey.

"Shout."

157

"This is Frank, from the other night. You bought some product from me."

"DC's boy. I remember. What can I do you for?"

"I need to move some more product."

"Same price?"

"No. This line secure?"

"Management sweeps it everyday. No need to. Damn mayor and police chief both are in here chasing trim every other night. I can assure you they don't want any taps, brother."

"Good."

"So what's the price?" Tyronne was a little suspicious.

"One telephone call. That's all."

"Why don't you make it?"

"The party involved needs to know the source. Has to be somebody who could have gotten the information, otherwise it won't do any good."

"Who you want me to call? What do you want me to say?"

"Straight up call. Call the Jokers. Tell them the word is out that the cops are looking to bust them on an arson rap. Say you got it from a source you have in the PD."

"Think they'll believe that?"

"It's true. The cops are looking to roll on them any time now. You play it right, they might advance you some jack for the nod."

"How do you know it's true?"

"I was the one that set the cops onto them."

"Straight up?"

"Straight up."

"How much product?"

"Four. Primo condition."

"How long until you get here?"

"Twenty minutes, but you got to make the call now for it to work."

"I'm supposed to just trust you about the product?"

"What do you have to lose?"

"Twenty minutes, out by my ride. You still in the same old truck?"

"That's me. See you in twenty."

Frank thought about tossing the stolen cell, but he would still need it for his plan to work. He pulled into the drive-through and ordered three plain hamburgers and a large water. People were dying, but a man's got to eat.

THE LAST SPARTAN

Twenty minutes later he rolled into the lot of Pandora's Box. He pulled around back to Tyronne's parking place. The burly black man stood beside his car. He smiled when he saw the truck.

Frank swung the truck around the car to let the headlights scrub the night away. There was nobody else there. Even Tyronne's car was empty. Might be somebody hiding in the trunk. Fuck it. You had to take some chances.

"Glad you showed," Tyronne said.

"I'm a man of my word. You make the call?"

"As soon as I got off the phone with you. They were glad to get the heads-up. Got a Franklin coming for it if the cops show."

"They will."

"Jokers looking for you?"

"They been around?"

"Asking questions. Looking for you and Bren."

"You give us up?"

"What's to give up? I don't know shit. They weren't offering anything anyways."

"I needed them off my back so I can complete my business."

"The set up, is it any good?"

"Solid enough."

"You got my product?"

Frank lifted the saddlebags from the front seat of the truck. He handed each gun in turn to Tyronne. The first three were identical army issue Berettas. The fourth was Bear's .44 caliber Colt Anaconda.

Tyronne checked the weapons quickly but with the same expert's ease as the first time.

"Full loads," Frank said.

"That's the way I like 'em. Makes them easier to move. My guess is I don't want to try to resale these to the Jokers when things settle down."

"That would be a good guess."

Tyronne opened the trunk. Frank felt a minute tensing of his muscles. Nothing happened. Tyronne slipped the weapons into a black bag in the trunk.

"You overpaid, brother."

"No. I got what I paid for."

"How you figure that?"

"It had to be somebody with some weight. Somebody the Jokers would believe. Had to pay enough to keep you straight. I try to punk you, then you set me up with the Jokers instead. Isn't that right?"

"Thought about it. For a second. No profit in it. Plus, I like your moves. You're a man. I don't mean any queer shit by that. I work with so many pussy-shit punks in this fuck hole that it's good to run into another man time and again."

"I appreciate the compliment. That's another reason I used you. I figured you'd stand tall."

Frank turned back to the truck.

"What if you had been wrong? What if the Jokers had been waiting. What would you have done then, Mr. Frank-with-no-last-name?"

Frank smiled. "I would have killed you." He tossed something toward Tyronne. Tyronne caught it in midair. It was the derringer. Frank had had it palmed all the time.

"Good plan," Tyronne said.

"Works for me. You can keep the popper. Consider it a bonus."

"Some other time, brother."

"Maybe."

Frank drove out of the parking lot. He wanted to get his stuff together. Get a clean shirt. Some clean pants. Shower. Then finish this stuff with Vincent. If the fucker was out, he would just camp until he came home. It was going to be over tonight. If it had to be the hard way, then it had to be. No one could say he hadn't tried to do it the other way.

Suddenly, he remembered Bren. She said one of her girlfriends might have a line on Jenny tonight. It would be simpler to just bust Vincent's head, but maybe there was still a chance to snatch Jenny and slip away. He pulled to the side of the road. He got Bren's number from his cell phone. He dialed it with the Jokers' stolen cell. No reason to leave any clues if you could help it.

THE LAST SPARTAN

Chapter 28

Vincent stumbled to the door. He was wearing only a black silk robe.

He looked through the peephole. It was Yusef. He opened the door with a grandiose sweeping of his arms.

"Come in. Come in. Welcome."

"Is the girl still here?"

"Yes. She is in the bedroom."

Yusef fought his anger. "You are a pig."

"I know. I know. I am weak. Did you bring the money?"

"Yes. The Ambassador says it is to be taken out of your final payment."

Vincent nodded. "It's not like I'm going to let her keep it anyway."

"Vincent," Bren called. "Is that my money?"

"Yes, dearest one," Vincent said. "I am getting it for you."

"Fix me another drink while you're up."

"Of course. It will be my pleasure," Vincent said then turned back toward Yusef. He whispered. "Here is the girl's address. She lives with a boyfriend who does things with computers. You must go there and see what he knows. He may be able to trace the Ambassador. Or he may be in league with the Israelis. I do not know."

"What about the girl?"

"After you are finished with her boyfriend, you can return here to pick up her body for disposal."

"You will do it yourself?" Yusef asked. He was skeptical. He did not trust Vincent to be able to kill her.

"Of course. It is the least I can do, but you will have to help me get rid of the body."

"American whores," Yusef almost spat. "I have a place near the railroad that is appropriate for leaving their bodies."

"You used the railroad yard before. Is it safe to return there so soon?"

"Yes. I use it sometimes because it is a place for discarding trash."

"Excellent."

"What about the one who is searching for the girl?"

"His name is Frank. It's all I know. He's staying with them. He will return there. You can be waiting for him. He may be there already."

"You are becoming sloppy, Vincent."

"A thousand pardons. It is not my fault, but I will be more careful in the future."

"Is that all? No one else?"

"Yes. They are the last loose ends."

"This new girl has been a great deal of trouble, Vincent."

"I am sorry, Yusef, but the Ambassador will like her. I guarantee it. When I saw her, I knew she would be perfect."

"I hope you are right. He seemed pleased with her."

"Perhaps he will wish to take her home with him."

"It is possible. Call me if you learn anything else."

"I will. Call me back after they are dead. I would like to enjoy my plaything for as long as possible."

"You sicken me."

"I sicken myself," Vincent said.

Bren strolled into the room totally nude. "So, this is the money man."

Yusef made a small bow and withdrew an envelope from his pocket. He passed it to Bren. She thumbed through the money, counting quickly, then she smiled.

"It's all there. You guys really came through, big time."

"I am glad you are pleased," Vincent said.

"Your big friend can stay and party with us if he wants to. You got any more money on you, big boy?"

Fear flashed across Vincent's face. "No, that would not be possible. Yusef is a devout Muslim. Such a thing is not allowed."

"Not allowed. What shit is that? What about it, big man? You want to stay and party?" She did a little turn for him. "See anything you like?" Bren giggled.

"I must go," Yusef said. His anger was rising.

"Come on," Bren continued. "I know what you Arabs like. For two hundred you can do my ass. You'd like that, wouldn't you?"

Yusef did not answer. His eyes seemed to glow with rage.

"Forgive her, Yusef. She does not understand your faith."

"Everybody knows Arabs are the biggest ass fuckers in the world. And mine's all nice and tight. Just like a young boy's ass." Bren started rubbing her hands along her own butt. She laughed. "On second thought, you're such a big boy you might have a really big dick too.

Better make it two-fifty to split my tail."

Bren turned and strolled back toward the bedroom. The rage swept over Yusef's face. His hand went to his gun.

"I will kill her now, for you."

"No, please, Yusef," Vincent begged. He tried to keep Yusef from drawing the gun. "Let me enjoy her infidel ways for a time longer. I promise I will strangle her with my own hands."

"You had better, or it will be I who strangles you."

"Where's my drink, Vinnie?" Bren shouted from the bedroom. She started giggling.

"Go," Vincent begged. "Find out what you can."

Yusef nodded and went to the door. He paused, as if reconsidering leaving the girl alive. He sighed and went outside toward the black Lincoln Town Car. Vincent could see the ambassadorial flags fluttering on the hood. The door opened, and he saw Jamal seated behind the wheel. Jamal was a sadist.

"Vinnie, baby," Bren called. "I'm getting lonely. Come back to bed. And bring some more of that fine blow, too. I want to do a line off your fat dick this time."

Vincent shivered. He had never met a woman like her. She was insatiable. It was too bad he was going to have to kill her.

Chapter 29

DC was busy working on his computer when he heard the knock at the door. He saved and shut the computer down.

Opening the door, he said, "Frank, where the hell have you been?"

Yusef punched him in the solar plexus. It ripped DC's breath away. He doubled over, gasping for breath. He couldn't get enough air to scream. The pain was like an explosion in a bottle, looking for a way out.

Yusef stepped past him. His pistol was in his hand. The supressor was screwed into place. He quickly scanned the room, tracking with his eyes as his swung the pistol. There was no one else there.

Jamal shoved DC to the floor and kicked the door closed behind him. He drew a similar pistol and pressed it against DC's forehead. He held one finger to his lips.

"Shhh."

Yusef moved into the other rooms, making sure they were empty. Finally, he checked the bathroom. It was empty. He picked up Frank's bag from the sofa. He rifled through it, but there was nothing inside that told him anything new. Jamal lifted DC by his shirt collar.

"Take him into the bedroom," Yusef ordered. "Restrain him to the bedposts."

Jamal shoved DC before him onto the bed. He tied him spread-eagle on the bed using strips he tore off a pair of t-shirts.

Yusef sighed. He hated this part. He was not an intelligence officer. He did not want to see the American suffer under their questioning. But as Allah was his witness, they had to find out what he knew. Yusef walked into the computer room. He thumbed through the pages beside the computer. Nothing of interest. He pulled the top sheet out of the printing tray. It was the end of a recent printed file. The heading said, "Vincent Street continued," then below it "occupation unknown." He searched the garbage can for more pages, but there were none.

He turned the machine on and watched it boot up. The screen asked for a password. Americans could be too clever sometimes. He left the room and went to the bedroom.

"Gag him," Yusef ordered.

Jamal stuffed a sock into DC's mouth and used another piece of cloth to secure it tightly in place.

"Take off his shoes."

Jamal tore the floppy sneakers off, then the white socks. Jamal was smiling.

Yusef stared into the terrified eyes of the American. He sat on the bed near his head.

"Look at me. Your name is DC. We are not here by mistake. We have been sent specifically to talk with you. You have information that we require. We will not leave until we have it. Do you understand this?"

DC nodded vigorously.

"No one is coming to rescue you. You are all alone."

DC's eyes swept the room in terror.

"You are scared now, yes? Your eyes say you will answer my questions."

DC nodded.

Yusef sighed. "Sometimes the eyes lie. You will try to hold something back. Something we might find useful will be withheld. It is the way you Americans are."

Yusef brushed DC's hair back from his face.

"Are you working with the Israelis?"

DC looked confused and shook his head.

"How did they contact you?"

DC tried to answer, but there was no way to answer except yes or no.

"What do they know of the Ambassador?"

DC struggled.

Yusef smiled. He patted DC on the shoulder. "The fear you have now is from the anticipation of pain. It is abstract. It must be concrete before we begin. You must know what to be afraid of. Do you not agree?"

DC shook his head violently.

"Trust me on this. Jamal is an expert." Yusef swiveled on the bed toward Jamal. "I was interrogated by the Israelis once," Yusef said offhandedly. "They are master at interrogation. Probably the finest in the world. It is terrifying to be in their custody because of this reputation."

DC tried to say something, but the gag muffled the words.

"Find me a cigarette," Yusef said.

Jamal passed a cigarette to Yusef. Yusef took the cigarette and lit it. He inhaled deeply. The tobacco sold in the United States was like the Americans themselves. It was weak. Still it was familiar. He turned toward DC. He blew on the tip.

"I have read that the tip of a cigarette reaches five thousand degrees. The Israelis would never stoop to such a barbaric device." He smiled. "It leaves marks, and the Israelis are very aware of world opinion. They never leave marks."

DC started thrashing on the bed, but Jamal had tied him well. Yusef blew on the tip until it glowed orange. He passed the burning cigarette to Jamal.

DC tried to scream.

THE LAST SPARTAN

Chapter 30

Bren's cell phone started ringing. It startled Vincent. His erection instantly disappeared. She started laughing.

"It's probably DC," she said. "Nobody else has this number."

Vincent doubted that. "Answer it," he said, passing her the telephone. "It might be important."

"As if," she snapped. Bren flipped open her cell phone. "Hello."

"Bren. It's Frank. Have you got anything for me?"

Bren giggled. She couldn't help it. She was so high.

"Something? I got it all for you. The guy. The girl. The whole nine yards. So maybe the next time, Frank, that you—"

Vincent took the telephone from her.

"Hey," she whined.

"Hello? Is this Frank?"

"Yeah. Who's this?"

"I am Vincent Street. Who are you?"

"Just Frank."

"Bren tells me that you are looking for the girl, Jenny. Is this so?"

"Yes."

"Why do you want her so badly, if I might be so bold?"

"It's personal."

"Truly? You are not with a law enforcement agency?"

"No."

"I do not wish to get into any legal trouble over any information I might have. Are you an attorney?"

"No. I told you. I'm just a guy. It's personal."

"If I were to know how to find this girl, you would be interested?"

"Of course."

"How much money do you have? The girl says you promised her money if she could locate the girl for you."

"That's right. I got about two grand left."

"The girl would cost you these additional monies as a consultant fee for me. I would be acting solely as an intermediary. Nothing else is to be implied."

"Fuck you. Quit acting like a pussy. I told you I'm not a cop or a lawyer. If you got the girl or can put me on to her, we can do business. If not, say so."

"If the girl is returned to you, unharmed in any way, you will go away? That will be the end of it? And you will not speak of how you found her to anyone?"

"Of course. That's all I'm interested in. Just the girl. Just Jenny."

"Where are you now?"

"In my car."

"Very well. Do you know where Pickle Park is?"

"Pickle Park? Never heard of it. Let me check a map."

Vincent laughed. "I am sorry. That is not its true name. Its true name is MacArthur park. It is called Pickle Park because of all the homosexuals that meet there."

"Clever. What time?"

"Not so fast. It will take me a little time to bring the girl. Say forty-five minutes to an hour. Take a taxi to the east side of the park. Walk west until you reach the last public restrooms. It is near a small parking lot. The lights will be on inside, but there will be a sign on the door that says closed."

"Got it."

"Let me finish," Vincent said, an edge to his voice. "Go to the last urinal along the front wall. The stalls will be directly behind you. Stand facing the urinal. I will contact you when I see you are alone."

"I'll be alone."

"Bring the money, and come unarmed."

"Anything else?"

"Yes. Do not speak to any other person. You never know when I'll be watching. Do not be late. The clock is ticking. I will not wait." Vincent hung up the telephone.

"What are you going to do now?" Bren asked.

"I will have my friend Yusef meet him there in my place."

"Will he whip his ass?"

"Most assuredly. Your Mr. Frank will not bother either of us again."

"Serves the bastard right."

Vincent went to his own cell phone and called Yusef. When he returned to the bedroom, Bren had a wicked look to her eyes.

"Have you got any more money?" she asked.

"No."

"Come on. Don't con me. I know you. You got another stash somewhere. How much you got left?"

THE LAST SPARTAN

Vincent remembered the three hundred dollars he still had hidden in another shoe. "I have another three hundred I keep for emergencies. Why?"

"Why don't you throw that into the pot for me, too. Then we can really party."

"What will it buy me?"

"Anything. Everything. You name it. You can tie me up. I can spank you. Golden shower, foot fetish, trampling. You name it. I'm so fucked up. I feel great. I'm open to anything. Let your perversion be your guide."

Vincent thought for a moment as his erection returned. He knew what he wanted.

* * * *

Yusef closed his telephone. He walked back into the bedroom. There was the stench of burned flesh. It smelled like cooked pork. Small circles on the soles of DC's feet were blistered and raw. Tears streaked DC's face. He had chewed his lips in agony, and the blood was wet around his mouth. Jamal stood watching him. Jamal was smiling.

"I have to go out, Jamal."

"Do you want me to continue questioning him?"

"No. He has told us all he knows."

"Then you believe him? They are nobodies?"

"Perhaps. A clever man could have tricked him. We will not know until I question this Frank."

"Should I—" Jamal opened his coat to reveal his gun. "While you are gone?"

"No. Wait until I return. The meeting may fall through. Frank may show up here. Stay alert. I will be back soon."

Yusef leaned over DC's body. "Rest. I am going for a little while. Soon all your suffering will be over." He patted DC on the head. "Use this time to make peace with your god."

He slipped his jacket back on and replaced the pistol in its holster.

* * * *

Frank drove to the nearest large hotel. He wandered into the hotel bar and ordered a Diet Coke. He drank as he watched his watch. He was close to the park and needed to kill some time before he showed. The deal with Vincent was obviously a setup of some kind. If Vincent was really going to trade the girl, he would have asked for more money. It didn't matter how much Frank offered, Vincent would have wanted more. That was the nature of deals. You had something someone wanted, you got all you could for it.

There was more than just the money angle that convinced Frank. Vincent should have given him more time to get it. You wouldn't set such a short deadline. There was no profit in it. The money was only a ruse to make it appear they were cutting a deal.

The same thing with the location of the trade. If it was on the up-and-up, why not have it at his apartment? Bren knew where he lived. It was reasonable to assume Frank did as well. Vincent didn't want the setup traced back to his apartment.

Frank rubbed his head. It still throbbed from where Bear had hit him with the pistol. He touched it lightly with his fingertips. It was swollen, but at least the bleeding had completely stopped. Head wounds could bleed forever.

It was obvious that Bren had sold him out. He wondered if DC had been in on it or not. Both were possible. Frank considered his options. If he got Jenny, he didn't care. If he didn't, he knew where to go to find some answers. You sleep with the devil, you get burned. That's what his mother used to say. No, wait. His mother never said that. Somebody had. He didn't make this stuff up. Maybe he heard it on television. Maybe Cyrus had said it. It didn't matter, he thought. The meaning of it was clear. Don't fuck with Frank.

"Hey," Frank signaled the bartender.

"Would you like another drink, sir?" the bartender asked.

"No, thank you. Have you got a rubber band I could have?"

The bartender had spent too many years catering to people to ever ask why. He got Frank several. Frank smiled and slipped them into his shirt pocket.

"Thanks."

"You're welcome, sir."

Frank went out to the front desk and had them call a cab for him.

He left his truck at the hotel and took the cab to the park. It was a Red Bird cab. Not much of an omen in that. Frank would keep his eyes open for the next omen.

Chapter 31

Frank followed his instructions exactly. He walked purposely across the wooded park toward the public restroom. He saw several male couples enjoying the solitude of the park along the way.

The public restroom was isolated in a small clearing. The lights were on inside. There was a sign on the door that read, "Closed for cleaning." He noticed that the supply closet had been opened. The lock had been forced. A mop and bucket were outside before the bathroom door. Someone had filled the bucket with Clorox bleach. The chemical smell was terrible. Frank opened the door and went inside. Once inside, the odor dissipated. He was impressed, it was a nice ruse. He would have to remember it.

Frank checked the stalls to be sure they were empty. He opened each door to make sure no one was perched on the seat to make the stall just appear empty. Frank knew what Vincent looked like. He had seen his picture and then later seen him moving around. He didn't doubt that he could take Vincent out if necessary. Something about this place didn't feel right. He got a tingling down the back of his neck. It felt like a hit. He didn't have much choice. He would play it out.

Frank went and stood in front of one of the urinals. He thought he heard something outside and stepped away. The urinal flushed. It startled Frank a little. The sound was loud. He had not been expecting it. He noticed that the urinals all had electronic eyes so they could self-flush. Our tax dollars at work. Since he was here, he might as well take a leak. He stood there with one hand on his privates and the other on the wall in front of him.

He heard the door open. He glanced over his shoulder but couldn't see around the corner.

"Do not look this way. Stare straight ahead," a voice said from the other side.

The voice was Middle Eastern. It was not Vincent's voice.

"Both hands on the wall in front of you," the voice said.

Frank put both hands on the wall. The steps were quick. He felt the metal barrel of a gun against the base of his neck.

"Hey, what's the gun for?"

"Silence," the voice said. "If you move, I will kill you."

Frank shrugged. He felt a hand expertly pat him down. When the man knelt, he drew the gun down with him. It never left contact with Frank. While the man frisked Frank's legs, the gun was lodged into the small of his back. This guy knew what he was doing. When he was done, the gun returned to the base of his neck.

The man lifted Frank's wallet from his back pocket. It was attached by a short chain to a loop of his pants. The man jerked hard and tore the loop. The wallet came free. Yusef flipped it open and studied the contents.

"Your name is Frank Smith?"

"That's right."

"What branch of the government do you work for?"

"None. I'm a mechanic."

"CIA?"

"No."

"FBI?"

"No."

"SBI perhaps?"

"No."

"Justice?"

"No. And I'm not DEA, or ATF, or a federal marshal, or a highway patrolman, or a sheriff, or a fucking mall cop. I told you. I'm a mechanic. I fix motorcycles."

"Why do you look for this girl?"

"It's personal—"

Yusef punched him hard in the left kidney. Frank crumpled. He regained his strength and stood again.

"Hands back on the wall. Why do you seek this girl?"

"She's a family friend. I owe her folks. I promised I would try to find her for them."

Yusef punched him again. Once more Frank stumbled to his knees. Once more he rose. He placed his hands on the wall in front of him again.

"Alright. All that's true, but there's more. They offered a reward as well. I could use the dough."

"How much?"

"Five grand."

"For this little girl? I don't believe you."

"They love her, man. She ran away from home, and they want her back. It's that simple."

Yusef thought about it for a few moments. It was possible. It could be that simple. No agency was aware of the Ambassador's activities. No political enemy. No foreign government hoping to blackmail him with his indiscretions. Not even the Israelis, may Allah curse them for a thousand years. Just a family looking for a runaway girl. Just a redneck trying to make some easy money. The story had the ring of truth to it. It always paid to be careful. He pressed the gun harder against the back of Frank's skull.

"Does anyone else know you are looking for this girl?"

"No. No one. Hey, can I ask you something? Was the stripper and her boyfriend both in on this set up?"

"The whore? She is a fool. She has already gone to the world that waits for her."

"What about the boyfriend?"

"No. Not yet. After I am done here. May Allah be merciful to him."

"You going to kill me, too?"

"Yes. Are you at peace with your god, my friend?"

"Whoa. Hold on just a second. I'm not exactly in the big guy's best graces."

"I will give you a minute to kneel and make peace."

Seconds passed before Frank spoke. "Can I ask you a favor?"

"What is it?"

"I know you're going to kill me. And I know there's not a thing in this world I can do about that."

"Yes."

"Can I finish taking a leak before you do it?"

"What difference will it make?"

"I just don't want to go to hell having pissed my pants, is all. Take my life, man, but don't take my dignity. Please."

Yusef sighed. "Be quick."

Frank tried to relax. He took his penis out and tried to piss a little more.

"Are you finished yet?" Yusef asked.

Frank sighed a deep contented sigh. "Just let me shake her off and slip her back into the barn."

THE LAST SPARTAN

Yusef shook his head. Americans were such animals.

Frank stepped back from the urinal. The sound of the knife opening was swallowed by the automatic flushing. Yusef's eyes shifted toward the toilet as Frank stepped back. Yusef stepped back as well, fearful of having Frank's urine splashed on his clothes. That's when Frank spun into him.

He drove the knife up through Yusef's belly, disemboweling him. It was a shock-inducing attack. Frank knew its effects. He remembered how it shut the body down and you couldn't respond. Frank hoped the man wouldn't recover enough to put a round through his head.

Frank sliced high until he had almost reached the sternum. He pulled the knife out and stabbed, aiming for the heart. The blade was incredibly sharp. It didn't cut flesh so much as slide through it. The first strike stuck in a rib. Frank stabbed again. This time it bounced off a rib and plunged into Yusef's heart.

Yusef had not made a sound. His eyes were wide in surprise. Already the light was gone from them. Frank half carried him into a stall and sat him on one of the toilets. The front of Yusef's shirt and pants were soaked with blood.

Frank wiped the knife on Yusef's pants and put it back into his pocket. The rubber band had held it nicely in place against his penis. Frank had been frisked many times in his life, and no one had ever touched his dick. The best would examine the fringes. But it was an unspoken taboo to actually touch another man's dick. Men were too homophobic. For an instant, Frank wondered if a homosexual frisked you if it would be different. Interesting question, he thought. The only risks had been that whoever he was meeting would just kill him straight off or that Frank would accidentally open the knife and cut his own dick off.

He searched Yusef and found his diplomatic attachÈ's passport. He took the pistol with the silencer and Yusef's spare magazine. He left the shoulder holster in place. He found Yusef's car keys in his left coat pocket. There was also a hotel key card. It was blank except for the magnetic strip across it. He took it as well. He left Yusef's cell phone and cash in his pocket. Frank closed the door to the stall behind him.

Frank got some paper towels and wet them with the Clorox. It was the best at quickly removing fingerprints. He wiped down the handle to the bathroom stall and the wall where he had placed his hands. He wiped down the handle of the door to the bathroom. He pulled the mop and bucket bucket full of Clorox inside and dumped it on the floor. There was no way to lock the door without a key, but he hoped the smell would discourage casual visitors. He placed the mop and bucket back outside the door. He flicked the light off and put the used paper towels into his pocket.

The front of Frank's shirt was stained red with Yusef's blood. Fuck it. There was nothing he could do about it now. He went out into the parking lot and saw the Ambassador's black car. He slipped into the driver's seat and turned the key. Vincent Street could wait. He would save DC if he could.

THE LAST SPARTAN

Chapter 32

Frank cut the lights on the car before he got to DC's apartment. He parked the car behind the building, near the stairs. He could see the lights were on in DC's apartment. There were lights on in other apartments on the other floors, but things were pretty quiet.

Frank took the thin knife out of his pocket. He didn't have any gloves with him. He cut a large piece off the front of the blood soaked shirt. He picked up Yusef's gun in his left hand and wrapped the piece of shirt around it. It wasn't large enough. Frank sighed and took off his shirt. He wrapped it around his hand. That was better. It was crude, but it would work. It almost made him look like his hand was in a cast.

He got out DC's spare key and crept up the stairs. He had Yusef's wrapped pistol hanging by his left leg so it was less obvious in silhouette. The second-floor landing was clear. He moved up to the third floor. It was clear as well. He could hear the television playing loudly inside. The station was set on CNN. Frank had only known DC a few days, but he was sure he never watched CNN. World news didn't seem to be high on DC's list of things to keep up with.

Frank moved as silently as a man his size can. Apollo used to call it noise discipline. He tried the door. It was locked. Gently, he inserted his key and turned it. The pop of the lock sounded like a gunshot to Frank. He paused, nothing happened. He turned the knob slowly. He inched the door open and peeked into the hallway. He was crouched below the door knob. If someone was waiting, they might fire a round at the door as it swung open. Hopefully it would go high, where he should be standing, not where he was. No shot. He opened the door a little more. The hallway was empty. He crab-walked into the apartment, easing the door closed behind him. It didn't latch.

The pistol was up now, sweeping the area before him. He saw the back of a head. The hair was thick and dark and shined with some kind of oil. The man was smoking a cigarette as he watched television. Frank did not see anyone else.

He tapped his gun hand against the side of the wall. The metallic thud of the barrel was muffled by the shirt. The head twitched, and the man glanced over his shoulder. When he saw Frank, his eyes grew large. The man stood up and faced Frank. Frank motioned for him to raise his hands. The man stared, dumbstruck. Frank understood the

177

man's confusion. In front of him, the man saw a half naked man crouched and pointing something. Frank realized the man was calculating. Was there a gun hidden beneath the white cloth? Was it a bluff? Was this the kind of man who could shoot another man?

Jamal darted a hand inside his jacket. Frank shot him twice in the center of his chest. Double tap. The man fell like a puppet with its strings cut. He crumpled to the floor. Frank waited.

No one else materialized. He shook his gun hand a few times to put out the fire that the shots had ignited. He eased farther into the room. He saw DC tied to the bed. He pulled his knife and cut the gag free.

"How many?" he whispered to DC.

"There were two, but one left to find you."

Frank smiled his humorless smile. "He found me."

Frank cut the strips of cloth binding DC's ankles and wrists. He stared at the burns on his feet. He went back into the main room and did a quick sweep just to be certain there was no one else. DC was right. He searched the dead man. His name was Jamal. He had a diplomatic passport as well. Frank rifled his pockets but found nothing else of interest. He unwrapped his bloodstained shirt from the pistol. He tossed it on top of the dead man's chest to soak some of the bleeding. He went back to check on DC.

He was standing at the bedroom door. He stumbled, trying to walk into the computer room. He was trying to walk on his heels, but the pain was obviously intense.

"Is he dead?" DC asked.

"Yes."

"Good."

Frank glanced toward his feet. "Can you walk?"

"Help me make it to the computer room," DC said, then stopped. He started crying. He bent at the waist and wept. Frank gave him an arm for support. DC took it. He struggled to move again.

"Are you alright?"

DC was crying, but he nodded yes. Spit bubbled up on his lips as he walked. Frank led him into the computer room. He helped him to sit in his chair. DC picked up his cell phone from beside the computer monitor.

"I got to call Bren. This fucker said another guy had her."

THE LAST SPARTAN

Frank jerked the cell from his hands.

"He's telling the truth. I called her and got one of them. He said they had her."

Pure terror showed on DC's face. "Is she okay?"

"I don't know."

"Where have they got her? We've got to call the police."

"It won't do any good. I think she sold us out."

DC was taken back. He shook his head to clear it.

"I don't care. I've got to know she's okay. She needs our help. They probably tricked her."

Frank thought quickly. Love was a bitch sometimes. He pulled the blank key out of his pocket. "Do you know what hotel this goes to?"

DC stared for a few seconds. "No. There is some kind of bar code, but I don't know what it means. And I don't care. We have to help Bren. That's all that matters. That's all that matters."

DC started crying again. Sobbing into his hands. Frank felt sorry for him. But not sorry enough to let him waste the only time they had left. It was too big a risk for Jenny. He slid DC's cell into his back pocket.

"DC. DC."

DC kept sobbing.

Frank shook him. "Listen to me. I think they have Bren with Jenny. If we don't get to them soon, something bad will happen to them. We may still have time to save them both."

DC looked up, trying to get control.

"They are at this hotel," Frank said. "We need to figure this out and damn quick."

DC wiped his nose and his eyes. He flipped the key around in his hands. "Let me see what I can do."

"That's the way. Cowboy up, DC."

DC stared at him. "Hey, you called me DC, not Donny. How come?"

Frank hesitated. "That Donny shit was just a way to establish dominance. Keep you down a little. Fuck with your head. I'm sorry about that."

"So why DC now?"

"You're a man now."

DC nodded as if it made perfect sense. "Give me some space. This is what I'm good at. Who are these fuckers?"

"Some kind of Arabs. The one who came looking for me said he worked for an ambassador. He had diplomatic attachÈ papers, but I couldn't read much more than that."

DC nodded, lost in thought. He booted up his computer and went to work. "One more thing. Can you get rid of the body? You'll have to."

"Sure, that's what I'm good at."

"Did they have a car?"

"It's outside."

"Bring me the license number, okay?"

"Consider it done."

Frank did a quick check outside and then quickly carried the dead Jamal down to the car. He tossed him into the back seat. The windows of the car were so heavily tinted he doubted anyone could see Jamal even if they tried. He locked the car and hurried back upstairs, working on a plan.

He recited the tag number for DC, who wrote it down.

Frank got a fresh t-shirt and a clean black pull over. He also took his last pair of leather gloves from his bag and slipped them into his back pocket. He ran different scenarios over in his head. It had to be simple and quick. He went back to check on DC.

"How's it going, DC?"

DC didn't answer. He stared at him. "Can I ask you something, Frank?"

"Sure."

"It's personal."

"We're friends. Ask away."

"How can you be so brave? When I was being tortured by those motherfuckers, I pissed my pants. I don't know if I was more scared or more hurt. I would have done or said anything to make them stop. I would have betrayed anybody, even Bren."

"But you didn't. You fought them. You were trying to protect Bren."

"Still. How do you do it?"

Frank paused as he thought how to explain it. "Five minutes."

"Five minutes?"

"Yeah. Five minutes. I realized a long time ago that you only have to be brave for a short time. Five minutes. If you can hang tough for that long, then whatever shit you're in is probably over."

DC thought about it. "Five minutes," he mumbled, more to himself than Frank.

"You get anything?"

"No problem. I was able to limit the search pretty easily."

"How?"

"I knew I was looking for a hotel. It had to be in the Atlanta area. It had to be five-star or better for an ambassador to stay there. It had to use bar codes for security. That cut the list down to three hotels—Ritz Carlton Atlanta, Four Seasons, and the Hilton Atlanta. The key is the wrong shape for most hotel rooms, so I searched for hotels that use them for elevators."

"You got a hit?"

"Four Seasons Hotel. Penthouse key. Presidential suite on the nineteenth floor. It allows you to take the elevator up. Opens into the foyer of the suite. A second key card opens that door. This key will only get you so far."

"You got all that from the Internet?"

"Yeah. I was able to crosscheck it against the rental car. That's the leasee's Atlanta address. Permanent rental. State Department pays the tab."

"I am impressed. Can I borrow your car?"

"What are you going to do?" DC asked, fishing the keys from the drawer beside the computer. He tossed them to Frank.

"In times like these, there's only one thing to do."

"What's that?"

"Order pizza."

Chapter 33

Frank parked a block away from the Four Seasons Hotel. He had no idea what type of security surveillance the hotel used. In his experience, those that used video cameras trained them on the potential trouble spots. Areas like the parking garage and the side entrances were common targets. There might even be one overlooking the check-in counter. He had never seen one watching the front door. Trouble didn't come in the front door. Not until tonight.

Frank walked through the front door like he belonged there. His Braves baseball cap was turned backwards and pulled down tight. He wore his sunglasses. Cities like Atlanta made allowances for wearing sunglasses at night. Small towns didn't. He wore a bright oven mitt on each hand. He was carrying five large boxes of pizza. Their aroma of onions and hot cheese followed him into the lobby.

He looked around, spied the bank of elevators, and hurried over. When one of the doors opened he stepped inside. There was another couple riding up. They were dressed nicely. The man pushed the sixth floor button.

"That smells good," the woman said. "What floor?"

He saw they had pushed six. "Ten."

The couple got off on six. There was no keycard slot on this elevator for the penthouse. Frank rode to ten and got off. There was no one waiting. He pushed the up button again. There was a bank of four elevators. The next elevator that arrived only went as far as the eighteenth floor. No penthouse. He waited and tried again. The third elevator had an unlabeled button with a slot for a key card. Frank sat the boxes down, pulled the key card from his pocket and swiped it through the lock. The key engaged. He pushed the button. He placed the key between his teeth. Put the oven mitt back on and lifted the boxes. Going up.

The elevator dinged open, and he stepped out. He let it close and retreat before approaching the door to the presidential suite. They would not be expecting him. That would help.

He kicked at the door. There was no answer. He kicked again.

"Pizza man," he called, slurring the words because of the keycard between his teeth. Nothing. He kicked again. "Pizza man."

The door opened and a large Arabic man stood there. He was

about six-foot-two and two hundred and fifty pounds with a thick dark beard. He had angry, suspicious eyes.

"What do you want?" he growled.

Frank let the elevator card fall from his mouth onto the lid of the top pizza box. "Pizza man."

"We ordered no pizza. Go away."

"Somebody ordered it."

"I did not. Go away."

"Look, they gave me the elevator key. Said to bring it right up."

"Who said this thing?"

"Are you Jamal?" Frank asked, as if he were trying to remember the name given to him.

"No. Jamal is not here."

"What's your name?"

"I am Ali."

Frank smiled. "Well, this guy. Yusef. That's it. Yusef, he said to bring these pies up here for Jamal and Ali. This dude, Yusef, gave me a note to give you. I got it here somewhere. Hey. Can you hold these for a second, and I'll get it?"

Frank pushed the pizza boxes toward Ali. By instinct, Ali accepted the boxes. Frank's right hand dropped, and the oven mitt fell to the floor. He was wearing thin leather gloves beneath it. Instead of reaching for one of his pockets, the gloved hand swung up beneath the bottom pizza box. He had cut a flap in it. The butt of the gun protruded from the open flap.

Before Ali could react, Frank had the gun in his hand. He pressed the barrel against Ali's stomach. Ali's eyes flashed wide.

"You know what this is. Now back into the room."

Ali did as he was told.

Frank kicked the dropped mitt in ahead of him. He dropped the other mitt. He wore a glove on that hand as well. He closed the door behind him.

The inside of the suite was huge. He walked Ali into the kitchen. He let Ali place the boxes down on the glass-top table. Ali's eyes burned.

"Who else is here?"

Ali did not answer.

"There are two ways we can play this. You can tell me what I ask.

Or I can shoot you in the fucking knee cap and find out for myself. Which way is it going to be?"

"I am here with the Ambassador."

"Alone?"

"Yes. But others will return soon."

"Take me to him."

Ali's eyes shifted around. Frank could see the bulge under his left arm. Frank removed his sunglasses and tucked them into the front of his shirt.

"Don't. I don't want to have to kill you, Ali. But I will if you force me. I must see the Ambassador. It is urgent. Yusef sent me."

"Yusef sent you?" Ali asked. The casual use of his friend's name kept him off balance. "Why?"

"It's not for you to hear. It's for the Ambassador's ears only."

Ali glared. He was still weighing his options.

Frank used his trump card. Always act like you know more than you do. "I know he's not alone. I know he's with some girl. Vincent told me. Is Vincent here? Or has he called?"

"No, Vincent is not here. He will not call until after midnight."

Frank sighed. "It doesn't matter. That's not important. I must see the Ambassador now."

"Can it not wait a little longer? His excellency is occupied. You understand these things."

"No. It is a matter of life and death. It is about the Mossad. They have sent a team."

Ali was confused. This could be important. Perhaps assassins were coming for the Ambassador. Disturbing the Ambassador was not wise. But getting himself killed for no reason did not seem prudent either. He nodded his head yes.

"Follow me."

Ali led him up the stairs to a double set of doors. He looked once more to Frank, silently begging him not to make him disturb the Ambassador. Frank motioned with the gun. Ali knocked.

"Ambassador. Excuse me, Excellency. I must speak with you."

There was silence. Ali knocked again.

"A thousand pardons, Excellency, but it is a matter most urgent."

The reply that came from inside was in some form of Arabic. The voice was deep and resonant. There was a tone of absolute authority.

THE LAST SPARTAN

Frank wondered if there was a special school you went to to learn to sound like that. Ali started to answer in Arabic. Frank pointed the gun at this head.

"Just open the doors, Ali."

Ali sighed and opened the doors. The lights were dimmed. A fire burned in the gas log fireplace. Middle Eastern music played softly in the background. The voice was still angry. Still speaking sharp, fast Arabic. Frank kept Ali in front of him. He could make out a gigantic bed. Frank found the switch and flipped the lights on.

The Ambassador was in the bed. A girl was lying beside him. Her hair was blonde. For an instant, Frank thought it wasn't Jenny. But she had Jenny's eyes. It was Jenny. She was lying naked beside him. She looked at Frank but said nothing. Her eyes were blank. A long, black dress lay folded neatly at the foot of the bed. Tiny shoes rested neatly on top of the pile. A small purse sat beside it. Frank's heart tried to burst, but he wouldn't let it.

"Mr. Ambassador. I must speak with you."

"Who is this man, Ali? Get out of my room at once. I will have you arrested."

Frank showed him the gun. "Calm down, sir. I just need a few minutes of your time."

"What? You dare threaten me? What is the meaning of this?"

"Not in front of this girl. Get her out of here. Yusef sent me."

The Ambassador hesitated. If Yusef had sent this crazy American, it could be important. The Ambassador spoke quietly to Jenny.

"Go wait downstairs for me, my little dove."

She smiled. "Alright." She rose from the bed. She was nude but seemed unembarrassed. She walked past Frank without a second glance.

Frank marched Ali over to the foot of the bed. His eyes swept the room. He noticed the small Visine bottle like the one he had seen in Vincent's apartment. It even had the same small red mark on it. He did not let his eyes linger. He continued to scan the room as if looking for something.

"Very well. What is it you want?" the Ambassador asked, trying to sound patient. He was not.

"I told you. Yusef sent me."

"Yusef. I know. Speak."

"Are we being recorded?" Frank asked, knowing the answer.

"Of course not. What do you wish to ask me?"

He pointed the gun at Ali. "Take your coat off. Slowly. I don't trust you. You might be in this with the Mossad."

Ali looked to the Ambassador. He nodded. Ali took his coat off and hung it on the back of a nearby chair. His shoulder holster was clearly revealed.

"Now the gun."

Ali complied, laying it neatly on the seat of the chair.

"Satisfied?" the Ambassador asked. His anger was barely in check. "What is this about the Mossad?"

Frank continued to stare at Ali. "Are you wearing a wire?"

"What?" the Ambassador barked.

"No," Ali said, looking at the Ambassador for confirmation.

"Take off your shirt," Frank ordered. "I have to be sure."

Ali removed his shirt. He was dark and hairy.

"Put it over your weapon."

Ali did.

"Turn around once more."

Ali turned.

"Now sit on the bed. Up near the top where I can keep an eye on you."

Ali sat. The Ambassador stroked a dark hand through his beard. Frank wondered what he was thinking.

"What did you need to speak with me about?" the Ambassador asked once more.

The words came quickly to Frank. He smiled.

"Yusef wanted me to ask you something. Something very important."

"Well? What is it?"

"Have you made peace with your god?"

Frank shot Ali twice in the head and then turned toward the Ambassador. The Ambassador's eyes were wide in horror. He started shaking.

"I am a diplomat. You cannot do this. I am a guest of your country. I have full diplomatic immunity."

Frank shot him through the left eye. He put the second round through his forehead as an insurance shot.

He moved over to Ali's body. He quickly stripped off Ali's shoes and socks. He pulled Ali's pants down. He placed the shoes neatly beneath the chair with the socks rolled up inside and folded the pants on top of them. He pulled the covers back enough to pull them over one of Ali's fat, hairy legs. So much for setting the stage, he thought.

Frank grabbed the Visine bottle and slipped it into his front pocket. He scooped up Jenny's clothes and carried them downstairs. She was waiting on a sofa. He carried the clothes to her.

"Put these on, and wait for me right here."

"Alright," she said and began dressing.

"I'll be right back."

"Alright."

Frank went back upstairs and did a quick search of the nightstand and bathroom for anything that could serve as a link to Jenny. He found nothing. There was a fresh box of condoms in the bathroom. Several were missing. He looked through the Ambassador's wallet. It held an array of credit cards. There was a money clip with nearly two thousand dollars. He left the money. Someone who knew the Ambassador well might know how much money he usually carried. This wasn't supposed to look like a robbery.

He checked under the bed and behind the pictures on the walls to be sure the Ambassador wasn't recording the escapade with Jenny to enjoy again later. Freaks were freaks. Frank knew modern spy cameras could be very small, and they could be hidden in almost anything. Frank took his time and did a thorough job. He found nothing.

The Ambassador's briefcase sat under a nearby desk. He checked the outside to be sure it didn't contain a camera then replaced it where he had found it. It had a combination lock. He didn't try to open it.

The Ambassador's suitcases were neatly stacked in the closet. His shoes arranged neatly below, the expensive suits hung above them. Nothing else.

He left the Ambassador's room and went downstairs. There were two more bedrooms down here. He glanced inside to be sure they were empty. They were. He found a white cotton shirt hanging in one of the closets. The sleeves were too short, but it was big enough. He changed shirts and put it on. He rolled the sleeves a couple of turns to disguise that they were too short. He left the collar unbuttoned and the shirttail out. He didn't examine their belongings at all. He went back to the kitchen area. He picked up the five boxes of pizza. They were all empty except the top box. He divided the pizza from that box among the four remaining boxes.

He found a paper grocery bag and put the pistol inside. He put the oven mitts on top of it and the Braves hat and his sunglasses. He balled up his black shirt and put it in the bag. He knew forensics could even detect the gunpowder residue on the shirt. It would have to go. He tossed the elevator key on top of it all. He went to find Jenny.

She was sitting primly on the sofa. Her dress was on, and she sat with her knees together. Her worn purse rested on her knees.

"Are you ready to go?" Frank asked.

"Sure," she said and stood up.

Frank stared at her. She smiled. He tucked the pizza boxes under his left arm and grasped the paper bag with his right hand.

"Let's go. Stay close."

"Alright."

She followed him out of the room. He closed the door behind them and heard it lock. He placed the "Do Not Disturb" sign on the knob. They took the elevator down to the eighth floor. Frank put the empty pizza boxes under a decorative table near the elevators. They rode the rest of the way down without speaking. Every time he looked at Jenny she would smile back sweetly.

Frank walked quickly across the lobby. Jenny followed along beside him, matching his pace. Another couple hurrying out for a night at Atlanta's famed Underground. They found DC's Acura and drove back to his apartment. Along the way, Frank made some calls to set up his next move.

Chapter 34

Vincent was leering wildly. Yusef would be proud of him.

Bren giggled. "Hell. This is going to be good, I can tell."

"You said anything."

"Let your freak side run wild, lover."

"I want to do it from behind."

Bren laughed. She looked disappointed. "Ooh, aren't we the wild man. Doggy style. Is that your big fantasy? I kind of hoped for something a little more extreme from you, Vincent."

"There is more. While I am making love to you, I would like to gently strangle you."

"Now, lover, that's something I've never tried before. And I've tried it all. What if you get a little too carried away with your little fantasy? I don't want to end up dead."

"We can use an escape signal. If I am choking too hard or you become frightened, just tap me on my forearm and I'll stop."

"But you want me to pretend that you are really choking me hard? That I'm terrified? That you're trying to kill me?"

Vincent smiled. "Yes. Only pretend. This way I will know if your actions are real. I don't want to misunderstand your acting and stop if I do not have to."

"Which arm?"

"Either one. Just a couple of taps, and I will stop."

"You are a freak."

"That sounds like a compliment."

"It is from me. I'm so sick and tired of the vanilla sex I have with DC, I think sometimes I will scream."

Vincent smiled. He entered her slowly. He was very gentle. He began to stroke back and forth as he eased his hands around her neck. As his thrust got stronger so did his grip around her slender throat. Bren was thrashing and writhing. She was a good actress. Vincent was impressed. He began to strangle her in earnest. It took a few seconds for Bren to become concerned. She tapped him on the arm. Vincent did not stop. He thrust harder. He choked harder. She started slapping his arms. Still, he thrust harder. Bren realized he was killing her. She started to flail in earnest, but she was nearly unconscious. She couldn't buck him off. She dug her nails deep into his hands. Vincent didn't stop. She could smell the blood on his hands where she had savaged them. Her last thought before she died was of DC. She wished he were there to save her.

* * * *

DC was kneeling on the floor beside the sofa when Frank got back. He was scrubbing up the blood stains. His feet were heavily wrapped with bandages. He had changed his piss-stained pants.

"Did you find her?" he asked.

"Bren wasn't there."

DC nodded, resigned. "I know. She's dead."

"Maybe not. I think I know where she is."

"It doesn't matter. She's dead. I can feel it. Inside," he said touching his chest. "She's gone."

Frank didn't answer. DC looked up. "I would have forgiven her anything. Even this. I loved her that much."

"I know you did, DC."

"There's nothing for us to do now."

"We can avenge her," Frank said.

DC smiled. "Yeah. We can do that."

Frank brought Jenny into the room. "DC, this is Jenny."

"How do you do?" DC asked formally.

"Fine," she answered.

DC gazed at her. "Is she stoned or something?"

"GHB. I think. It will wear off soon. I need your help."

"Just ask."

"First, I got questions. Whose name is your apartment in?"

"Tom Farr. The lease is in his name, but Bren took it over from a dancer that moved to L.A. We don't even know the guy. We just pay the rent when the monthly bill comes."

"How do you pay it. With checks or credit cards?"

"Checks. We each paid half. Bren liked to keep everything separate."

"What about the cell phones?"

"We got those together. It was a better deal. I pay them online. It's simpler. Bren makes it up by paying for something else like the cable TV or the Internet hookup."

"What about your other bills?"

"I pay them online too."

"Good. I think it might work."

"What?"

"There are going to be some people looking for you. How hard, I don't know."

"Who would be looking for me? I haven't done anything."

"The Jokers for one. They spotted me with Bren last night."

"So what?"

"I have a history with them. They are back on their heels for right now. I'm not sure if they can still put me together with her now, but they might try. I think it will be safer for you to be out of Atlanta. At least for a little while until things cools down."

"Okay. Anybody else?"

"After tonight there could be other people. That's the real bad news. Government types, depending on how motivated they are. I've hidden our trail pretty well. They even have an out if they want to use it. You just never know with the Feds."

"You think they'll come looking for us because you had to kill that Arab guy? They started it. We didn't do anything wrong. It was self-defense. That asshole was torturing me. He was going to kill me. They'll have to listen to reason."

"Yes, he was trying to kill you. Doesn't mean they'll see it that way. They might want to make an example of somebody. They might have to."

"You mean us."

"No. I mean you. Bren is the link that can draw them here. Even if they get to you, there's no way they can connect the next step to me. You can't help them find me, even if you wanted to."

"So if they come, they'll just be looking for me?"

"Yes."

DC looked down at the dim pink stain on the floor.

"Shit. You could just kill me and torch the apartment, then you wouldn't have to worry at all. It would simplify things for you."

"I thought about that option. I'm not that guy anymore."

"The fuck. What kind of guy were you?"

"Very bad. You got to decide where you are going to stand, because after tonight there's no going back. You want to turn yourself in, that's your call. You think you can hold it together and play silent, that's cool, too."

"Why would I turn myself in?"

"Guilt. A man's dead. Let me be straight with you. Several men are dead."

DC rubbed his bandaged feet. He thought about it hard.

"Fuck them," he said finally. "If they're dead, they deserved it. I'll play along. What do you need?"

"You got to pack up. They may trace Bren back here. I doubt it. But you can't take the chance. Load all the shit you want to take in your car. Anything else that's yours that you don't want, toss in the dumpster out back. Remember, travel light. You can always replace things later. Wipe the apartment down as good as you can. Door knobs, faucet handles, toilet seats, refrigerator door. Anything you can think of."

"Shit, my fingerprints are all over this place. I'll never get all of them."

"I know. You just have to make it harder for them. Do the best you can."

"What about Bren's stuff?"

"If I find her, I'll come back and pack it up. I'll bring her. If she'll come."

"Thanks for saying it, Frank. Even if it is a lie."

"Come on, get to work. Jenny will just sit on the sofa until you're ready to go. Isn't that right Jenny?"

"Sure," she said and smiled.

"DC. You don't have much time. Get it done and then motor."

Frank handed him a piece of paper with a name and address.

"Here. I will meet you there tomorrow morning. Tell them you are there to meet with Mr. Robinson. That's all you know. Mr. Robinson will take care of everything tomorrow morning including the bill."

"What if you don't show?"

"Then I'm dead. You're on your own, but you should be safe."

"And Jenny?"

"She has to make her own decisions. Tell her what's happened."

DC folded the paper into his pocket. "You can count on me."

"I know."

THE LAST SPARTAN

Chapter 35

Frank pulled the dark Town Car over behind the grocery store. He tossed the oven mitts, his black shirt, and his baseball cap into the dumpster. He snapped the elevator key into two pieces and tossed them into a second dumpster along with the paper bag from the Ambassador's suite. He had stashed his other shirt, the one he had used to wrap around his gun, inside it. He stomped the cell phone he had gotten from the Jokers and threw the pieces into the dumpster. He threw DC's spare key into the woods behind the grocery store. He knew he wouldn't need it. He didn't want the evidence too close to DC's apartment or to Vincent's. Sometimes the cops could be very thorough.

He drove to Vincent's apartment. He cut the lights on the car and cruised into the parking lot. He parked in the back. He looked in the back seat. Jamal had rolled around onto his stomach. He almost looked like a drunk sleeping it off. He locked the car's door behind him.

Frank carried his overnight bag. The pistol lay inside on top of his remaining clothes. He pulled out the spare key he had stolen from Vincent's apartment earlier. When he reached the door, he removed Yusef's dark pistol with the supressor from the bag and tucked it into the front of his pants. It felt weird. Must be what it felt like to have a really big dick.

He unlocked the door and stepped inside. Music was playing on a Bose Wave radio. He placed his bag by the door and closed it. He set the security chain. It was time to wrap things up.

He scanned the loft. Someone was in the bathroom. He could hear water running in the sink. He walked into the kitchen and laid the Ambassador's car keys by the sink and covered them with a dish towel. He waited quietly. There were no other sounds. The water stopped. The door swung open. He was looking at Vincent Street. Vincent was wearing nothing except a dark silk bathrobe. It was untied in the front.

Vincent's eyes were rheumy. His hair was mussed. His hands were badly scratched. He did not speak. He just looked at Frank and his gun. Frank watched him, let the realization settle in. Let Vincent realize that his position was hopeless. Vincent tied his robe and ran a shaking hand through his hair.

"Where is Bren?" Frank asked.

"Who are you?"

"Where is Bren?"

"You're Frank. You're the one she told me about."

"I won't ask again. Where is Bren?"

Vincent's eyes darted toward the bedroom and back toward Frank. His mind was racing.

"She's in there," Vincent said, pointing toward the bedroom. "She's asleep."

"Show me."

Vincent hesitated. His shoulders slumped, and he walked into the bedroom like he was walking to a gallows. Bren lay on her stomach on the crumpled sheets. Frank slipped past Vincent and moved toward her body.

"She may be passed out," Vincent said. "We were partying pretty hard."

Frank used his teeth to pull off the glove on his left hand. He placed the back of it against her neck. That way he would be sure not to leave fingerprints or a palm print. She was dead. She had been a sorry excuse for a human being, he thought. She had set in motion a chain of events that had caused a lot of people to die. If she had played it straight, things might have been different. So what? If pigs could fly. You get what you get. She lived her life. She had a past. Somebody had loved her and now she was gone. End of story.

Her death simplified things. It trimmed the loose ends down to one.

Frank pulled the tight glove back on. He used it to wipe her neck, just to be safe. The sight of the gloves seemed to strike Vincent with unnamed dread. He started to tremble uncontrollably. He knew Frank had come to kill him.

Normally, Frank would have killed Vincent. A quick double tap and then an insurance shot to the head. Keep it simple. Yet, Frank was puzzled. He didn't understand what was going on with Vincent and the Ambassador. He wanted to know. Frank was not an abnormally curious man, but he felt that if he understood the situation a little better, he could control it and its aftermath more efficiently. So he decided to lie.

"Did you kill her?" Frank asked.

"It was an accident. I didn't mean to."

Frank picked up the envelope of money on the nightstand. Vincent cringed. That was his money. Frank thumbed the contents. He stuck the envelope in his back pocket. He looked up at Vincent.

"I'm glad she's dead," Frank said. He motioned with the pistol. "Let's go into the other room where we can talk business."

Vincent turned to go.

"Wait," Frank said. "Put your clothes back on. I don't like talking to a naked guy in a faggoty bathrobe."

Vincent picked his clothes off the floor. He put them on.

"The shoes, too?" Vincent asked.

"Hell, yes, the shoes, too. I don't like looking at your dirty feet either."

Vincent put his shoes on and led Frank into the main room. He was confused and off balance. That was what Frank wanted. Now to let him have hope so he would tell what he knew.

"Sit," Frank said.

Vincent sat on the sofa. Frank sat on a chair across from him. Vincent sat rigid with his palms flat on his thighs. He was trying to think.

"So, what's the deal, Vincent?"

"What do you mean?"

"Look, Vincent. There are a couple of ways we can play this. You can jerk me around and try to play dumb. In which case I shoot you in the fucking head. Or you can tell me what kind of scam you're running. If there's profit in it, I let you cut me in."

The relief showed instantly in Vincent's face. This was something he could understand. He might be going to escape after all.

"I thought you were searching for a girl?"

"I was. I am. It is a job. I was paid good money to do it. The girl doesn't mean anything to me. If the money's better on the other side, I could be tempted to cross over. So, why don't you tell me the deal?"

Vincent was still wary. "What happened at the restrooms with Yusef?"

"You mean the fucking setup at the restrooms, don't you? I hid out and watched that big fucking rag head go in. I'm not dumb enough to walk into such an obvious trap."

"Yusef is still there waiting?"

"For all I know the queers are having a go with him. I didn't stick around to find out."

"That is not possible. Yusef is a devout Muslim."

"If you mean serious muscle, I agree. If you mean he's straight, I wouldn't know about any of that. I don't care."

"He should have called me."

"Should, could, would. With that and a dollar you still can't get coffee. I don't give a fuck. Maybe your phone's off."

Vincent started to rise to go check his cell phone. Frank pointed with the pistol again.

"Sit down. This isn't your show. Now tell me how it works."

Vincent sighed. If Yusef had been unable to reach him by telephone, eventually he would come to the apartment. If Vincent could stall long enough, Yusef would come.

"How much do you know?"

Frank pointed the pistol at his face. "I know I've about had it with your shit, Vincent. I know what I know. If what you tell me doesn't jibe with what I've already learned, then I know I'm going to shoot you in the fucking head. You understand that, Habib? From the fucking top."

The insult and threats worked. Vincent leaned forward. "It is a long tale."

"Be brief."

"My mother was of the royal line in Kuwait. After my American father died, she moved us to America. When I learned of my heritage, I left home to live with some of my cousins who had come to Atlanta to school. They were new to this country. I knew the ways of America, and they did not. I was skilled at finding them American girls for sex. They paid me. It was easy. They introduced me to others. Three years ago I was approached by an influential Arab who shall remain nameless."

"The fucking ambassador from Kuwait. I know."

Vincent's shock was real. "How do you know this?"

"Maybe I should just shoot you in the head to shut you up. The license plates on Yusef's ride. I traced them. What do you think I've been doing for the last few hours, holding my dick? Go on."

"The Ambassador has certain special needs. He is very particular about the type of girls he desires."

"What kind?"

"His Excellency fears the taint of American women and their diseases. He requires virgins. Young virgins only."

Frank fought to show no emotion. "And you find them for him?"

"Yes. Atlanta is a beacon for many young runaways. It is easy to find girls who claim to be virgins, but I confirm it through a doctor to be certain."

"Why does he come down here? There have to be girls like that up in New York."

"True. But up there he is closely watched by your government and by the Israelis. There are many risks there. When I find the girl, he announces that he is coming to visit a nephew in college here. He visits briefly, for the beard, as you say. In Atlanta he is free to do as he wishes. It is only a few times each year. Nothing to raise suspicions."

"Is that what happened with the girl, Jenny?"

Vincent watched Frank's eyes for some tell. There was none. "Yes. She was a small town girl. Unspoiled."

Frank leaned back in the chair. No reason to show too much interest in one girl. "Not bad. What's the pay?"

"Ten thousand per girl," Vincent said.

Frank cocked the hammer back on the pistol.

"You are going to make me shoot you in the head, Vincent, if you keep fucking with me. I was getting five grand to find her. You don't go through all this shit for a lousy ten grand. Hell, you killed the other girl."

Vincent raised his hands with the palms toward Frank. "No, wait. It is as you say. I get sixty thousand per girl. More if she finds special favor in the Ambassador's eyes."

"What's that mean?"

"Some of the girls he takes back with him to Kuwait to serve in his harem."

"How much extra for them?"

"Another forty."

"Sweet. What happens to the others?"

"What do you mean?"

"What happens to the other girls? After he leaves?"

Vincent laughed. "It does not matter. Some continue to work for me through my contacts. Some go out onto their own. Some leave. Some die. They are nothing. They are dogs. It does not matter."

"Like the bitch in the bedroom?"

"Yes. Sometimes I am a little rough," Vincent chuckled. "I get carried away."

"You got a good place to dump the body?" Frank asked. "Or is that something I need to take care of?"

"I have a good place. Yusef will take care of this one for me. The Ambassador is happy to do little favors for me."

Frank nodded as if thinking over the information. "Might be something I can work with," he said. "How about you fix us a little drink, and we talk about my cut."

Vincent got up and went to the wet bar. "What will you have?"

"Whatever you're drinking is fine."

Vincent fixed them both gin gimlets. Bombay Sapphire gin, very dry. He mixed them strong, three to one. His back was to Frank as he mixed them. He dropped a few cubes of ice into each glass with silver tongs. He passed one glass to Frank and kept the other.

While Vincent was fixing their drinks, Frank had removed the bottle of GHB from his pocket. It was palmed in his hand with the gun. The top was off. When Vincent handed him his drink, he acted like he was trying to get the glass situated in his hand and squirted some of the clear liquid into the glass.

Vincent took a sip of his drink. He was smiling. Frank wondered if Vincent had doctored Frank's drink. Wouldn't surprise him. It was what Frank would have done. What Frank did.

Frank hesitated before drinking his gimlet. "Let's trade glasses," he said, extending his toward Vincent.

Vincent looked hurt. "You don't trust me?"

"No."

"How can we be partners if you do not trust me?"

"You'll have to convince me. Now drink."

Vincent took a deep drink out of the glass and sat down. Frank wondered if he had doctored his own drink, suspecting Frank of switching glasses. It was confusing.

"Drink up," Vincent said.

Frank sat there holding the drink. "How do you think your boy, the Ambassador, will take me working with you?'

"I will not tell him."

"And Yusef?"

"I can handle Yusef. Do not worry about him." Vincent took another drink, almost draining the glass. Frank passed him his own glass. "Drink this one next. I'll make my own."

"You Americans are very suspicious."

"Cautious. Tell me about your father," Frank asked for no particular reason.

"He was an evil man. Very cruel. I hated him. My mother was a princess, and she gave up everything for him."

"What did your dad do in Kuwait?"

Vincent laughed. "He told me he worked on the oil lines as a manager."

"That's funny?"

"He was in the CIA."

"Really?"

"I learned the truth by accident. I heard him talking to another American while I was playing."

"That must have been an eye opener," Frank said. He poured straight gin into another glass. He did not turn his back on Vincent.

"I told some older boys I knew. They had friends in the underground. One night they sent men, and they killed my father."

"What did they do to you and your mother?"

"We were away at the time, as I had arranged. That is why she brought me to America. I loved Kuwait." Vincent seemed to stare off into some distant place in his own mind. Perhaps it was the deserts of Kuwait. He didn't speak.

Frank watched him. He stopped pouring gin and recapped the bottle. He like the smell of gin. After you drank it, your sweat smelled like pine cones.

"Vincent. Vincent. Vincent."

Vincent slowly looked over at him. He didn't speak. The dope worked pretty fast.

"Stand up." Vincent did. "Go into your office." Vincent did. His movements were slow like Jenny's had been.

"Sit down in your chair. That's it. Sit the glass down. Very good. Are you alright?"

Vincent blinked at him and nodded.

"Are you alright?'

"I'm fine," Vincent answered.

"Take off one shoe."

Vincent bent to the task. He unlaced the black shoe and pulled it off. He set it beside his chair. He looked up at Frank.

"I hope you can understand me, Vincent. I want you to know. I want you to suffer."

Vincent blinked.

"Take this pistol," Frank said, guiding it into Vincent's hand. He wrapped Vincent's fingers around the handle. He placed his own fingers over Vincent's. Frank's other hand was on Vincent's wrist. The gun was pointing toward Vincent. Frank waited. Any resistance and he could snap Vincent's wrist.

"Open your mouth. Now put the barrel inside against the roof of your mouth."

A tear formed at the corner of Vincent's right eye.

"Press it hard against the roof of your mouth. That's right. Say good-bye."

Frank pressed the trigger. The top of Vincent's head exploded.

Frank released his grip on Vincent's hand and let it and the gun fall to the floor. Vincent's legs twitched and then were silent.

Frank pulled the spare magazine from his pocket and dropped it on the desk. He took the exquisite switchblade from his sock. He hated to give it up. It was the sweetest little knife he had ever had. But he had to. It had Yusef's blood on it. No amount of cleaning would remove all the traces. He slid it into Vincent's front pants pocket.

He walked into the other room. He took his glass of gin and dumped it into the sink. He searched under the sink and found a black garbage bag. He stripped off all his clothes and gloves and stuffed them into the bag. He even changed socks. He put on his other pair of clean pants. He was out of shirts except for a sleeveless red nylon t-shirt. He pulled it on. He pulled his corduroy jacket on over it. He stuffed the garbage bag and the cash into the gym bag.

He scanned the living room and found Jenny's picture. The one he had given to Bren. He smiled at the girl in the photograph. He slipped her picture into his back pocket.

He started to leave and then thought of Bren's telephone. He walked into the bedroom. He recognized it immediately. He checked the number to be sure it was hers. It was. He slipped it into his gym bag as well. He went through her purse. He stuck her unidentifiable apartment key and car key into her pants that were balled up on the floor. He also put her tube of lipstick and a twenty dollar bill in her other front pocket. Maybe she traveled light. He stuck her purse with her driver's license and other personal information into his gym bag. No reason to make things too easy for the cops. Let them earn their paychecks.

He left the lights like they had been when he came in. He locked the door behind him. No reason to try and get fancy with the security chain. He started down the street.

Chapter 36

Frank figured he was almost safe now. Check out at the Four Seasons was twelve o'clock. If the Ambassador was due to check out and didn't, they would be hesitant to check on him for fear of offending him. They would give him at least an hour or two of grace. Probably send a cleaning woman up first. If he was supposed to stay longer, all the better. It could be days before the cops traced the clues to Vincent. Time helped distort forensics. He had made the crime scenes very compelling. He had tied Yusef's death to Vincent as well as to the death of Jamal parked out back. The same gun could be tied to the deaths of the ambassador and Ali.

The meeting in the restroom had given him an idea. He might as well exploit the homosexual angle. Yusef was killed in a bathroom frequented by gay men. The knife was found in Vincent's pocket. It raised questions. Ali and the Ambassador found dead in bed together. The questions were piling up. There would be telephone records that would link them further to Vincent. Bren was murdered by Vincent. The forensics would prove that. He even had the wounds on his hands. There was probably trace tissue under her nails. It was good she had at least fought a little.

Vincent's suicide was a nice touch. It closed the circle. No signs of forced entry. The apartment locked. No sign of a struggle. The same pistol for each murder and Vincent's suicide. No one to contradict the evidence.

If they did a toxicology check, the lab would show a witches' brew of drugs in Vincent's body. It might hide or distort the GHB. But hell, in the straight world, you never knew the combos druggies did. They were always mixing new things. Maybe the GHB had been for the girl. Even removing the one shoe was a good touch. It was odd. Cops loved odd bits of evidence. It made it seem more real. Not so perfect. The cops and feds would be confused by the evidence. Overwhelmed possibly. Murder and suicide. Homosexual triangle. They would go crazy working all the angles.

Frank thought he could call a cab safely after a couple of blocks. He decide to make it six. No one would walk six blocks from a crime scene before panicking and calling a cab. There was a slim chance the

THE LAST SPARTAN

Jokers might stumble onto him before he got back to his truck. You could only control the things you could control.

He heard the laughter before he reached the alleyway. He heard the clink of a bottle. Whispers. Two white teenagers bolted from the darkness in front of him. They were what he used to call gutter punks. Street kids.

There is an aura a man gives off, especially a violent man. Animals can pick up on it easily. It is something in the way the man moves, in the way he holds himself.

The gutter punks' smiles faded when they saw Frank. He was not the innocent victim they had been hoping for. Some feral sixth sense told them what he was. Frank waited.

They looked at each other, then ran in the opposite direction.

Who says the youth of today are stupid? It was probably the single most intelligent thing they had done all day.

Frank used a pay phone outside a Korean market to call a cab.

* * * *

Frank dumped the garbage bag into the dumpster behind the hotel where his truck was. He tossed Vincent's spare key down a drainage culvert along with the smashed pieces of Bren's telephone and the contents of her purse. He climbed into his truck. He was tired. His head still hurt.

He smiled. He had left the feds some prizes. They would clamber over the Ambassador's briefcase like dogs with a bone. Vincent's computer files should be interesting as well. Who knew where it might lead? What good might come from it? It should take the focus off searching for mystery people who might be involved. Leaving the Ambassador's cash behind was another distraction. It was open-and-shut with a cherry on top.

And Jenny. She was safe. He slipped her picture out of his back pocket and leaned it over the area where the radio should have been. The dials helped hold it in place.

Frank cranked up the old truck. He wished he had kept the radio now. He could use the company. It was going to be a long drive. Maybe when he got home he would buy one. The Spartans like music, he reasoned. They regarded singing as the best virtue next to those of a warrior. There needed to be a little more joy in his life. He had been too hard on himself. He missed the sounds of music.

* * * *

Wilmington, North Carolina, was quiet. By the first of November the beach had died down. The sun was still a half-hour away. Frank sat gazing out at the ocean. Thalassa. That was the Greeks' cry. Every school boy knew the story. Cyrus had led an army of ten thousand Greek mercenaries in a bold attempt to seize the throne in Asia. He had died in the decisive battle. The Greek army had agreed to a truce with the Persian king in exchange for safe passage out of his kingdom. He had broken the truce by seizing and slaying all their leaders. Trapped by the unknown country as much as by the king's vast army, the Greeks had turned to a man called Xenophon. Xenophon was a friend of the Spartans. He marshaled the remaining troops and led them across a thousand miles to safety. They fought the Persian king and barbarians every step of the way until at last one morning Xenophon heard the cry of his scouts. Thalassa. Thalassa. The sea. The sea. To the Greeks it meant safety. Now they could return home again.

Frank took off his boots and socks. He wanted to feel the sand with his toes. It was cool, but he removed his jacket anyway. He wanted to feel the bite of the crisp sea air. Hours crept by.

Frank sensed her before he saw her. She didn't speak. She just stood in silence.

The sun crept up. A pair of die-hard surfers in wet suits sprinted past them, heading for the morning glass. Frank turned to look at Jenny. She was cradling her stuffed dog, Scampy. He remembered it. She had left it at the foot of his bed when he had been at their home. She said it would protect him at night while he slept.

She looked so young. Her eyes seemed older.

"DC told me what happened," she said. "When I came around."

"How are you doing?"

"I'm okay. What about you?"

"Alright."

"I prayed you would come. Rescue me like a knight in one of those story books."

"You should have called. I would have come sooner."

"I couldn't. I don't know why. I just couldn't."

"I understand."

"It wasn't supposed to be like this. Vincent lied to me. He conned me, and I fell for it."

"We all get conned sometimes. You're only human."

They stared at the sun rising over the ocean. The steel gray waves turning blue and green in the sunlight.

"I have never seen the ocean," Jenny said. She could not hide the awe in her voice. "Not for real. Only on TV."

"It is wondrous to behold," Frank said.

She sat beside him without speaking. They watched the water for what seemed like a long time. Jenny started again.

"Will I ever forget the things I've done?"

"No. But you'll learn to live with it. There are a lot of worse things to have to live with."

"I feel dirty. You know? Who'll ever want me now?"

"Some good man," Frank said. "Someone who learns to love you. Someone you love. Remember, we are all damaged goods. We are all imperfect and messed up in different ways. It's just how you choose to deal with it that matters."

"I guess."

"What are you going to do?" Frank asked.

"I called home last night. I know it was late, but I had to let them know you found me and that I was alright."

"Good. And you really are alright?"

"I think so. I hope so."

"Are you going to go back home?"

"Not yet. I can't. There are other factors I have to consider."

"Like what?"

"That's what I need to talk to you about. We have a problem."

Frank did an odd thing. He smiled. It wasn't a bad smile for a man out of practice at smiling. It was heartfelt.

"You know me. I'm a problem solver."

Jenny snuggled up beside him and wrapped her arms around his waist. Frank draped his jacket over her shoulders.

"I'm glad you came," she whispered.

"So am I."

Chapter 37

Frank watched the ocean in silence. He remembered back to when he had been conned. Back to the day Sybil and Lamar and Jenny had found him. Back to the day he had been killed.

They had ridden hard all morning. Cyrus had sent Frank and Spanish Johnny ahead to check to be sure the next safe house was secure. Their organization was falling apart. The compound in Asheville was wiped out, as were most of the Spartan elite. Those that remained were being hunted by law enforcement and their outlaw enemies as well. They needed sanctuary.

Cyrus had foreseen such a possibility and arranged isolated safe houses all over the country. He was waiting for Frank's call before moving again. The Spartans had been reduced to a small handful of members that Cyrus could trust.

Frank idled his motorcycle at the turnoff road. He scanned the area for signs of a trap. It looked deserted. He moved cautiously down the long dirt road. An old gravel driveway led off to the right. The safe house should be there. Spanish Johnny pulled up beside him.

"What do you think, Frank? Think it's safe?"

Frank did not answer.

"Atlas and his boys are suppose to have secured it for us. What you want to do?"

"Check it out and see," Frank said.

They drove down the driveway. The house was hidden behind a stand of trees. Frank saw the side of a gray van parked out back and at least one motorcycle. Didn't mean anything one way or the other. The lights were on.

Frank left the .45 Colt wedged into his pants at the small of his back in place. He slipped the other .45 Colt from the front of his pants out. He made sure the safety was off and there was one in the pipe. He rolled closer to the front of the house. He saw nobody. Spanish Johnny revved his engine a couple of times. Frank looked back at him. Spanish Johnny was smiling. The dumb ass thought this was some kind of game.

A head peeked out from one of the windows. It disappeared. The front door opened, and Atlas lumbered out. He signaled them to cut their engines. Three other Spartans followed him outside.

"It's secure," Atlas said. He motioned to the three men with him with the large bore Remington shotgun he carried. It was a twelve gauge. It would hold four rounds. "These are Spartans I can vouch for. Mondo," he indicated a dull-eyed boy wearing a black beanie, "Earl," another country bumpkin in bib overalls, "and Fritz."

"Come inside and get some coffee," Fritz said. "It's getting too cold to stand out here."

Spanish Johnny got off his motorcycle and and embraced Atlas in a bear hug. "Glad you're here," he said.

Atlas grunted.

Inside, the house was nearly empty. There was old worn out furniture abandoned by the original owners years ago when they moved out. The place felt dusty and sad. There was a fresh pot of coffee brewing in the kitchen. Frank got a Styrofoam cup from the stack nearby. He poured a cup. There was an open bag of sugar. Frank didn't see a spoon. He scooped some up with his fingers and dumped it into his cup. Frank swirled the coffee around to mix in the sugar.

Spanish Johnny and the others were talking in the living room. Frank gazed out the side window at the empty fields. A police scanner squawked from an old table near the other Spartans. Frank went over to them.

"Hear anything on that thing?"

Atlas shrugged.

"Pretty quiet," Fritz said. "If they're on to us, they haven't let on."

"It's not them I'm worried about. Are you sure we are secure here?"

Atlas nodded. "It's safe."

"Anybody outside watching the perimeter?" Frank asked.

Atlas looked a little embarrassed. "No. Didn't seem to be any need to."

"If we are safe, let's keep it that way. We don't want Cyrus walking into an ambush."

"There's nobody else here," Mondo said, "but us. There's nothing to worry about out here."

Frank was wired. The gun battle at the estate in Asheville, the running and hiding, other safe houses blown, more gun battles, and more running, it had him understandably on edge. He didn't like this retard's attitude.

"Fuck you, hillbilly. You weren't there. We've lost a lot of good men. Better men than you."

Mondo didn't answer.

"I want to know this place is secure before I call Cyrus. You got that?"

"Yeah," Atlas said. "I'll get back out on the perimeter."

"Take the hillbilly with you," Frank said. "You got any food in here? Spare gasoline? Ammo?"

"We got ammo in the van," Fritz said.

"Doesn't do us much good out there. Bring it in, and sort it in case we need it. What about the food and gas?"

"Some of our guys went to stock up on provisions. They should be back anytime. We didn't expect you guys so soon."

"I'll get the ammo," Mondo said. His voice held no emotion.

"We passed a gas station a few miles back," Spanish Johnny said. "I'll make a quick run. I'm sure they have some gas cans I can score to haul it back in. Shouldn't take long."

Frank stared at Spanish Johnny. "Then do it."

"I'll be right back. I'll take the van. You call Cyrus and give him the okay."

Frank didn't answer. Everyone wandered off to their tasks. Frank went and stared out the window at the field. Apollo had hidden invisible in plain sight, in a field like that. He scanned the rows for anything suspicious. There was nothing. Fritz wandered in from the kitchen with a cup of coffee. He stood vigil near the police scanner.

A flock of crows rose suddenly from the dead field. Something had sent them skyward. Or nothing. Crows were never a good omen. They were associated with death. Frank felt more than heard the gun rising toward his back.

There was the roar of a pistol, but he was already moving. Frank dipped and spun. Each hand seeking a different gun. The bullet tore a trough across the top of his shoulder. A few inches lower and Frank would be dead. Fritz' face was set hard for his task. It didn't have time to register surprise that he had failed.

Frank's first shot punched a huge hole in his stomach. The second and third caught him above the knee cap as he fell, tearing the leg off. Frank heard sounds and saw Atlas and Earl running toward the house. Atlas kicked the back door in. He had his Remington pump shotgun pointing upward. Fool, Frank thought, a shotgun didn't do you any good if you didn't have it in play. Frank shot him four times in the chest. Atlas toppled back into Earl. Frank continued firing at both men until they were down.

Frank whirled back toward his right. It was too late. Mondo was outside the window with his gun raised. Frank was a fraction too slow. Mondo's automatic flared as it released the .9mm rounds in the magazine. Frank fired wildly without aiming for a particular spot as he had been trained to do. The window blew inward as the rounds tore their way through glass and screen and thick curtains until they caught Frank in the left side of his chest. He staggered backward onto the couch. He didn't try to get up. He wasn't sure he could. He didn't need to. He had seen his own bullets tear the window back outward as they tore into Mondo. There was no way Mondo was still alive.

Frank's left arm seemed to be going numb. The .45 automatic fell from his grip. He had to get up. Had to warn Cyrus. Atlas was turned. It wasn't safe. They had to find another place. He concentrated, building his strength. He rose unsteadily to his feet. The room teetered and then righted itself.

Spanish Johnny came running through the front door. He was unarmed. Frank lowered his pistol. His eyes were wild.

"Ambush," Frank snarled. "We've got to go before the others get back."

"You're in no shape to travel, Frank. Let me try to get you patched up."

"There's no time. We have to go now."

Spanish Johnny shook his head. "Come on. I'll help you. You are a hard man to kill, just like they say."

Frank grunted as Spanish Johnny lifted his right arm over his shoulder and stepped in close to help support Frank's weight. Frank was concentrating on each step. He didn't expect the knife. Didn't even feel it at first. Spanish Johnny shifted slightly, and the knife was in his hand. The move was meant to disembowel Frank. But the position was a little awkward. Spanish Johnny could not get all his weight behind it. The blade caught itself in Frank's jacket. The blade moved in slow motion as it sliced his stomach open and curved upward. The blood poured from the wound as it opened behind the knife's passing. Frank seemed to lose all strength. That was shock setting in, he knew.

He slumped toward Spanish Johnny. His own falling weight added to the power of the knife. He was dying. He was ready. He looked into Spanish Johnny's dark face. He was smiling. The knife slowed to nothing as it cut man and jacket as one. Spanish Johnny leaned in close to Frank's ear and whispered.

"For Aphrodite."

Something happened inside Frank. Perhaps from a lifetime of forging his will, it wound not let him stop. His blue eyes flashed, and the knife stopped completely in its path. The smiled faded from Spanish Johnny's face. He tried to move the knife upward. It would not move. Maybe it was caught in the jacket's thick material. He looked downward. Frank had gripped his right wrist. He couldn't move the knife. It was impossible. He grabbed the blade with both hands. Frank's Herculean grip held firm.

Spanish Johnny looked back up into Frank's face. His eyes were on fire.

"Your life is mine," Spanish Johnny snarled. "Give it to me."

"Molon labe," Frank answered. It was Greek. Although Frank did not speak Greek, he knew these words. They were the words spoken by the great Spartan king Leonidas when the Spartan three hundred had stood before the might of Xerxes and his Persian army. The Persians had sent an emissary to Leonidas. They offered him many things—riches, power, the lives of his people—if he would lay down his weapon. These words had been his simple response. Molon labe. Come and take it.

Frank smashed a savage head butt into Spanish Johnny's face. Spanish Johnny staggered, his hand loosely on his knife. Frank smashed him with another head butt. Spanish Johnny toppled to the floor. The knife came out with his fall. Frank gasped at the fresh, hot pain that burned through his abdomen. He clutched the wound closed with his left hand.

Spanish Johnny lay on the floor. He didn't move. He might be dead. He might only be unconscious. Frank raised his pistol. He centered the sites on the middle of Spanish Johnny's forehead. His hand was trembling. He squeezed the trigger. There was the dull click of an empty chamber. Frank pulled the trigger a second and third time to be sure the gun was empty. He let it fall to the floor. He thought he might have heard an engine approaching. It could have been the roaring of the blood in his ears. He was out of time. The others were coming back.

Frank stumbled outside. His motorcycle was gone. He climbed onto Spanish Johnny's BMW 1200. The engine turned over with a smooth, deep purr. He had to escape. Once he had put some distance between them, he could warn Cyrus. There would be time for revenge later. He roared away down the road.

Even now, five years later, Frank wondered what Spanish Johnny had meant. "For Aphrodite." Did he mean in retribution for Frank having saved her all those long years ago? Did he mean because Spanish Johnny wanted Aphrodite for himself? Did he mean she had sent him to kill Frank? There was no way to be sure. It didn't matter anymore.

Frank looked over at Jenny. She was resting her head against his shoulder as she watched the sea. She was safe. He had done good.

Chapter 38

It was late morning by the time Jenny and Frank left the beach. Frank knocked on the door of the hotel room. A nervous DC opened it and quickly hobbled back to the sofa.

"It's not my fault, dude. There was nothing I could do."

"He's right," said Caron. "We made him take me along. I didn't want to stay in Atlanta."

"Caron's got no one and no where to go," Jenny said. "She can't go home, she's only sixteen. I couldn't leave her behind. "

"And my feet were killing me, dude. There's no way I could have made the drive. I needed Caron to do the driving."

Frank didn't speak.

"It was like this," DC said. "When Jenny came down from the dope, she was worn out. I told her what was what. Straight up like you told me to."

Jenny nodded. "Straight up," she confirmed.

"She said she needed to pick up some things from her apartment before she left."

"Scampy. You know I couldn't leave Scampy behind. He's my oldest friend. I just couldn't leave without Scampy."

"Then when we got there, my feet were killing me. I decided to wait in the car while she got her stuff. Honest. That's what I was going to do. Get her stuff. Toss it into the car and roll thunder."

"Caron was waiting for me," Jenny said, pointing to the other girl in the room.

"Nice to meet you," Caron said.

Frank nodded back.

"I told her what had happened and what I was going to do," Jenny continued. "She wanted to tag along. I couldn't say no."

"It's like I told you. I made them take me along," Caron said. "Anywhere was better than there."

"So, you see. We got to figure out what we do next. I mean all of us. We're all at the crossroads, dude," DC added.

"Please," Jenny said. "You got to help her. She's my friend."

Frank looked from face to face. His own face was unresponsive. He smiled. He was getting pretty good at smiling.

"It's a problem," he said. "But I fix problems."

"Then she can stay?" Jenny asked.

"Of course," Frank said.

"See, I told you," DC said. "I told you Frank would work things out."

Caron came up and hugged Frank. He clumsily tried to pat her on the back. It felt awkward. Displays of affection were not his strong suit. He was still working on smiling.

"I won't be a bit of trouble. I promise," Caron said. "I'll do whatever you tell me."

"First thing we got to do," DC said, "is fix your hair. We add some auburn highlights, it would be killer. Frame your face, bring out your eyes. The whole package."

"Red?" Caron said.

"Not red. Auburn. Just a hint to mix in with the blonde. Trust me on this."

Jenny moved beside Frank. "She is a great girl. I couldn't leave her."

"Always stand with your friends. I'll work it out."

"Promise?"

"I promise."

They stayed in Wilmington enjoying the rare Indian summer. The weather turned unusually warm and stayed that way for the entire week. Frank thought it must be an omen. Frank read the *New York Times* and *USA Today* every day looking for word on the Ambassador and Vincent.

Three days into their stay there was an article about a tragic car accident in Atlanta. It seems the ambassador's car went off a bridge and burst into flames. The ambassador and his three aides were all killed. Forensic teams were on the site. Although the bodies were severely burned and badly mutilated, there was no indication of foul play. It was an accident. Some speculated that the driver may have been drinking. After autopsies were complete, the remains would be returned to Kuwait. A memorial service was scheduled for the ambassador in New York.

It seems the feds had their closed case. There was no mention of Vincent's suicide. In a month or two, he would have DC do a computer check of the Atlanta newspapers for a more detailed check on Vincent.

Frank was glad to see the ocean again. He had missed it. The others were joyous, too. They played in the surf. Even DC with his bad feet. They built sandcastles. They ate seafood and went to arcades to play video games. Frank left them alone to bond. He was waiting for a sign, something to let him know the gods felt it was safe to return home.

When he saw the headline he made up his mind. The sports page heralded the upset soccer victory of UNC at Greensboro over UNC at Wilmington. The headlines could not have been more prophetic. "Spartans defeat Seahawks." And under it the subheadline read, "Return home, ranked number one."

It was time to go home.

THE LAST SPARTAN

Chapter 39

Frank contacted attorney Charles Foster in Greensboro. He had Caron and Jenny both emancipated and declared legal adults. Frank had set certain rules for the girls that they had both agreed to in advance.

Jenny's school records were transferred, so she could continue high school in Greensboro. Using Jenny's records as a guide, DC was able to obtain documents through the Internet proving that Caron had completed the ninth grade in Atlanta with a B average. They even looked genuine.

Jenny and Caron were enrolled in Westchester Academy, an expensive private school. Their classes would start after the Christmas holidays. Through Foster, a mysterious benefactor, a Mr. Robinson, provided money to cover their tuitions. The girls were not thrilled at the prospect of returning to school. It was one of Frank's terms of their being allowed to stay.

They also got part-time jobs together as waitresses at a local Steak and Shake restaurant. That was another condition for them to stay. They had to contribute to the upkeep of the car Frank bought them. It was a used Volkswagen Beetle. The girls had chosen the bright yellow one. They thought it was adorable. Adorable was a word Frank could not ever remember hearing before.

DC moved into Frank's home and paid him a monthly rent that was exactly the same as he had paid for his half of his old apartment. Frank got DC a job overseeing the bookkeeping at Elite Motorcycles. Within three weeks, DC had complety redone their computer system. He modernized and simplified their billing system and tracking procedures. By the end of the month, profits were up eleven percent.

Frank moved out of his home. He bought a larger three-bedroom house on the same street on the corner. The family who sold it was happy to move. They made a hefty profit. Frank took the two smallest bedrooms as his bedroom and library. The girls shared the largest bedroom with its own master bathroom. The new house did not have a deck, and Frank forced DC to help him build one. To make matters worse, after they had completed the deck, Frank forced DC to help him roof and screen in part of it. DC apparently had never done physical labor in his life. He seemed truly amazed with his first callous.

Frank bought himself a new larger hot spa. He also bought several bathing suits for himself.

With DC's help, Frank was able to locate a small Japanese weapons maker in Kyoto. The company was called Busido Blades. They made a unique assortment of handmade weapons. They were very expensive. One of the most unusual was a small knife. The thin ceramic blade opened straight through the handle. The blade was described as being ten times sharper than steel. The blade was inscribed in Japanese. It said, "Death before Dishonor." Frank ordered one for himself under DC's name. He really liked that knife.

Frank went back to work customizing motorcycles. He would never admit it, but he liked having Jenny and Caron in the house. They seemed to wake the place up. Everything was a thrill for them, whether it was choosing furniture or painting the bathroom. He settled back into his old routine. No one came looking for him. Everyone had forgotten about the last Spartan.

THE LAST SPARTAN

Epilogue

The wind was icy as it blew off the river. The river was trying to freeze, but it just wasn't quite cold enough yet. Ice-slush had built around the edges and struggled to extend its dominion. The woman huddled by the window, watching the water. She brushed her short blonde hair back from her face. Absently, she fiddled with the string of white pearls at her long throat.

In the other room a telephone rang. It was the private line. She could tell by the ring. She heard him pick it up. She heard a muffled conversation but couldn't make out any of it. She didn't care anymore. At length the man hung up the telephone. She heard his footsteps approaching. She continued to stare out the window.

"Helen," he said.

She continued to stare at the water.

"Helen. You'll never guess who that was."

She turned toward the man at last. She smiled wanly. She could not care any less. It did not concern her.

"Who was it, dear?" she asked politely.

"Voice from the past. Guess who's back from the dead?"

"I haven't a clue," she said and meant it. She really did not care.

"Frank Kane," the man said. He watched her face for a reaction.

She smiled wanly again. There was no other sign that she recognized the name. Her face was aloof as always.

"That's impossible. He's dead."

"That's what I thought, too. Seems we were both mistaken."

"Are you sure?" Helen said. She seemed only vaguely interested.

"Seems legitimate. Frank has been busting heads down in Atlanta."

"Is that where he is now?"

The man shook his head. "I'm afraid it won't be that easy, my darling. He seems to have disappeared again."

She turned back toward the window and the freezing river.

"Don't worry, I'll find him," the man said.

"You'll have to, won't you?" she said with a thin smile. "He might start asking questions. Then he might decide to come looking for you."

"We wouldn't want that, would we, my darling? I have to go out for a while."

"Be careful."

The man's smile was cruel. "You can count on it, Aphrodite."

She shivered at the mention of her other name. "Please, don't call me that," Helen said.

The man laughed.

She watched him get his long camelhair coat from the closet. It was a warm tan color and stretched down to his calves. She watched him slip a pistol into the front right pocket, then he was out the door. She listened as the garage door opened. She heard the distinctive snarl of the Jaguar. She got a glimpse of the dark blue car as he drove away past the river. Helen stood for a long time listening and thinking.

When she was sure he was gone, she went to her own closet. She removed an old black suitcase from the back. It had sat hidden behind the others for years. It was the one she had taken from the Ghost Riders' clubhouse many long years ago. The man let her keep it for her nostalgia. She laid it on the bed and opened the latches. It was empty. Or so it seemed.

The suitcase had been used for smuggling. She knew its secrets. Helen flipped the secret catch, and the bottom opened. Inside was an old black vest. There was a Greek lambda burned into the back. Three bullet holes punctured the vest. She picked it up and held it to her face. She breathed in the scent. She imagined she could still smell him, but she knew it was only her imagination. It was her only remembrance of him. She had told Frank she had thrown it away, knowing even then she would keep it always. She rubbed the dark black leather. She felt its softness. She noticed for the thousandth time how it had conformed to the shape of Frank's body. Even now, the vest remembered and held those contours. Helen wondered what it all meant. Frank Kane was alive.

She looked out across the water. The clouds were building to the east. The wind had picked up and lashed at the water with renewed fury. A storm was coming. A terrible, dark storm.

Other Savage Press Books

CHILDREN'S BOOKS

Out of the Rainbow by Jay Ford Thurston
Luella by Melinda Braun
Kat s Magic Bubble by Jeff Lower

OUTDOORS, SPORTS & RECREATION

Curling Superiority! by John Gidley
Off Season by Marshall J. Cook
Packers "verses" Vikings by Carl W. Nelson
The Duluth Tour Book by Jeff Cornelius
The Final Buzzer by Chris Russell
The Year of the Buffalo by Marshall J. Cook

ESSAY

Awakening of the Heart, Second Printing by Jill Downs
Battle Notes: Music of the Vietnam War by Lee Andresen
Color on the Land by Irene I. Luethge
Following in the Footsteps of Ernest Hemingway
       by Jay Ford Thurston
Hint of Frost, Essays on the Earth by Rusty King
Hometown Wisconsin by Marshall J. Cook
Potpourri From Kettle Land by Irene I. Luethge

FICTION

Burn Baby Burn by Mike Savage
Charleston Red by Sarah Galchus
Keeper of the Town short stories by Don Cameron
Lake Effect by Mike Savage
Lord of the Rinks by Mike Savage
Marks of the Forbidden by Olaf Danielson
Northern Lights Magic by Lori J. Glad
No Peace in Exile by Olaf Danielson
Sailing Home by Lori J. Glad
Something in the Water by Mike Savage
Spirit of The Shadows by Rebel Sinclair
Summer Storm by Lori J. Glad
The Devil of Charleston by Rebel Sinclair
Voices From the North Edge by St. Croix Writers

REGIONAL HISTORY, MEMOIR

Beyond the Freeway by Peter J. Benzoni
Crocodile Tears and Lipstick Smears by Fran Gabino
Dakotaland by Howard Jones
Fair Game by Fran Gabino
Memories of Iron River by Bev Thivierge
Stop in the Name of the Law by Alex O'Kash
Superior Catholics by Cheney and Meronek
Widow of the Waves by Bev Jamison

BUSINESS

Dare to Kiss the Frog by vanHauen, Kastberg & Soden
SoundBites Second Edition by Kathy Kerchner

POETRY

A Woman For All Time by Evelyn Gathman Haines
Eraser's Edge by Phil Sneve
Gleanings from the Hillsides by E.M. Johnson
I Was Night by Bekah Bevins
Pathways by Mary B. Wadzinski
Philosophical Poems by E.M. Johnson
Poems of Faith and Inspiration by E.M. Johnson
Portrait of the Mississippi by Howard Jones
The Morning After the Night She Fell Into the Gorge by Heidi Howes
Thicker Than Water by Hazel Sangster
Treasures from the Beginning of the World by Jeff Lewis

HUMOR

Baloney on Wry by Frank Larson
Jackpine Savages by Frank Larson
With Malice Toward Some by Georgia Z. Post

OTHER BOOKS AVAILABLE FROM SP

Blueberry Summers by Lawrence Berube
Dakota Brave by Howard Jones
Spindrift Anthology by The Tarpon Springs Writer's Group

TO ORDER ADDITIONAL COPIES OF

THE LAST SPARTAN

Call **1-800-732-3867**

or

Purchase copies online at:
www.savpress.com

Visa/MC/Discover/American Express/
ECheck/accepted via PayPal.

All Savage Press books are available through all chain and independent bookstores nationwide. Just ask them to special order if the title is not in stock.

Coming Soon:

THE SPARTAN NEGOTIATOR

Frank Kane returns in another thriller to arrange the release of a friend's wife from Russian criminals. This time, Frank takes on MS-13 gangbangers, a sexy thief, a pair of vengeful enemies, the police, and terrorists. It's time to negotiate like the Spartans — kill everyone in your way and let the gods sort it out.
Lock and Load...